Demand Generation

A Church & Troy novel

by Gary Elmes

Published by Canewdon International Ltd., Auckland.

This book is a work of fiction. Names, characters, places and incidents are products of the author's imagination or are used fictitiously. Any resemblance to actual events or locales or persons living or dead is entirely coincidental.

Merkel-cell carcinoma is a real disease. However, aspects of its epidemiology have been fictionalised in this book.

ISBN: 978-0-473-42712-2

For Betty and Brian

without whom, this author would not have been possible

One

"I loved my office" — Francesca Boyle

Bailey Troy looked briefly at the woman she had come to see. Then her training took over, and she started scanning the room.

It was large for an office, maybe 30 feet square, but with only the one simple desk tucked in a corner. Plain and utilitarian, the office had about it a sense of slightly haphazard efficiency — untidy without being disorganised. The desk was littered with the detritus common to any commercial organisation — piles of invoices and delivery dockets, rows of lever-arch folders with indecipherable scribblings on the spine, a battered old 14-inch computer monitor behind a coffee stained keyboard.

The walls were plain and unadorned except for one large and much scribbled-on wall planner. A window stretched along the far wall, set high enough simply to let in light without distracting the occupants with any kind of view. On the wall immediately to Bailey's left was a row of old filing cabinets. To her right was a photocopy machine, its tangy metallic ozone aroma mingling with the other odours that Bailey had come to expect at these encounters.

She gave her attention once more to the woman in front of her. Sat in the room's only chair, pushed slightly away from the desk, Francesca Boyle faced out at the room with her head resting lightly against the light tan paintwork of the wall. She was young — early twenties, Bailey guessed — and dressed in a simple but upmarket business-casual skirt and blouse that spoke of a nonchalant refinement devoid of any slavish adherence to fashion. Her clean-scrubbed and intelligent girl-next-door looks were, Bailey noticed, carefully enhanced with the expert and restrained application of eye shadow. Her physique was what Bailey would describe as "athletic" — a body kept trim and finely toned through exercise rather than emaciated by dieting.

Bailey created a quick mental character-sketch of the young woman before her. Refined and intelligent? Certainly. Confident and independent? Most probably. A young woman who had, perhaps, recently aced a respectable degree through natural aptitude and the sparing application of hard work. And doing so, Bailey speculated, while splitting her spare time between volleyball, pizza and the playful navigation of the rites of passage to adulthood.

In the back of her mind Bailey mused that, under other circumstances — in the right kind of bar, perhaps — Francesca Boyle might just be the sort of woman that she would make a pass at. The sort of woman who might just have been curious enough and playful enough to be coaxed into bed with a glass of Merlot or two and the lure of some new and unexplored forms of intimacy.

But Bailey Troy would not be making any passes at Francesca Boyle. Not here or in a bar, not now or later. Because Francesca Boyle was dead. The small hole an inch below her left eye and the lumpy red splatter down the wall behind her made that abundantly clear. A subtle head-shake from the paramedic a few minutes previously, after a token search for a pulse, had simply confirmed the obvious. The ozone from the photocopier mingled with the smell of firearm discharge and the faint but unmistakable stench of shit — signalling that the victim had, as was often the case, suffered the final indignity of death.

Bailey took one last look around — at the starkly utilitarian office, at the incongruously elegant and even more incongruously dead Francesca Boyle, at the scene-of-crime examiners crawling their way across the floor. Too young for a husband, she thought, better start with the boyfriend.

And with that, Detective Inspector Bailey Troy turned and left.

Two

"Poor Isaac. He was such a cutie." — Francesca Boyle

Isaac Church sat and looked out across the city.

For once, the faint brown smoggy haze that usually blurred the view was absent — washed away by the overnight rain — and Isaac had a crystal-clear view. Across the wooded hills to the edge of the urban sprawl five miles away, on to the huddle of towers that was the central business district 15 miles further on, and out across the sea to the distant and slightly indistinct horizon.

Isaac settled back in his chair and rested his feet on the balustrade that marked the edge of the balcony. He could feel the morning sun on his face and the earthy smell of moist woodland mixing in his nostrils with the aroma of freshly ground coffee.

It was, without doubt, Isaac's favourite chill-out spot.

This hour of tranquillity was a treat he granted himself most Saturday mornings. The Café sur la Colline was a short but slightly hilly one mile walk from his home in the leafy semi-rural fringe of the city. The unhurried walk there and back, the time spent meditating over the view, and the extra strong coffee that he had ordered a few moments ago were all part of the ritual.

"Double-shot flat white?" enquired a young female voice from behind him.

"Yep. That's mine," he confirmed, turning to smile at the woman bringing his first caffeine fix of the day. She returned his smile and gently clattered the cup and saucer down on the wooden slatted table beside him, slopping a little of the froth down the side of the cup as she did so.

Isaac was pretty certain he hadn't seen her before. The waiting staff here came and went pretty quickly — the proprietor was, he knew, a hard taskmaster and a lousy payer. He took a second to enjoy the sight of this latest employee. She was dressed unadventurously in old jeans and t-shirt, with the uniform black apron of the establishment over the top. The words "Café sur la Colline" were printed conspicuously across her breasts, an area that Isaac examined with approval as she leant over to retrieve the small stand into which his order number had been inserted.

He put her age at around seventeen or eighteen. Young enough to still be at school, old enough that he could admire her curves with a clear conscience.

Isaac allowed himself to stare unashamedly at the young woman's denim-clad buttocks as they gyrated their way back inside the café, then turned his attention to his coffee. He tore the end from the sugar tube, upended the contents into the cup, picked it up and returned to his slouched, feet-up position. Taking in the view across the city and stirring his coffee absent-mindedly, he slipped easily into a semi-hypnotic contentedness, and allowed the minutes to drift by.

Definitely his favourite spot.

"You're admiring the view, I see."

Isaac recognised the rhythmic *Marseillais* accent of Raphaël, the proprietor, just as his peripheral vision detected the Frenchman perching himself on the balustrade to his right.

Isaac nodded slowly in agreement, still staring out across the hills towards the city. "You certainly have a pleasant spot here, Raph," he replied.

The proprietor gave a quiet chuckle. "Ah, no. I meant... the view." He pointed back to the interior of the café. Isaac swivelled round in his chair to see where Raphaël was pointing. Inside the café, the young waitress could be seen leaning over a table, wiping away the crumbs and coffee rings left behind by an earlier customer.

Isaac laughed and turned to look directly at his host. Raphaël was, Isaac assessed, in his mid fifties. A small man; no more than 5' 3". He wore Black Levi 511 jeans and a black t-shirt; both faded to an uneven dark grey by age and too many turns through the laundry. His body was thin and wiry; a physique maintained, Isaac knew, by the combined effects of red wine, Gitanes, and a bottomless well of nervous energy.

"You are an incorrigible old lecher, Raph. She's far too young for you."

Raphaël shrugged. "*Peut être.* This one certainly still has too much of the teenager in her, you know? Talks too much about too little, brain full of air. Too much *commérage*, not enough work. But still..." he gave an approving gesture back towards the interior of the café, at what Isaac assumed was a view of the undeniably captivating young waitress.

"Maybe you should be looking for a woman your own age, Raph. Someone who isn't immediately going to realise what a licentious old scoundrel you are."

The Frenchman laughed again. "Ah, *non.* Even the older women, they can see what I am. This one," he pointed back into the café again, "she is not for me, I know. But perhaps you, now that your woman has..." He made a walking motion with his fingers.

Francesca. Yes, she had indeed walked away.

"No, Raph. As pleasant-looking as your latest employee is, she's not really my type. You know my rule."

"Yes, yes. I know," the older man replied. "Older women only. And you are right, of course." This was, Isaac knew, a topic that the Frenchman would inevitably wish to expound upon at some length. "As with all things in life, confidence in the bedroom comes with practice, yes? A woman without her thousand hours experience of *baiser* is too clumsy, too nervous, to be a good *amoureux;* we both understand this. But your Francesca, she was young, no? Too young to have her thousand hours, I think. Too young to teach you very much about *l'amour physique.*"

It was a valid point, Isaac admitted to himself. Francesca was young, barely out of university. Her approach to sex had certainly been tinged with all the uncertainties and insecurities of inexperienced youth — eager to please him but not understanding how; tentative and confused in seeking her own pleasure; unsure of her own boundaries, afraid of exploring his. But what she had lacked in competence, she had more than made up for in enthusiasm. Determination, even. Before she had left him, that is.

Isaac turned to look at the café proprietor, and let out a long sigh. "Yes, well. Lesson learned there, eh. But it's not just about the sex, you know," he added; aware, even as he said it, of how defensive it sounded.

The Frenchman looked at him dubiously. "How old are you, Isaac?"

"Twenty eight. Why?"

"And what's the longest you've ever been in a relationship?" Isaac didn't answer. "You've been coming here and telling me about your life long enough that we both know your *affaires d'amour* last a few weeks at most. When you meet the woman you're going to fall in love with and want to spend the rest of your life with, you'll know. But you haven't met her yet. So for now, admit it: it *is* all about the sex."

Isaac raised an eyebrow. "Says the middle-aged single French lecher."

"Yes, well," Raphaël replied, with a faraway look. "Life is complicated, and sometimes even love is not enough. But anyway. What happened with you and Francesca? Did you fight?"

"No, we didn't fight. She just... stopped. Didn't want to see me after work, or over the weekend. Wasn't going to explain. Just wanted me to just leave her alone; goodbye. I can't make any sense of it."

"Probably for the best. She was the boss's daughter, after all. And fathers are very protective of their daughters. It could have been costly for you, no?"

Dick. Francesca's father. Not Isaac's boss, exactly; but certainly his biggest and most important client.

"Oh, Dick didn't seem to mind," replied Isaac. "I think that, as long as Francesca was happy then he was happy. Well, maybe not happy, exactly — Dick didn't really do happy. Just unconcerned. He and I got along well enough."

Raphaël gave another of his Gallic shrugs, signalling the end of his interest in the topic. "No matter. I'm sure that your tolerable looks will lure some other poor woman into your clutches before too long. But enough of *les femmes*," he continued. "Tell me, how is business? You are still charging our local enterprises outrageous fees for the use of your modest technical talents?"

"My charges reflect the excellent value that my IT services provide," replied Isaac in mock indignation. "And besides, they allow me to earn enough to pay the exorbitant prices you charge for your indifferently prepared coffee."

Raphaël laughed. "Well, if *Monsieur* would prefer to walk to a different establishment..."

Isaac smiled and tilted his head in mock surrender. The coffee was, they both knew, excellent. And there was no other café even remotely within walking distance of his home.

"Actually, business is pretty good right now," said Isaac, returning to Raphaël's question. "Dakin Boyle Pharmaceuticals need to upgrade their core systems, which will keep me lucratively employed for a while. They've been putting it off for ages, of course, as all companies do. But now they have no choice; the European Commission has updated all its rules for the pharmaceutical industry, and Europe is one of Dakin Boyle's biggest markets. Just utter the magic words 'EudraLex compliance' and I'll be able to buy your over-priced coffee for months to come."

"You're lucky that old Dick Boyle didn't mind you seducing his daughter, or he might have given all that work to someone else."

Isaac shook his head. "I get on all right with Dick. And honestly, they don't really have a choice. There's nobody else in this city that understands that Pharmazeutika system of theirs like I do. It's a bit of a niche product, and I'm the only guy in town who can upgrade it for them in time."

Raphaël shook his head, then looked up as something inside the café appeared to catch his eye. "Well, some of us need to earn an honest living, and I have another customer." He pushed himself off the balustrade and walked back inside the café.

Isaac slouched back in his chair and returned to quietly surveying the view across to the city and beyond. He sipped his coffee, and slowly allowed his mind to empty. The minutes passed.

"Double-shot flat white?"

"Eh?" he offered in reply, turning to look over his left shoulder at the teenage waitress, bearing another cup and saucer.

"Yes, perfect. Thank you." Another female voice, this one from his right. He swivelled round to find that he was now sharing the café balcony with another customer, leaning with her butt perched against the balustrade. The teenager handed her the coffee and left.

"Great minds," said the newcomer, raising her coffee cup and nodding towards his.

"I guess so," he replied, at a loss for anything more engaging to say as he struggled to bring his mental focus back to the present.

Isaac took a moment to survey this new presence. She was petite, but not overly so — it was hard to tell from sitting down, but he guessed about five three. Long, straight, blonde hair framed a pretty face that was textured with a light and weathered tan. She had the kind of build that was curvy enough to be sexy but wiry enough to give the impression of a woman who could, Isaac reflected, probably look after herself in a fight. She was wearing a man's casual shirt that was tight in all the right places and which hung down over jeans that were ripped just above the left knee. Old ripped, not fashion ripped. Working jeans that had seen plenty of hard use. He placed her age at somewhere in the early thirties, maybe five years older than him — no bad thing. Just beyond the reach of his consciousness, the reptilian part of his brain flashed its approval.

This was, Isaac decided, how Avril Lavigne might look if she worked out and got outside more. And she was looking directly at him with a smile that said: no promises, but talk to me and see how you get on.

"Do you come here often?" Isaac couldn't believe he'd just said that. It was so far beyond lame it wasn't funny. His subconscious had simply needed to fill the silence, and that was all it had to offer. But she laughed, taking her gaze briefly off him to look down at her coffee and shake her head.

"No. No I don't." She resumed her gaze, and now the smile had a hint of mischievousness. "You?"

"I like it here. It's quiet, the view's great, the coffee's drinkable, and I live just down the road. I treat myself to a break up here from time to time."

The woman balanced her coffee cup on the balcony and held out her hand. "My name's Bailey," she said.

He stood, took the offered hand and shook. "Isaac," he replied. "Isaac Church." Her hand was small in his, but had a casual strength about it. Not the tight bone-squeezing grip of a guy trying to impress, just the vague sense of a hand controlled by muscles accustomed to hard work.

"So, what do you do for a living, Isaac?" she asked, turning and staring out across the city.

He turned and did the same, vaguely aware that this was a posture more common to two guys chewing the fat than to two strangers starting to flirt. He looked sideways at her, but she continued to look out at the view.

"I have my own business" he said, and was immediately aware of how lame that sounded. He was completely off his game today — this was not a woman who was going to be impressed with clumsy pretensions to eminence. "Actually, the business is just me. I do IT support for a few local companies."

"Computers, eh? You must do well out of that." He turned and looked at her again. She was still looking straight ahead. But the mischievous smile was back. She was playing with him.

"It keeps the wolves from the door, most of the time," he said. "What about you? What keeps you busy, erm..."

Shit! Her name was completely gone from his mind. And he'd gone and made it obvious that he couldn't remember. What an idiot! "I'm sorry, I've completely forgotten your name. You'll have to remind me, I'm afraid. Very rude of me"

The woman smiled and shrugged in a display of forgiveness. "It's Bailey," she replied. "Bailey Troy." She turned to show him something. It was an identity card. "Detective Inspector Bailey Troy. And I'm afraid that you, Isaac Church, are under arrest for the murder of Francesca Boyle."

Three

"It must've been horrible for him." — *Francesca Boyle*

Police interview rooms are not intended to make people feel comfortable. They're deliberately designed to be harshly Spartan in every conceivable way. The tables are cheap and tattily laminated, though firmly secured to the floor. The chairs are plastic, hard and uncomfortable. The acoustics are echoing and unforgiving, every sound jars the senses. And the rooms are always just that little too cramped. Just small enough to create a vague sense of claustrophobia — especially in someone with a good reason for wanting to be elsewhere.

And Isaac Church, Bailey could tell, really did not want to be here.

She looked across the table at the frightened young man opposite her. He was tall and lean. More filled out than the average gangly teenager, but not by much. In his mid to late twenties, she guessed. He wore olive-green cargo pants and a plain white v-neck t-shirt. His hair was medium length and had been gelled into a calculated unkemptness. A millimetre or so of carefully cultivated stubble covered an unblemished pale complexion that had seen less sun and more skin-care product than he would probably care to admit to.

He sat there, slumped in the uncomfortable chair. And he had The Look.

Bailey knew that look. In every murder investigation she'd ever been involved with, she had interviewed people with The Look. It was the look of fear, of confusion, of finding oneself suddenly, completely, and inextricably out of one's depth. It was the look that said "this just can't be happening" overlaid with the certain and dreadful knowledge that, actually, it was.

In a murder investigation, there were two types of people who got The Look.

Victims got The Look. Victims for whom, like most people, serious crime had previously been an abstract concept — for whom rape, murder and casual thuggery was something that happened somewhere else, to other people. Victims whose comfortable lives had been shattered by the sudden and inexplicable slaying of an innocent loved one. Victims who found that violent death, previously only experienced at the reassuring distance of the newspaper headlines and television news, had burst with crimson brutality into the sanctity of their homes. Those who were the innocent collateral damage of murder and reprehensible mayhem; they had The Look.

Killers got The Look too.

Not the fully paid-up members of the criminal underclass, for whom murder was just a tool of the trade and arrest and imprisonment an occupational hazard. You rarely saw that look in their faces. Whatever terror the career criminal may have felt at the prospect of a life sentence, they kept it hidden, deep down. For them, arrest and interrogation was a time to display little more than a bored indignation at being held to account for their chosen trade.

But those who had led, if not blameless, then respectable lives before snuffing out that of another — they got The Look. Those who had, over the years, earned seniority in their careers and respect in their communities while cheating on their expenses and their spouses with impunity — coming to believe as they did so that consequences were for other, lesser, beings. Those who had one day found the continued existence of another human being to be a financial inconvenience or an emotional indignity, and had subconsciously assumed that murder would be just another quick fix. Those who found themselves in the unaccustomed position of being held to account, and for the most heinous of misdeeds. Those who sat on that uncomfortable chair in this small room behind that locked door, and realised with a sudden flood of dread that their future was going to be one of small rooms and locked doors for many, many years to come. Such people — cornered and suddenly very, very alone — they got The Look.

Bailey Troy looked across the desk at Isaac Church, and saw The Look. The question was, she asked herself, was he collateral damage or was he a killer?

The evidence so far was shaping up to make for a smoking gun, slam-dunk, open-and-shut case. This guy Church had got all bent out of shape over being dumped by a hot chick, and dealt with it by blowing her away. It was stupid, it was pointless, it was a completely inexplicable waste of two promising young lives. But it was where the evidence pointed, and it happened a thousand times a day all over the world.

But her instinct wasn't backing the evidence.

Bailey knew from long experience that, if it came down to choosing between the evidence and her instinct, she would go with the evidence. Real life wasn't like the movies. In real life things were usually, she had found, pretty simple and more or less exactly as they seemed. But she had also learned when to let her instinct off the leash for a while to sniff around. She was going to do so now.

She lent over to the recorder, pressed the record button, and recited the date and time.

"Detective Inspector Bailey Troy interviewing. With me is Detective Constable Finlayson."

As she said his name, she turned briefly to look at the officer beside her. His bulk dwarfed her diminutive frame and dominated the small room. He was dressed in sharply pressed charcoal business trousers, an impeccably ironed white shirt, plain blue tie, light grey blazer. His face was clean-shaven, but mean and faintly chubby, his hair cropped close to his skull. Bailey guessed that he dressed that way each morning thinking that it made him look like a Secret Service agent — she imagined him practising talking into his cuff-link in front of the bathroom mirror. In fact, she thought, it just made him look like a gone-to-seed bouncer.

Constable Finlayson was, in Bailey's opinion, a complete half-wit. She was trying to get him off her squad — giving him a constant stream of shitty jobs to goad him into applying for a transfer, while at the same time giving him a good write up at each formal review so that he would be accepted when he did. It was a widely used strategy known euphemistically as "packaging for export" and which, unfortunately, had not yet worked in Finlayson's case. But he would serve his purpose today, she thought. He would sit there silently, his brain a docile thought-free zone, exuding just a hint of menace, and making up the required number of interviewing officers as stipulated by police procedure.

She returned her attention to Church. "Please state your name for the tape."

"Isaac Church."

"Middle name?" He shook his head. "Out loud please, for the tape."

"No. No middle name. Just Isaac Church."

"Date of birth?"

"April third."

"What year were you born?" He told her.

"You understand that you're under arrest for the murder of Francesca Boyle?"

"I didn't kill her. I can't believe she's dead."

"We'll get to that. But you understand that's why you're here?"

"Yes. No. I mean — yes, I understand that I've been arrested because you think that I... That she..." His elbows were resting on the table. He dropped his forehead down onto his hands, closing his eyes. "I know that I'm here because you think that I murdered Francesca."

"OK. Do you remember that I read you your rights? Do you understand those rights?"

"Yes. Yes."

"Good. I'd like to ask you some questions. You don't have to answer them, but it would help me if you do. Are you OK to answer some questions for me, Isaac?"

"I guess."

"Do you want to have a lawyer here when I ask my questions? You can have one if you want, I can wait until we get someone here for you."

"What? Erm — no. No, I don't want a lawyer. I don't need a lawyer. Go ahead, ask your questions. I didn't kill Francesca. I didn't kill anyone."

"As I said, we'll get to that." That was all the check-boxes ticked off for the tape. He was under arrest for murder, he knew his rights, he'd waived his rights to silence and to a lawyer. It was time to see what she could get from him.

"You said your birthday was in April, is that right?"

He nodded. "April third."

"Aries," she said.

"Sorry. What?"

"You're an Aries. Your star-sign."

"I guess. Yeah. Aries. I'm Aries, yes." His forehead was still resting on his hands, his eyes still closed.

"Aries people are supposed to be headstrong and impulsive, aren't they? Is that you, Isaac? Would people describe you as being headstrong and impulsive, do you think?"

"I don't know. No, not really. I wouldn't describe myself that way. I don't think other people would, either. I guess you'd need to ask them."

"Because killing Francesca was a pretty headstrong and impulsive thing to do, don't you think? Murder is a pretty headstrong business. I think the killer must have been an Aries, don't you?"

Isaac's head jerked up. He stared straight at his interrogator. "Are you kidding me? You've pulled me in here because of my star sign, is that what you're telling me? That's your evidence?" Bailey saw the fear and confusion in Church's expression take a step back, making way for a resentful indignation. As it did so, her instinct whispered a quiet *I-told-you-so.*

"We'll come back to the evidence in a minute. First, tell me how you spent yesterday evening."

"I finished up at Dakin Boyle around four. Headed home. Stayed there until this morning when I walked up the road to the Café sur la Colline and got arrested for murder."

"A bit quiet for a guy like yourself on a Friday night, wouldn't you say?"

"Yeah, well. My date had fallen through." The reply was delivered with a measured sarcasm. In Bailey's experience, suspects trying to prop up a flaky cover story did it with impromptu embellishments and wheedling assurances that it was all true. They did not deliver their story with a simple "this is it, take it or leave it". Another point for instinct.

"You didn't go out at all."

"No."

"Nobody came round."

"No."

"Nobody borrowed your car."

"My car? No. The car was on the driveway all night."

"What did you do?"

"Watched some DVDs."

DVDs. Not so good, she thought. If it had been broadcast television, she could have grilled him about the programmes, checked his answers against the schedule, asked about the story lines. If he'd claimed to have been watching a streaming service, she could have got the logs from the streaming provider. But DVD watching was hard to verify.

"DVDs? Do people really still do that?" He smiled at that. Not what she had intended; careless. She didn't want to make him comfortable.

"The boxed set cost me two hundred bucks back in the day," he replied. "I need to get my money's worth."

"Fair enough. Which DVDs, what were you watching?"

"Star Trek. Next Generation. Series 3 to be precise. I watched the first disc, the first four episodes." Bailey smiled inwardly. She had that same boxed set herself; it cost her $200 too. She scribbled a note to check which disc was in his DVD player. Time to probe a little deeper, see if he was really watching Star Trek...

"Tell me about the first episode that you watched. What happened?"

He sighed and rolled back on the chair, looking up at the ceiling. "Let's see. Wesley accidentally lets a bunch of little nanites escape, and they start eating the computer. Somebody pisses off the nanites by trying to kill them, then Picard gets them all rounded up and sent off to a nearby planet, and they all live happily ever after."

That sounded about right, from memory. Maybe he really did watch it. Or maybe he's just a really avid Trekkie who had committed all the episodes to memory. Time to try another angle.

"Did you have anything to eat last night?"

"Pizza and beer."

"Did you order in?"

He shook his head. "Beer from the fridge, pizza from the freezer. Pepperoni, to answer your next question."

"So, in short, you went home and stayed there all night. Nobody saw you, and you didn't see anyone. Nobody can vouch for you. You have no alibi at all for the time when Francesca was being murdered. Do I have that right?"

Isaac shrugged. "I guess so. I stayed home, I watched DVDs, I ate pizza, I drank beer. I didn't kill anyone."

Although she'd played it for what she could, Church having no alibi didn't really help her much. An alibi could be checked out, could be broken. Inconsistencies could be uncovered. So far, the interview had given her nothing. But there was plenty more to cover.

"Do you own a gun, Isaac?"

"Yes. You know I do. It's all legally registered." This much was true, she had the details in front of her. "It's at home in my gun safe."

That, though, was not true.

"Actually it's upstairs, bagged, in the evidence room. That's why you were arrested by a chick armed with a latte and not by a swarm of police ninjas with stun grenades and assault rifles." That, she thought, and the fact that the team were across town scaring the living shit out of a house full of crack kiddies, and she wanted to move immediately.

Isaac smiled again. "It was a flat white, not a latte." That was not the response of a murderer under interrogation. Another point to instinct.

"Tell me about the gun."

"It's a Glock 34 pistol. Similar to the Glock 17 you guys use, but modified for competition use. Longer barrel, slightly lighter trigger pull, a few other things. A nice gun."

"You use it a lot?"

"I'm at the club most weekends. Shooting, training new members, hanging out."

"Would you say you were a good shot with the Glock?"

"Good enough. I make A grade in competition, and I can hit a dinner plate at fifty yards pretty reliably. You?"

Bailey was, she would be the first to admit, a lousy shot. If she hit a dinner plate at ten yards she would feel pretty pleased with herself. She ignored the question.

"Your 34 — what calibre is that?" She already knew the answer, but she wanted to hear it from him.

"It's a Nine mil."

"Nine millimetre Parabellum?"

"That's right."

"*Si vis pacem, para bellum,*" she left the quote hanging in the air.

"Sorry?"

"It's where the name Parabellum comes from. It's Latin — if you seek peace, prepare for war. You'd be prepared for a little war with that Glock, wouldn't you Isaac?"

He smiled and shook his head, as if it was an accusation he'd dealt with a hundred times before. "It goes to the range, then it goes in the safe. It's a hobby, that's all. I use the gun to make holes in pieces of cardboard."

"Well somebody made war with Francesca Boyle last night. With extreme prejudice, and with a nine millimetre pistol. We recovered some nine mil shell casings from the scene. And we'll be checking to see if they were fired from your gun."

"And when you do, you'll find they weren't. My gun and I were both at home last night. Me on the sofa, the gun in the safe. You're barking up the wrong tree." Not a hint of doubt in his voice. Another point for instinct.

"Tell me again about where your car was last night."

"Like I said, on the driveway. All night."

"It's a Mazda 3, is that correct?"

"A Mazda 3, yes."

"Blue? A blue Mazda 3?"

"Blue, yes. A blue Mazda 3."

"More specifically, it's this particular blue Mazda 3, is it not?" She pushed an A4 photograph across the table at him. "For the benefit of the tape, I'm now showing Mr. Church a photograph taken by a red-light camera at the junction of Edmund Road and Strand Avenue, around one hundred yards from the premises of Dakin Boyle. The data imprinted on the photo shows it to have been taken at eight-oh-seven yesterday evening. Tell me what you see in the photo, Isaac."

"It's a Mazda 3."

"It's *your* Mazda 3, Isaac. Can you make out the registration plate?"

Quietly, "Yes."

"Is it your registration?"

Bailey could see the fear and the confusion back in his face. This was the point where the murderer realises they've been cornered and tries for a desperate last-minute elaboration of the cover story, some just remembered fact to try to square away, however untidily, the new and inconveniently incontrovertible evidence. Or sometimes they will simply descend into panic, swearing profusely on their mother's grave or some other convenient relic that it's all been a big mistake.

Isaac's voice was deathly quiet. He lifted his eyes and looked directly into hers, shaking his head almost imperceptibly. "I'm sorry," he pushed the photograph back towards her. "But I can't explain this. I went home after work last night, I ate pizza, I drank beer, I watched DVDs. I left my car on the driveway. It was still there this morning. I don't understand how it could be in this photo."

Bailey waited for him to say more. To elaborate, speculate, try to add some credibility to his story. But he said nothing more. Seconds ticked by.

A quiet tapping sound broke the silence. She turned to Finlayson and nodded towards the door. Finlayson lumbered up out of his chair, opened the door and stepped out, returning a few seconds later with a single piece of A4 paper, folded in half. He handed it to Bailey.

She opened it. A hand written note from Goff, one of the more useful members of her team. She quickly scanned the message, refolded the paper and placed it on the table.

She closed her eyes briefly to gather her thoughts, to assimilate this new information and reformulate her game plan. Then she nodded to herself, opened her eyes and looked across at the man who, until a few seconds ago, had been her suspect.

"No, Isaac. But I think I can. You're free to go. Thank you for your help, I'm sorry to have put you to this inconvenience."

Four

"Daddy always liked Isaac." — Francesca Boyle

Isaac walked through the front door of his house to the sound of his phone chirping for attention. He hurried through to the kitchen and picked up the receiver.

"Hello."

"Isaac? It's Dick."

Dick Boyle. Co-owner of Dakin Boyle. Francesca's father.

"Dick. My god, I... I don't know what to say. I'm... I'm sorry. For your loss. About Francesca..." He tailed off. At twenty eight years of age, Isaac had as yet had little need or opportunity to learn the art of comforting the bereaved.

"I know, Isaac. I know. Hey look, I just called because... Well, I heard what happened — with you and the police, this morning. I just wanted you to know that, well... I never thought for a moment that... that you could have... you know."

Typical Dick, Isaac thought. Even in the midst of coming to terms with the killing of his only child, his first thought was for the feelings of someone else. Isaac felt himself letting out a deep breath as he guiltily acknowledged his relief that Dick harboured no lingering suspicion that maybe — just maybe — he had killed his daughter.

"Jesus, Dick. I can't believe what's happened. You must be... well, I can't even imagine how you must be feeling. I'm so sorry. If there's anything I can do..."

"I know. Thanks. I'm just kinda numb right now. Empty. I don't really know what to do or what to feel. I can't believe... She was just... just..." There was a pause, and then Dick's voice started again — quieter, and with just a hint of tremor. "She was just so full of promise, you know? I was so proud of her, and now..." Dick's voice faded away, the silence on the line filled with the older man's grief and bewilderment.

"Dick, listen. Do you have anyone there with you? Do you need me to come over, or maybe call someone for you? Is there someone there for you, taking care of things?"

"Eh? Oh, yeah. No. Yes, I mean. My brother's here. I rang him as soon as... When the police called and... y'know. He's here now. I'm OK, really I am. I'm fine."

Isaac doubted that. Being fine was not Dick's strong suit, even at the best of times.

"Well OK, if you're sure. Just let me know if there's anything you need, OK? Anything at all."

"Actually, there is one thing. I know that you and Francesca had been, well, close recently. And I just thought... There's no hurry, of course, but..."

Not quite up with the play there Dick, thought Isaac. But there was no need to go into that now. Or ever, in all likelihood, he thought. There would be no point in making Dick's memories of his daughter any more... complicated than they needed to be.

"Just tell me what you need, Dick. Of course I'll do whatever I can."

"It's her stuff, that's all. In her apartment. The police say they've been through and won't need to go back. And I guess the landlord will probably, you know, now that Francesca's..." It would be a while, Isaac guessed, before Dick would be able to bring himself to say that word.

"Well, I was hoping you could go round and sort out her stuff. She didn't have much, I know. Clothes, TV, books, music. I thought maybe you could... perhaps there's a charity that needs that kinda stuff. Honestly, I don't think I could face doing it myself."

The City Mission. Clothes, appliances, books — they'd take it all, find good homes for it all. Isaac had the request all squared away in his mind in less time than it took to answer. "Sure Dick. No problem. Leave it with me, I'll take care of it."

"And if there's... you know, you find one or two things that are a bit — well, perhaps a bit more personal to her, you know? A bit special. Things that I might want to hang on to. I don't know, maybe photos or something."

"Anything like that I'll hang onto, and bring them over. Leave it to me."

"I really appreciate that, Isaac. Really. And that Pharmazeutika upgrade will still need to go ahead of course. Bill will look after that with you from here on, I guess." Bill Dakin, the other half of Dakin Boyle. And, in Isaac's opinion, altogether the more obnoxious half of the duo. "I'm not really... I'll need to..."

Isaac wondered at Dick's ability to think about work at a time like this. He had yet to learn how commonly people will, in the depths of an all-consuming heartache, grasp whatever shards of their old normality they can find for comfort.

"It's OK Dick. I'll work with Bill, and we'll take care of Pharmazeutika. You need to concentrate on... well, you need to concentrate on taking care of Francesca."

Taking care of Francesca. Isaac pondered the ease with which he had slipped into the euphemisms that skirt around the reality of death. Francesca was beyond the need for any care. It was Dick who needed taking care of, who needed to grieve for his daughter, to come to terms with her having been wrenched from the world. And to bury her — once the forensic examiners have finished picking over her remains for clues, Isaac thought to himself.

"Of course. Thanks, Isaac. I really do appreciate that. And I'm sorry about the police thing. I don't know how they could ever think that."

"They're just doing their job, I guess. Call me if there's anything else you need, OK?"

"Will do. Thanks, Isaac."

"Goodbye, Dick."

Isaac hung up the phone. He stood for a moment, propped against the kitchen unit, trying to summon up some sense of what Dick Boyle must be feeling. But it was, he realised, far beyond anything his experience had equipped him to imagine.

There was a knock at the front door.

Startled back from his thoughts, Isaac walked through to the front of the house and opened the door.

"Inspector Troy. Long time no see," he said with forced irony. He felt his nerves tighten as he wondered whether he was about to be re-arrested.

She smiled up at him — a friendly, non-threatening, not-here-to-arrest-anyone kind of smile. "Call me Bailey, please. Only my constables get to call me Inspector. I thought I should return this." She held up a clear plastic evidence bag, the distinctively angular outline of a Glock semi-automatic pistol clearly visible within.

"My gun." He took the bag, opened it, took out the gun, and pulled back the slide to confirm that it was unloaded. "Shouldn't there be some kind of paperwork involved before I get it back? Forms to fill in or something?"

"Yes, there should. It'll catch up sooner or later, I'm sure. May I come in?" she nodded at the handgun. "You should probably put that away."

So he wasn't being arrested, he thought. It was just a somewhat improbable courtesy call from an enigmatic — and, Isaac noted approvingly, far from unattractive — police inspector with a *laissez-faire* attitude to procedure. Well, being enigmatic, attractive, and *laissez-faire* will get you a fair way with Isaac Church, he admitted to himself; even at times such as this. Probably quite a shallow reaction on his part, all things considered, he reflected. But he decided to play along anyway.

"You're right," he said, holding up the gun. "I should stash this in the safe." He stepped back from the door and gestured towards the back of the house. "The lounge is along there, make yourself comfortable. I won't be long."

He left her to make the short walk to the lounge while he took the gun to the study. Once there he opened the cupboard door, knelt down and punched the combination into the small gun safe hidden in the bottom left corner, opened the door, tossed the gun inside, and closed up.

As he walked back to the lounge, he wondered whether he would find the Inspector leafing through his mail looking for clues. Instead, he found her sitting patiently and apparently incurious on the sofa.

"Can I get you something? Coffee?"

"I've got a better idea," she replied, coming effortlessly to her feet. "How about I buy *you* a coffee? Café sur la Colline? I've a vague recollection that I may have caused you to leave your last coffee there unfinished."

She had indeed. And that was barely five hours ago, he mused. Just three hundred minutes since his easy going weekend had been submerged in the grizzly murder of a beautiful young woman who, he grudgingly admitted to himself, he had been quite fond of. This morning seemed a long, long time ago.

And here he was now, at home offering his hospitality to Detective Inspector Troy. Or Bailey to her friends — among whom, it would appear, he now numbered. This woman who, in one short morning, flirted with him, arrested him, accused him of murder and was now offering to buy him coffee.

In amongst all the emotions of this extraordinary day — the shock of Francesca's death, the (admittedly fading) indignation at his arrest, his concern for Dick — Isaac found he still had room to start developing something of a fascination with the intriguing police inspector. Not, he reflected briefly, the most empathic and mature state of mind to be in, given the day's events. But he was young, single, and a guy; it was what it was.

She looked at him impatiently. "Well? Coffee? My treat? Café sur la Colline? Nod for yes, shake for no."

As he contemplated the idea of some time in Bailey's company, he felt his mood lift. Plus one for shallowness, he thought to himself. "Sure. Why not. Let's go. But just a coffee's not going to cut it, I'm afraid. False arrest gets you shelling out for dinner too. It's a bit early, but I'm sure they'll be able to serve us something."

She conceded to the request with a smile. "Yeah, OK. Fair enough. Come on then." She got up and headed to the front door. Isaac followed along behind.

As they stepped out into the late afternoon sun, Isaac asked, "shall we take my car?"

"That's probably not a good idea," she replied. "I think you've been in enough trouble with the law for one day, don't you?"

"Eh?"

She pointed at the Mazda on the driveway. "Take a look."

"OK. I see my car. What am I looking for?"

"Not from there. Come round and look at the back."

Puzzled, Isaac stepped out onto the road and looked back at the rear of his car.

"The plates are missing," he said, with a slightly embarrassed sense of stating the obvious. "How did that happen?"

"I'll hazard a guess that somebody stole them," Bailey replied.

"Who?"

"If I knew that, I'd be off handcuffing them now for the murder of Francesca Boyle. But I don't, so I'm buying you dinner instead. I think we'd better take my car." She nodded in the direction of a late model Prius parked across the street.

The indicators flashed, the doors thunked themselves unlocked, and they climbed into the Prius. As Bailey drove away, Isaac pondered the significance of the missing plates. His awareness of his surroundings became indistinct as his mind slipped into problem solving. Problem solving was what he did well. Problem solving was how he earned his living.

"You think whoever stole my plates murdered Francesca."

"Yep."

OK, he thought, so what's the connection?

"Someone stole my plates, fitted them on another Mazda 3 — same model, same colour — which they drove to Dakin Boyle. Then they shot Francesca."

"Pretty good. And they ran a red light. Don't forget that."

They pulled up outside the café. The ride was over almost as soon as it had begun, and Isaac realised that this was the first time he had ever driven there. They crunched their way across the small gravel car park and went inside — where they were greeted by the same waitress who had served them both this morning. The same waitress who had looked on in bewilderment just a few hours previously as Bailey had led Isaac out of the café in handcuffs. She showed them to an unoccupied empty table for two, in silence and with a facial expression that shouted "whatever!"

Bailey offered Isaac the wine list. "Drink?"

Without taking the list, he turned to the bemused waitress. "Heineken, please." She nodded and turned to Bailey.

Isaac watched as Bailey ran her finger down the Merlots on the list. He knew from memory what she would find there: Backstone, Penfolds, Casa Lapostolle, Alpha Domus. A good but unpretentious selection. She nodded in silent approval. "A glass of the Alpha Domus Merlot. Thanks."

"Sure. I'll be right back." The youngster turned and headed towards the bar.

Isaac picked up his menu and started reading. Bailey did the same. "The steak is always good," he offered.

"I can't eat steak, I'm vegetarian," she replied. "I might have the chicken."

Isaac suppressed a surprised laugh. "Chicken, right. Good choice for a vegetarian."

"Yeah, yeah. I'm a vegetarian except for chicken, OK? I like chicken."

"OK. Vegetarian except for chicken. Got it."

"And fish. I like fish too."

"Right. Vegetarian except for chicken and fish. No problem." As female irrationalities went this was, in Isaac's experience, pretty low on the scale. "If you don't mind me asking, what made you choose to become vegetarian?"

"I guess I don't really approve of killing animals."

"Except for chicken and fish."

"No, I don't really approve of killing them either. But I do enjoy the taste."

"And that contradiction doesn't worry you, at all?"

"No, I'm good with it. You?"

"Hey, if it works for you then it works for me."

The waitress returned with their drinks. "Would you like to hear the specials?"

"No, thank you," Isaac replied. "I think we're ready to order."

"I'll have the chicken," said Bailey.

"And I'll have the fish," said Isaac. "We're vegetarian, you see."

The teenager's polite smile told Isaac that the comment wasn't nearly as funny as he had thought it was going to be. She scribbled down the orders. "Your meals will be out shortly," she said, with scrupulous indifference.

Isaac caught his companion's eye and raised his glass in an unspoken toast to nothing in particular. She did likewise. They chinked their glasses gently together and sipped before she broke eye contact and looked away with a smile.

Isaac let the moment linger, until his curiosity reasserted itself and his mind slipped back into problem solving mode.

"Why would someone do that? Steal my plates, I mean."

"And run a red light, don't forget."

So it's a test, he realised. She knew the answer, and he was expected to work it out.

"OK, so someone runs a red light on their way from a murder. That's understandable, he would want to get away pretty quickly, I imagine."

"Except he didn't. Or she didn't. Women can be killers too, you know."

"Didn't what?"

"Run a red light getting away from a murder."

"What do you mean? You've got the photo."

"You're a bright guy. Work it out."

She was still playing with him. But that was OK, he though. He was kind of enjoying it. Isaac let his mind go blank, and mentally separated what he knew from what he'd just thought he knew.

"The photo was taken on the way *to* the murder."

"You got it."

"So the killer was anxious to get there and get it done, and got careless."

"Then why did he — or she — steal your plates? I'll give you another clue. The camera records how long the lights have been red when it snaps the car. Take a guess how long these lights had been red when our killer decides to jump them."

"No. Go on."

"Five seconds."

"So?"

"Count it out. Five seconds is a long time to be approaching a red light and not realise."

"So…" as he started the sentence all the pieces fell into place. "The killer steals my plates then *deliberately* jumps the lights, knowing that there's a red light camera there. Leaving evidence of my car heading towards the scene of the murder."

"Full marks!" Bailey raised her glass in salute.

Isaac felt a mild tingle of elation at having solved this part of the puzzle. Then he remembered that what they were discussing was the murder of Francesca. Someone was dead, and someone else had gone to a lot of trouble to try to make sure that he took the blame for it.

But that part of their plan hadn't worked. Maybe they had a plan-B. If they did then, whatever it was, it was unlikely to have anything good in store for him.

All of a sudden, it wasn't such a good feeling.

"It sounds like quite a professional piece of work," he said quietly.

"Well, yes and no," she replied. "Pretty sloppy in the detail."

"How so?"

"Think about it. Where did it go wrong? What should they have done to make sure you stayed on the hook?"

Now that she had asked the question, the answer came to him easily. "They should've put the plates back. That was the note you got during the interview, wasn't it? Your guys had found my car with no plates. If they hadn't found that, then I'd still be locked up."

"That was part of it, yes."

"Which reminds me — you searched my house?"

"The team did, yes. We had a warrant. Do you want to see it?"

"I'll take your word for it. How did you get in to the gun safe? How did you know the combination?"

"We didn't need the combination, we just needed the key. You know, the one you keep in among all the other keys in the kitchen drawer."

"Oh yeah. Right. Very clever."

"We do this kind of thing a lot," she replied with a mock reassuring sincerity.

"Are you always so tidy when you execute search warrants? I was expecting to come home to find the place trashed."

"Ordinarily you would have done, but I felt sorry for you. I sent Finlayson round ahead of you to tidy up. That's why the desk sergeant was so tardy in getting you a cab — Inspector's orders. You should expect to find things in unusual places for the next few days, I'm afraid."

"Now that you mention it, the place did look spookily tidy. Your constable clearly has a talent. But," he shrugged, "domestic chores, who needs 'em. He would have loved the assignment, I'm sure."

"I hope not."

Their meals arrived, delivered by the poker-faced waitress. She enquired as to the state of their drinks and, having been assured that what they had was still sufficient, left.

There was a loose end somewhere. Isaac struggled briefly to recall it as they both took their first mouthfuls.

"What else was there? You said that not replacing the plates was only part of it. What else did the killer overlook."

"The bullet cases. Remember I mentioned them in the interview?"

"Yes."

"They were nine millimetre. You own a nine millimetre. We thought the cases were from your gun, but they weren't."

"I know they weren't."

"No, you're missing the point. I knew they weren't, this morning when I let you go. They couldn't have been." She took a mouthful of chicken.

"You got the results back from the lab?"

"I wish! No. Lab results take much longer. Goff spotted it. Those shells weren't fired from a Glock, couldn't have been."

The obvious question started to form in Isaac's mind. But this was a subject that he knew. He pondered briefly, and made a guess. "The striker indentation on the primer."

Each make of gun, he knew, made a slightly differently shaped indentation on the primer at the base of the bullet when it fired. And Glocks made a quite distinctive rectangular indentation.

"Got it in one! The primers on the casings recovered from the scene had circular indentations — they couldn't have come from a Glock."

"Your guy Goff spotted that? He'll go far."

"He did better than that. Both indentations were round, but one was noticeably larger than the other. They were shot from different guns."

"So two killers?"

"Well, two guns at least. But probably two killers, yes."

Not jumping to conclusions — Isaac was impressed. He was liking this Inspector Troy call-me-Bailey more and more. Then he remembered again that the only reason they were talking was because Francesca was dead and somebody, somewhere, had been trying to frame him for it. He concentrated on scooping up some fish as he let his emotions return to an even keel.

"But wouldn't the whole frame-up have come unravelled sooner or later anyway, when the lab results came back showing that the casings hadn't come from my gun."

"Yep. As I said before, pretty sloppy in the detail. What should the killer have done differently there?"

Easy. "He should have followed me to the range one day, picked up a handful of my spent cases. Scooped up his own brass after shooting Francesca, and left mine behind."

She smiled. "You, if I may say so Isaac Church, are a criminal mastermind. If the killer had been as bright as you are, then you'd be in a lot of trouble right now."

"But what about the bullet itself?" he asked. "The tests would show that it didn't match the gun, surely?"

"The bullet smashed through a lot of bone" — as she said the words, Isaac shuddered inwardly at the image that they conjured up — "and then slammed into a brick wall. It'll be pretty thoroughly beaten out of shape. I'm guessing any results on the bullet itself will be inconclusive. And we haven't found the second bullet at all yet. I wouldn't count on anything there getting you off the hook."

"So, with a little more thought the killer could well have succeeded in setting me up for this?" Not a nice thought.

"Probably, yes," she agreed. "But still," she raised her glass, "here's to criminals being not-so-bright." He raised his glass in reply, and they both sipped and reflected.

They grazed quietly on their meals for a few minutes. Then Bailey looked up.

"Tell me a bit about Francesca. And about Dakin Boyle."

"OK. Pick one."

"Francesca first. What can you tell me about her?"

"She's... she was... lovely; fun to be around. She'd just finished her journalism degree, and was making a bit of loose change doing some admin work at her dad's firm while she looked for the perfect first career step."

"And you and she were...?"

"An item for a while. But not for the last week."

"Why? What happened?"

"You're asking me? I'm the guy, how am I supposed to know? All fine and dandy one day, all cold and prickly the next." He shrugged. " It happens, I'm over it."

"No you're not."

"Eh? Well OK. So I liked her. I'd have been happier if she hadn't dumped me. And I'd certainly have been much, much happier if she wasn't dead. So no, perhaps I'm not over it. But it wasn't serious. It was just fun. She was very... well, never mind that."

"No. Please — go on. It could be helpful."

As he tried to frame his answer, Isaac realised that there was really only one aspect of Francesca's life that he was properly qualified to comment on. He smiled to himself and started thinking out loud. "Well, she certainly wasn't shy in bed." Nor, he continued to himself, was she shy in the shower, or on the dining table, or on the damp grass under the stars in Grenville Park...

"You were saying..." the Inspector's interjection snapped Isaac back to the here and now.

"Oh. Yes, sorry. Well, it was just that, I don't know, she seemed quite determined that the relationship was going to be all about the sex. As if she had a tick list of every position, every location, every kink, and she wanted to try them all. Was in a rush, even. Some kind of sexual bucket list."

"It must have been terrible for you," Bailey replied, deadpan.

"I coped," he replied, refusing to take the bait. "But it was just a bit unusual. When we did talk it was about work, stuff that was already common ground. We were together for three weeks, and I'm pretty sure I didn't learn anything new about her in that whole time."

Bailey shrugged. "Everyone's different. And I don't see much of a motive for murder, there. Is there *anything* else you tell me about her?"

Isaac looked down at the remains of his meal as he tried to frame his next observation. He had the feeling he wasn't presenting Francesca in such a good light — not what he wanted to convey.

"Well, she wasn't afraid of moving on, after ending a relationship, if you get my meaning."

"Meaning what, exactly?"

Isaac paused before continuing. "Before we were together, she was seeing Gus Dakin."

"Gus Dakin? As in *Dakin* Boyle?"

"Gus is Bill Dakin's son — Bill started Dakin Boyle with Francesca's father."

"And she was seeing Gus before the two of you got together?"

"Yeah. Actually, there may have been a bit of an overlap."

"Nice."

"I wasn't particularly inclined to feel guilty about it. Gus is just like his Dad, an eighteen carat bastard. She was well rid of him."

"He treated her badly?"

"He didn't get the chance. As soon as he started easing off the charm and reverting to form, she dropped him like a hot potato."

"How did he react to that?"

"The same way he responds to everyone he doesn't like — like a complete prick. He went out of his way to try to make life impossible for both Francesca and me at Dakin Boyle. If Francesca's father hadn't been who he was, and if I didn't know Dick so well, he could well have succeeded."

"Sounds like he deserved to be dumped. What about you, did you deserve to be dumped?"

He looked across at her. She was smiling — teasing him.

"Well, she obviously thought so. But, as I've said, I've no idea why she dumped me. I thought we were doing quite well."

"Did she... Were you... overlapped, with anyone at all?"

Isaac smiled grimly and looked away. "I don't know." He did know, perfectly well. "But you might want to talk to Russell Bridgeman. I think he and she might have had a thing going."

"Russell Bridgeman, who's he?"

"He's the plant manager. I wouldn't have picked him as being Francesca's type. But you live and learn, I guess."

"You don't like him?"

"He's Bill Dakin's man. Bill decides what needs doing, and Russell makes it happen. So a bit of the Dakin shit rubs off on him, by association. But he's OK, I supposed. Just a bit... unsophisticated. I'm surprised Francesca saw anything in him." Even as he said it, Isaac knew it sounded lame.

The waitress came over to clear away their empty plates. "Would you like to see the dessert menu?"

Bailey raised an eyebrow at Isaac, giving him the option. "No, thank you," he replied. The waitress turned and left.

"Tell me about Dakin Boyle itself."

"What do you want to know?"

"Well, I've read the headlines, of course. Biotech success story. Wonder cancer-drug. Millions in profits. Give me more detail."

"What you've got is about it. Over five hundred million dollars in revenue every year. A private company, so it doesn't publish profit numbers. But pharmaceuticals is a high margin business; you can bet that a substantial portion of that half a billion goes straight to the bottom line. And it all goes into the pockets of the two owners, Dick Boyle and Bill Dakin. Dick's the oncology genius who came up with the cancer cure. Bill's the commercial mastermind who turned it into a massive money fountain. The company does some generics as well, though I've no idea why — the money's in the cancer drugs."

"Why do you need a commercial genius to turn a cancer cure into money? I'd have thought the world would beat a path to your door."

"The drug only treats one type of cancer. And there's a lot of crap to wade through in actually getting a product out — regulatory approvals, manufacturing, distribution. That's all the stuff that Bill takes care of. The regulatory approvals were a hell of a mission apparently. Pushing them through was Dakin's big contribution to getting the company to the point of making money."

"But it's made them both stinking rich. At least if you believe the headlines."

"Oh, it's made them rich all right. Rich, but not happy. Bill is just completely cheerless, doesn't have a happy bone in his body — I'm glad his money makes him miserable. But Dick's a nice guy."

"What makes him miserable? Dick, I mean."

"He's never been the same since his wife died, apparently. Francesca's mother. Just as they were getting Dakin Boyle off the ground, I gather. Died of cancer, ironically enough. Dick's struggled with depression on and off ever since."

"How long ago was that?"

"Since she died? I'm not sure, it was before my time. Ten years, maybe."

Bailey drummed her fingers together thoughtfully. "Money," she said. "Where there's money, there's a motive for murder. Come on, I'll give you a lift home."

She settled the bill, and they headed out to the car.

"What kind of cancer?" She asked, as they climbed in to the Prius.

"Which — the cure, or Francesca's mother?"

"The cure, the wonder drug."

"Merkel cell carcinoma."

"Never heard of it."

"It's pretty rare, apparently. Some kind of skin cancer. I don't know the details — not my kind of science. You should talk to Jenny, if you're interested in the detail. She can tell you all about it."

"Jenny?"

"Jenny Watson. She's the chief technologist. She lives and breathes that stuff. And Francesca was basically working for Jenny, so you should talk to her if you're interested in what Francesca was doing there."

"I might just do that. Here's your place now." She brought the car to a halt outside his house.

Isaac paused briefly to weigh his options. He looked at Bailey — smiling, looking straight ahead, waiting for his move.

Well, he reflected to himself, once you've given yourself permission to be inexcusably shallow, you might as well reap the benefit.

"Would you… like to come in?"

Bailey chuckled and turned to look at him. Her amusement was kindly, but left Isaac with the distinct impression that he wasn't in on the joke. She shook her head without losing eye contact. "I'm afraid you're out of luck tonight, young Isaac. But I like your style. Now go and watch some more Star Trek."

As Isaac stood on his driveway watching Bailey's Prius disappear into the distance, he wondered to himself: was that a "no", or just a "not yet, keep trying"?

Five

"People laughed at me for redecorating a rental. But, y'know, it's only money" — Francesca Boyle

Isaac awoke at 10:30am. Late for him, even on a Sunday morning, but it had been a restless and largely sleepless night.

He got up, showered, dressed, and headed down to the kitchen. It took barely five minutes for Isaac to assemble his breakfast — coffee, juice, and a bowl containing the last remnants from the cornflakes packet. He poured milk into the bowl and started eating, idly reading the milk label as he did so. The "use by" date was two days ago. He pondered the significance of this, and decided there was none — it was still clearly milk, not yoghurt, so he would keep using it. As if to emphasise the point to himself, he poured another dash of milk into his coffee.

As he munched on his cornflakes, Isaac wondered how he would spend his day. Ordinarily, his Sunday mornings were spent out at the gun club. But the weekly club match would be starting about now, and he was in no mood to hurry. There were plenty of things he could make himself busy with — as in most bachelor pads, there was a comprehensive backlog of chores to be tackled — but he discarded the option of housework with barely a thought. He had enough food and clean underwear to last for a few more days yet, so he saw no reason to waste his day on domesticity.

His mind was, in any case, consumed with the events of the previous thirty six hours — the horror of Francesca's murder, the grief of her father, and his introduction to the somewhat stimulating Inspector Troy. He lingered over his coffee, allowing his thoughts to wander freely across the uneven and contrasting terrain of these three topics.

He recalled his promise to Dick and, as he drained the last of his coffee, decided to make a start on clearing out Francesca's apartment. The City Mission Op Shop wouldn't be open on a Sunday, and he didn't want to risk driving his car with no plates, but he could walk over to her place and start sorting things out. He clattered his breakfast crockery into the sink, and went back to the bedroom in search of a jacket and shoes.

Having attired himself for the outdoors, he set off for Francesca's apartment. It was a three mile drive, but just a little over thirty minutes' walk if he cut across Grenville Park and climbed over her back fence. It had rained overnight again, although morning had brought clear skies, and the air felt clean in the mid-morning sun.

As he walked, he thought through the minutiae of his mission. He would need cardboard boxes — the supermarket would have plenty that they would let him take, he guessed. He'd need tape too, he could buy that at the supermarket while he was there. There were some books and CDs of Francesca's that he would like to hang onto for himself, and he wondered whether he should ask Dick if it was OK to take them. But he knew what the answer would be, of course — he would just keep them and make a donation at the Op Shop to cover the money it would have made from selling them.

He reached Grenville Park and started walking across the turf. The ground was soft underfoot from the night's rain, but not muddy. The direct route across the park was blocked by a kids' Sunday morning soccer match, which was being observed from the sidelines with slightly forced enthusiasm by a sprinkling of parents. He watched the game as he walked around the edge of the park. The players were young — five or six years old at most — and it appeared that notions of tactics and positional play were, at that young age, beyond them. The soccer ball twitched around the field in a kind of drifting Brownian motion, the teams streamed out behind it in a single elongated swarm as each player focussed on their own attempt to reach the ball and kick it in the direction of the opposition goal. Next to his own concerns, the game seemed inaccessibly mundane.

He reached the wire-linked fence that marked the edge of the property that included Francesca's apartment. The fence was about six feet high, but he was able to scramble over it with no more than a moderate loss of dignity. His entry on to the property was, in any case, witnessed only by the elderly widow — Agnes, he thought her names was — to whom Francesca had introduced him ten days or so ago and who observed him now from the kitchen of her ground floor apartment. He waved at her casually, and she gave an uncertain and disapproving nod in return.

It was a three-storey building, with Francesca's apartment making up the middle floor. There were steps leading up to a small balcony outside the back door of her apartment. Isaac took the steps up two at a time, then reached up to retrieve the spare key from its hiding place in the hanging flower basket that swayed lightly just above head height. As he unlocked the back door, he recalled fondly the one and only other time he'd had occasion to use that key — under instructions from Francesca to let himself in and make himself comfortable ahead of her arriving home for a long and vigorous night together.

As he stepped into the kitchen, he realised that his promise to clear out the apartment was a bigger commitment than he had thought. Dick had indulged his daughter with a substantial allowance, which had provided Francesca with the means to equip her home comprehensively and expensively. The kitchen reflected both Francesca's elegant taste and her access to ample funds. The fittings were a slightly creamy white, edged with brushed chrome. Halogen lights spotted the ceiling. The sink, oven, hob and hood were all Smeg, top of the line. Francesca's landlord would barely have been able to believe his luck, Isaac reflected, when he found out that Francesca wanted to put all these fixtures in.

The rear of the bench top was populated with an array of matching appliances — microwave, juicer, coffee maker, toaster, kettle. Behind the shutters of the wall mounted cupboards, Isaac knew that he would find plain white crockery stacked in abundance. It would take an hour just to box up the crockery and kitchen utensils, he guessed. And he would need to add a stack of old newspapers to his shopping list, to pack the breakables safely.

Isaac walked from the kitchen through into the lounge, and surveyed its contents. The contrast with his own lounge was striking. Where his living room was centred around a large wide-screen TV and conspicuously complex music system, this was a room designed for socialising. The elegant Lucerne sofa and chairs of the lounge suite were organised in a circle. One wall was dominated by a lengthy hardwood bookcase, the books neatly organised so that the spines lined up with the edges of the shelves.

It would, he reflected unhappily, take a lot of packing and a lot of heavy lifting to empty this apartment.

His mobile phone chirped in his pocket. Isaac took it out and examined the callerID number on the screen — it wasn't one he recognised. With a shrug, he pressed the answer button with his thumb and lifted the phone to his ear.

"Hello."

"Isaac?"

He recognised the voice immediately. "Inspector Troy! How are you this morning?"

"I'm fine. But I thought we were on first name terms. I'm just checking, are you at Francesca's apartment right now?"

"I am, as it happens. How did you know that? And how did you get this number?"

"That's OK then; though you shouldn't really be there — it's still officially a scene of interest to the police."

"Why's that?"

"My prime suspect managed to wriggle off the hook. Don't you remember? So we're kinda back to square one. Francesca's apartment might still provide us with useful information about her killer. What are you doing there, anyway?"

"Someone told Dick — Francesca's father, that is — that the police had finished here. I promised Dick I'd sort out Francesca's gear."

"That would have been Finlayson, I bet. God, that man's hopeless. Just don't touch anything, OK. I'll be there soon. I just have a quick errand to run."

"Sure, no problem. You still haven't told me how you got this number." Isaac had no objection to the inspector having his phone number — far from it — but he was quite interested to know what had motivated her to unearth it.

"From the phone company. They're pretty good with us about that sort of thing. And I like to make a point of having my suspects on speed-dial." There was that flirtatiously mocking tone again. Isaac smiled as he imagined her raising her eyebrows as she said it. "Have you moved anything? Did you start packing?"

"No, apart from a couple of door handles, I haven't even touched anything as far as I can remember. It's going to be quite a job clearing it out though, she's got — she had — quite a bit of stuff."

"I don't imagine the father will be much interested in trying to sell it off — he doesn't exactly need the money. Just give the address to the City Mission. They'll send round a couple of guys with a truck and take it all away. They do that kind of thing — deceased estates — all the time."

That, thought Isaac, was a much better plan than his.

"How did you know I was here, anyway? In her apartment."

"I've just driven past, and saw you were there."

"You saw me through a window?"

"No. I saw your car outside."

"But my car isn't outside. My car's at home. I walked over here."

There was silence at the end of the phone. One second. Two. Then: "Isaac, listen to me. You need to get out of the apartment. Now."

"What? Why? What's going on?"

"Don't argue. No questions. Just get out of there."

"But..."

"Now, Isaac! For God's sake, just *get out of the fucking apartment!*"

"Okay, okay. I'm going."

He stabbed the button to end the call, and turned to head back to the kitchen.

The man in the doorway was muscular and mean. His scarred and bitter face was centred around a nose that had been broken too many times. Isaac felt a rush of adrenaline send his heart pounding, his limbs quivering and his abdomen tightening. Then, though he didn't see it coming, he felt a fist slamming like a freight train into the right side of his face.

After that, he saw and felt nothing.

Six

"I don't know why I kept all that Uni stuff. I guess I'm just a hoarder." — Francesca Boyle

Bailey stabbed at the end-call button on the phone in the cradle, cursed her own stupidity and swung the Prius round in a tight U-turn. It was a manoeuvre that the car was unaccustomed to — the tyres screeched, the car body swayed unsteadily, and the traction control light blinked angrily in protest at the undignified handling. Bailey stabbed again at the phone — fast-dial, button number 2 — and called in for backup, possible armed offender with hostage. The unflappable dispatcher on the other end of the line promised four general duties cars immediately, and a tactical squad within twenty minutes.

It took Bailey barely a minute to get back to Francesca's apartment, but there were two patrol cars already there. Each one was set back fifty yards either side the apartment and sprawled untidily across the road in the manner much loved, it seemed to Bailey, by young officers who have watched too many Hollywood cop movies. In spite of the urgency, Bailey consciously decided to park the Prius carefully against the kerb.

As she got out of the car, she was unsurprised to see one of two young uniformed constables running towards her in a crouch, as if expecting to come under fire any second. She held out her ID as he stopped in front of her — flushed, slightly out of breath and obviously excited.

He glanced at the ID and very nearly, it seemed to Bailey, snapped to attention. "We've established an initial perimeter at the front, and there are two cars approaching across the park to the rear of the property, ma'am. Tactical are fifteen minutes away." Bailey smiled briefly at the thought of the patrol cars bouncing their way gracelessly across the soccer field behind the apartment building. Then she looked up the road towards the apartment.

The Mazda was gone.

She looked back at the young officer. "Was there any sign of a blue Mazda 3 when you arrived?" They should, in any case, have been looking out for a Mazda with Isaac's plates; they would have been briefed at the start of their shift that it was "of interest" in relation to Francesca's killing. But there was always plenty to try to remember from a shift briefing, and it would doubtless all have been forgotten in the excitement of a call to a possible armed hostage situation.

"The one from the Dakin Boyle murder? No, ma'am. We've only seen two Mazda 3s all morning, and the plates didn't match either time. And none near here."

Bailey noted the name on the officer's name badge — Rayner. Pretty switched on for a young guy, she thought to herself. She made a mental note to put a good word in with the duty sergeant.

No Mazda meant no suspect. But what about Isaac? She took out her phone and rang his number. It rang four times. Five. "Hi, you've reached the voice-mail of Isaac Ch..." She punched the end-call button. She ran through the possibilities in her head. Incapacitated, separated from his phone somehow, or under threat. But which?

The protocol in this situation was clear and unambiguous: wait for the tactical squad, go door-to-door evacuating anyone who could be in the line of fire, let the tactical guys go in and secure the apartment. All to protect against the threat of an offender who was, Bailey knew, long gone.

And in the meantime, she thought, Isaac could be in the apartment, injured or worse. To hell with the protocol.

"OK, Rayner, here's what we're going to do. You're going to radio in and call off the tactical squad and the cars around the back — we won't need them. Me and your partner — what's his name?"

"Lorne, ma'am."

"OK. Lorne and I will go and check the apartment."

"But ma'am…"

That's the trouble with young smart cops, Bailey thought — too many exams and not enough experience. Clever enough to have memorised the protocol, not enough years on the job to know when they can and should ignore it. She gave Rayner her best don't-argue-with-me look and then turned to his partner, who was still standing over by the patrol car.

"Lorne! With me!" she shouted, and strode off towards Francesca's apartment. Out of the corner of her eye, she saw the two officers exchange uncertain glances before Lorne started trotting after her.

The front entrance was, like the rear, accessed via a short but wide set of steps up. Bailey took the steps two at a time, with Lorne behind her struggling to keep up. She found the front door ajar and stepped through it into a hallway that seemed gloomy after the bright morning sun outside.

The hallway was about five yards long. Immediately to Bailey's left was an elegant hardwood coat rack. The rack had five pegs, but was home to only one coat — a black, mid-length, Burberry trench coat. There were three doorways on the right and one, at the far end of the hallway, on the left.

Bailey moved quickly to the first door on the right. A bedroom. It was well appointed and decorated in pastel colours. Lace-trimmed linens adorned a made-up queen sized bed. Everything was tidy, nothing was out of place. There was a faint aroma that Bailey recognised as Christian Dior Addict Eau Fraiche. There was no Isaac. She moved on to the second door. The bathroom — tiled, spotless. The many accoutrements essential to any young and single female were aligned tidily on glass shelves beside the vanity unit. Again, no Isaac.

Bailey moved quickly to the last door on the right. A home-office. The contrast with the other rooms was striking. Like all the rooms so far, it was well appointed. A large Apple-branded wide screen monitor dominated the workspace of the hardwood desk that comprised the only furniture in the room. But the room was far from tidy — papers were strewn all across the desk and over the floor, box files lay upended and empty. The room had been trashed.

But still no Isaac.

Bailey turned and stepped through the only doorway in the left wall of the hallway, into the lounge. In the middle of the room was sprawled a body, its right leg hooked untidily up on the sofa. Bailey stepped forward and saw that it was Isaac Church. As she knelt beside him, he began to stir.

She turned to Lorne. "Ambulance," she barked, then turned her attention back to Isaac as the officer stepped out into the hallway and started talking into the radio microphone hanging from his lapel. There was, she knew, an ambulance station barely half a mile away over on Great West Road. With a bit of luck, paramedics would be here in barely a minute. Isaac opened his eyes and tried to raise his head.

"Isaac, it's me — Bailey. Don't try to move, just lie still." She reinforced the instruction by pressing down firmly on his shoulder, and caught his head in her other hand as he gave up the attempt to raise himself. The right side of his face was heavily bruised, his right eyelid swollen closed. She scanned his body for any other sign of harm, examined the floor for any creeping bloodstain that might signify a gaping exit wound from a gunshot, but saw nothing to indicate any further injury.

"Isaac, can you hear me?"

"Wha…?" His good eye was open but unfocussed, his gaze wandered aimlessly.

"Isaac, listen to me. Do you know where you are?"

"I ah… yeah. Yeah, I…" His one-eyed gazed roamed the room, searching in vain for Bailey as she kneeled beside him.

Concussion, Bailey thought. Maybe worse. She heard the wailing siren of the ambulance in the distance. "It's OK, Isaac. Just take it easy."

"It's… I'm… I think I… Francesca?" His one good eye was still hunting randomly and in vain for anything to make sense of.

"It's Bailey, Isaac." She knew better than to try to impose too much reality on a concussion victim. "You look like you've had a knock to the head. The ambulance will be here soon, the paramedics will take care of you."

"Ambulance? No, I'm fine, really. I just…" Isaac tried weakly to lift himself up on his elbows, but was again defeated by the gentle pressure that Bailey exerted on his shoulder.

"Don't try to get up, Isaac. Just relax until the ambulance gets here." He nodded weakly and closed his eyes.

Isaac lay that way for around thirty seconds — eyes closed, breathing slowly and evenly. Then he opened his one good eye and looked directly at Bailey with what she thought might be a flicker of recognition. "Can you remember what happened?" she asked. It was a long shot, she knew, she doubted if he could even remember his own name.

"I was… here. I was going to… I was going to do something for Francesca. Where's Francesca? Is she here?"

She heard the ambulance arrive, and the paramedics clattering their way into the apartment. As she stood up she saw Constable Lorne gesturing the leading paramedic — a stocky, no-nonsense woman of about Bailey's age — into the lounge.

The woman brushed past Bailey with barely a glance and knelt beside her patient. "What have we got here?" The question was loud enough to be obviously directed at Bailey, though the paramedic's attention never wavered from Isaac.

"His name is Isaac Church. We found him," Bailey glanced at her watch, "eleven minutes ago, at 12:13. He was unconscious initially, but became responsive after a few seconds. Responsive but not coherent since then. Apart from the bruising on his face, I didn't find any other sign of injury. I have reason to believe he has been attacked by an intruder."

The second paramedic, a young wiry guy with a face still carrying the remains of adolescent acne, stood in the hallway and diligently wrote in his notebook as Bailey spoke. Once she had finished, he flipped his notebook closed with a flourish. "Leave him to us, he'll be fine," he said with a tone of authority that, to Bailey's ears, sounded laughably bogus. Not enough experience yet, she reflected, to have experienced that cavalier "he'll be fine" promise coming back to bite him in the backside.

Bailey stepped out into the hallway and took another look into the study. Whatever it was the intruder was looking for, they clearly expected to find it in there.

Without stepping into the room — if there was going to be any forensic evidence, then chances were it would be in this room — she crouched down to get a better look at the paperwork strewn across the floor.

About two feet away, Bailey could see a ring binder lying open. Inside was a stack of A4 sheets containing handwritten notes. The handwriting was distinctly feminine, with a neat and looping cursive style, though with a hint of having been rushed. "Gutnick v Dow Jones — o/seas Internet sites still accountable for libel," read the first line of the topmost page, and continued on in the same truncated English. It was a style of writing that Bailey recognised immediately as lecture notes.

A few inches beyond the ring binder was an empty box folder. About a foot beyond that began a small but untidy sprawl of documents that looked, to Bailey's eye, as if they had all been tipped from a single source. From where Bailey crouched, they all looked similar — photocopies of invoices. Bailey couldn't make out the name of the company, but on the four sheets where it was visible the company logo was the same.

The shelves on the far wall were still approximately half filled. Bailey stood up to examine their contents, still careful not to step into the room. The highest of the three shelves was populated with ring binders, with topics neatly printed on each spine — "News/media procedures", "PR mgmt", "Lang & Comm", "News gathering Fundamentals", "Intro to Bus Communications", and a dozen more abbreviated titles. Course notes from Francesca's journalism degree, Bailey guessed.

The middle shelf contained a row of textbooks, and appeared to be undisturbed. Whatever the intruder was looking for, Bailey surmised, it wasn't academic enlightenment. A few of the authors caught her eye. John Pilger's name she recognised, but the book itself — "Tell Me No Lies" — wasn't one she had heard of. Eleanor Mills was another familiar name, although Bailey suspected that the author of "Cupcakes and Kalashnikovs" was not the same woman as the one murdered in the "Hall–Mills murders" case-study that she vaguely recalled from her studies for her Postgraduate Diploma in Criminology.

The bottom shelf was the most thoroughly trashed. There were only three untouched items, all of them box files. As with the ring binders on the top shelf, each one was neatly but slightly cryptically labelled. The boxes had fallen sideways and were now lying flat or nearly so, and Bailey had to tilt her head to make the subject lines readable: "Deliv dockets: substrate", "POs: substrate", and "Wade Park Desp Notes".

Delivery dockets, purchase orders, and despatch notes. It was the sort of paperwork that you might find at the home of a small businessman who did all his own paperwork. But not, Bailey noted, what you would expect find in the apartment of a young woman doing holiday work for a company big enough to have a fully staffed admin department.

The computer was switched on, the large screen looking uncannily bright in the dimly lit room. The screen was dominated by a large login dialog-box containing a button icon with a head-and-shoulder silhouette and the description "me" next to it. Beneath the button was a field labelled "password", and beneath that a message in bright red: "Invalid password!"

"Coming through," called the female paramedic. Bailey turned to see that they had put Isaac onto a narrow wheelchair — the type designed to fit through the narrow doors and tight turns typical in homes. His head was held in a tilted-up position with a neck brace, and he was tightly trussed up in a cream coloured blanket. Rather than disturb the study, Bailey stepped briefly into the hallway then out of the paramedics' path into the bedroom door.

"Where are you taking him?" she asked as he was wheeled past by the stocky female.

"Western Shore Hospital," replied the young paramedic as he bumbled past carrying slightly more equipment than he could easily manage. "They'll want to keep him in overnight for observation at least," he added with an air of knowledgeableness that, Bailey reflected with a barely suppressed smile, only the young can bring to a statement of the blindingly obvious.

Once Isaac was gone, Bailey refocused on the question of what the scene could tell her about the case. "Lorne! Get out here," she called. The young officer emerged from the lounge and looked at her expectantly. "Seal off the apartment, and call in a scene-of-crime squad. Tell them to concentrate in here, and get it done first." She gestured towards the study. "I'm sending one of my guys — his name's Goff — over. Apart from scene-of-crime, nobody goes in until Goff gets here. You got that?"

The young officer nodded nervously and reached again for his radio mike. Bailey walked out of the apartment, down the steps and onto the small lawn at the front of the building. She took her cell phone from her pocket, punched "3" and held the phone to her ear. She listened as it rang once, twice, three times before being answered.

"Boss?"

"Goff, how quickly can you get over to Francesca Boyle's apartment?"

"I can be there in about twenty minutes."

"OK, don't break any speed limits. Just get here some time in the next hour. There'll be a scene examination going on. Once they've finished in the study, get the computer over to technology forensics and get them to copy the contents of its hard drive to somewhere where I can look at it. There's also a whole load of paperwork I want photocopies of. Anything that looks like documents to do with Dakin Boyle — invoices, stuff like that. Got that?"

"Copy of the computer hard drive, copies of paperwork to do with Dakin Boyle. No problem."

"And make sure you don't mess up my chain of evidence when you do it. We might need this stuff."

"I'm not an idiot, boss," came the slightly pained reply.

"No, you're right. Sorry. But since we're on the subject of idiots, find Finlayson and tell him that I want to see him in my office at two o'clock. And warn him not to expect to enjoy it." She pressed the end-call button without waiting for a reply.

Detective Inspector Bailey Troy stood in the midday sun in front of Francesca Boyle's home and, under her breath, posed a question to the ghost of the murder victim: "Well, Francesca — my young, beautiful, wealthy, wannabe journalist, promiscuous friend — just what *did* you do to get yourself killed?"

Seven

*"It can be amazing if you do it right. But he crossed the line. He just
wanted to hurt me." — Francesca Boyle*

As apartments went, this was about as good as money could buy.

Bailey stood in front of the entrance to Gus Dakin's bachelor-pad
home in the plush waterside suburb of Knight's Point. Ordinarily, her
occupation being what it was, she was accustomed to announcing her
presence by pounding heavily on the front door. But these solid-looking
double doors, forming an entranceway nearly six feet wide, somehow
created a sense of being impervious to the mere hammering of police
officers. So instead she pressed the brass doorbell mounted
conspicuously to one side.

Her action generated no sound that she could hear, but after about
20 seconds one of the doors swung silently inward to reveal a tussle-
haired, stubble-chinned and slightly puzzled looking man.

"Angus Dakin?" she asked.

"Yes," came the reply. The monosyllable was delivered on a rising
note, as much a demand for Bailey to explain her presence as an answer
to her question.

She held out her ID. "Detective Inspector Bailey Troy. I'm
investigating the murder of Francesca Boyle."

The change of attitude was immediate. "Oh, yes of course. Terrible business. Please, come in." He pushed the door further open and stepped back to make way for her to enter.

She walked through the door and into a display of casual and slightly dishevelled affluence. The entranceway comprised a raised platform at one end of a large single living area, maybe forty feet square. To the left was a semi-circle of cream coloured sofas around a large, low glass coffee table, upon which rested an empty fruit bowl and a scattering of motoring magazines. Just beyond the sofas, stairs led down to what Bailey assumed were bedrooms and bathrooms. The corner immediately to Bailey's right comprised a kitchen area, dominated by brushed steel appliances and separated from the rest of the room by an L-shaped granite-topped breakfast bar. Beyond the kitchen area was a large and solid looking wooden dining table, with a dozen or so items of unopened mail sprawled across it. The far end of the room consisted entirely of floor-to-ceiling sliding windows, beyond which Bailey could see a balcony extending about 20 feet to a waist-high glass barrier, with the shimmer of the open sea beyond.

"I've just made some coffee. Would you like some?" Dakin headed towards the kitchen area without waiting for a reply.

"Thank you, yes. Milk, no sugar." Bailey took the two steps down from the entryway, then walked over and perched herself on one of the stools that ringed the breakfast bar. She sat and watched as Dakin prepared the coffee with a nonchalant but slightly rushed clattering of mugs, milk jugs and coffee pots.

Her host was, she guessed, about the same age as her — early thirties. He wore khaki cargo pants and a black v-neck sweater. He was barefoot. His hair was dark and short — just long enough to need combing, which it hadn't been. His face was thin without being gaunt and peppered with, Bailey guessed, around two days-worth of stubble. Although the sweater was loose-fitting, Bailey could clearly see that

Dakin had the lean and slightly V-shaped torso of a man who regularly worked out — heavy weights, low reps.

Down from the kitchen, Bailey could see on the wall beside the dining table a large and, to Bailey's eyes, somewhat nightmarishly chaotic portrait — an abstract, head and shoulders representation of a forlorn looking woman. Dakin looked round and saw her staring at the piece.

"Are you much of a modern art lover?" he asked. "I'm a bit of a sucker for it myself."

"It's not something I know too much about," she lied. She recognised the work as an Auerbach, one of the artist's many representations of his lover Stella West. And, she suspected, an original. She waited for the brag, for Dakin to try to impress her with the wealth and discerning taste that ownership of such work implies. It never came.

"Strong, or milky?" he asked, gesturing at the coffee mugs. He spoke and moved with the casual assurance of a man who had nothing to prove. Not arrogant, just pleasantly and disinterestedly confident. She recalled Isaac's unashamedly judgemental character-sketch of Dakin, and contrasted it with the restrained and courteous man before her. She had wondered at the time whether Isaac's assessment of Dakin might have been coloured by their competition for the attentions of Francesca. Maybe so, maybe not. Too soon to tell.

"Just a little on the milky side. Thanks." She took the mug that he proffered and sipped at the hot brew. Then she set the mug down gently on the granite surface of the breakfast bar and pulled her notebook from her handbag. "There are some questions I have to ask, you understand."

"Of course. Go ahead."

"To start with, tell me about your movements Friday evening — between say five o'clock and eleven."

"I was out of town, I'm afraid. Travelling back from Munich, actually." He paused, looking briefly lost in thought. "I'm not sure about the time-zones and so on, but I think at that time I would have been on the first leg of the flight, from Munich to Dubai. I got home about midnight last night. Picked up the voice-mail from Dad about Francesca when I checked my messages during the stop at DXB. Terrible business — such a lovely girl. Do you have any idea, you know, why...?"

"It's still very early in our investigation. It's too soon for us to be speculating about motive." Especially, Bailey thought to herself, since the usually reliable "lovers' tiff" theory wasn't yet delivering the goods. If Dakin's story checked out — which she was pretty sure it would — that left Russell Bridgeman, the plant manager and most recent beneficiary of Francesca's rowdy affections, as the last remaining candidate for a *crime passionnel* killer.

Unless Dakin had hired someone else to do the job. He was certainly wealthy enough. In Bailey's experience, jilted lovers typically preferred to do their own dirty work, but she would not discount the possibility.

Unlikely as it was to be a fabrication, she would get his story checked out. "Which airline did you fly?"

"Emirates. They're very good, have you ever flown them?"

She shook her head to dismiss his question as she noted his answer in her notebook. "And why were you in Munich?"

"To meet with our European distributors. I go every six months. Pricing, volume commitments, regulatory matters, promotional activity. You know the kind of thing."

She shook her head again, still writing. She wondered to herself what kind of promotional activities a cure for cancer might require. "Not really something I have much experience of, I'm afraid. Who exactly did you meet with in Munich?"

"Most of my discussions were with Lukas Gruber. He's the marketing director for Therapeutische Logistik, our distributor. Nice guy, Austrian." His pronunciation of the German seemed well practised and effortless.

"Can you spell all that for me, please." She scribbled as he did so. "Now, what can you tell me about Francesca Boyle?"

"I'm not sure what you want to know. I've known... that is, I knew... her for ages, since Dad and Dick first started up together. Not especially well, I have to admit. Not until recently, that is. She was just a kid when they first started up, of course — all braces and pigtails. Didn't really have much to do with her then, she was just some kid who showed up around the office now and then. I vaguely recall her being quite precocious. I do remember that Dick spoiled her rotten. Especially after Muriel passed away."

"Muriel?"

"Dick's wife, Francesca's mother. Died of cancer, when Francesca was still just a kid."

"What about more recently?"

"After school, she went away to college. Got an honours degree in Journalism, finished it just this year. She was working with us temporarily while she looked for her first real job. She had turned into quite an attractive woman. We, ah... we were a bit of an item for a while. Until recently."

"Tell me about that."

"It was the usual thing. You know — boys, girls. Nothing particularly serious. It was fun while it lasted."

"The usual thing. Just that? Nothing — unusual?"

Dakin laughed and looked down at his coffee, not replying. Bailey tilted her head to one side and lowered it in a conspicuous attempt to catch his eye — making it clear that she was aware of him avoiding eye contact. After a few seconds, he looked up and smiled weakly.

"No, nothing to speak of. Not really. A bit of role playing, maybe."

Bailey chose to play dumb. "Role playing?"

"Yes, you know the sort of thing, I'm sure. Dominants, submissives, that sort of thing."

"Are you telling me that you were violent towards her, sexually?" It was an unfair question, and she knew it. But Bailey Troy did not crack murder cases by playing fair.

"No! No. Not violent. Not really. Just... She liked... She liked a bit of discipline. Just playful stuff. That's all."

"She did, or you did?"

He looked straight at her. "We both did, Inspector. She... well, she was keen to explore. And I," he spread his hands and gave a you-know-how-it-is shrug, "was happy to oblige. It was all a bit tame really, as these things go, I'm sure. Just two consenting adults, behind closed doors. Doing no harm to one another, or to anyone else." A hint of a playful smile crept across his face. "Maybe you should try it some time."

Maybe, she thought to herself. But not on the receiving end, and certainly not with you. She forced her face into its most solemn investigating-a-murder expression, and made a mental note to double-check the post-mortem report for any remaining signs of Dakin 'doing no harm' to the victim.

"Someone did a great deal of harm to Francesca on Friday." She let the statement hang in the air. It worked; Dakin's flirtatious grin faded into a faintly sheepish embarrassment.

"Yes. Of course. Sorry."

"Why did it end between the two of you?", she continued.

The sheepishness evaporated, replaced with a businesslike expression to match Bailey's. "I don't like to speak ill of her, now that, you know... But, well, there's a computer contractor chap that does some work at the office."

"Isaac Church?"

"Yes, that's him. She just decided one night to jump in the sack with him. I've no idea why. She didn't even try to be discreet or make much of a secret about it. And I'm not really one for sharing."

"So you dumped her?"

"I think it was more by mutual consent. We didn't really discuss it, but we didn't go together after that. I was probably a bit frosty towards her around the office. I was a bit annoyed by it, to tell you the truth; I'd thought we were quite good for one another."

"How annoyed?"

"Just annoyed, Inspector. Not murderous. And I was out of the country when she was killed, remember? I don't know what she saw in him, though. Church, I mean. An uninspiring kind of guy, to be honest. Not even all that good with computers, really. I'd have got rid of him if it was down to me, but Dick seems to like him."

Bailey suppressed a smile at this. So the dislike was mutual.

"Can you think of anyone who would have had a reason to kill her?"

"Well she didn't last long with that Church guy. He seemed to get pretty miserable about being dumped. And I'm guessing he would have been in town that night. Maybe you should talk to him."

"Anyone else?"

"Not that I can think of. She was an OK kid. Not the sort to make enemies. Not seriously. She was a bit, I don't know, careless about people's feelings. Maybe there was someone else in her past, from college maybe, who took it all too much to heart. It seems like a pretty trivial reason to kill someone, though."

People got killed over much less every day of the week, Bailey reflected. But she kept that thought to herself. She drained the last of her coffee, picked up her notebook and swung herself off the stool.

"You've been very helpful," she said to Dakin, who smiled and nodded a small acknowledgement in reply. "If I need anything else, I'll be in touch."

Eight

"I've really come to hate hospitals." — Francesca Boyle

A visit to the emergency department is not, unless one is obviously at death's door, a hurried experience. Arriving by ambulance did give Isaac the benefit of an immediate brief triage assessment, but when it became clear that his injuries were not life threatening the pace of events slowed markedly. He waited for an hour before being assessed and sent for an x-ray, another hour for the x-ray to be performed, and then over two hours for the radiologist to deliver the verdict that there were no bones broken. At the end of which a harried looking doctor who had played no prior role in the proceedings had declared to Isaac that, as a precaution, she was going to "keep you in overnight for observation".

This announcement conjured up in Isaac's mind a picture of a restful night in a dimly lit room, sleeping tenderly on crisp and newly laundered linen as young and beautiful nurses hovered over him looking anxiously for any sign of complications from his injury.

But that wasn't quite what the doctor had promised. Weekends were not the best time to be expecting a bed in the Western Shore emergency department, especially if your bones were intact and you showed no obvious signs of imminent death. Instead, Isaac was to be left all night fully clothed on a narrow gurney in a busy and starkly lit hospital corridor, to be largely ignored by staff unless and until he started to fit or throw up blood.

He had passed the night without having a fit, throwing up or, for the most part, sleeping. It was now 7:00am, he still had a faint trace of a headache, his face was tender to the touch, he could only see out of one eye, he was hungry, and he needed to take a piss. He swung up into a sitting position and looked around for any sign of either a cafeteria or a lavatory. He saw neither.

Instead, he saw Bailey Troy walking along the corridor towards him — looking annoyingly bright and well rested.

"Good morning. How are you?" she chirped. "On second thoughts, don't answer that. You look like shit."

"Thanks for the compliment," he grumbled. "What're you doing here?"

"I thought you might need a ride home. Have the doctors said you're well enough to leave?"

"I haven't asked. Come on let's go."

"I think they'll want you to complete some paperwork if you're going to discharge yourself."

"They can shove their paperwork. I'm going. Is that offer of a lift still there, or are you worried about aiding and abetting a fugitive from the emergency room?"

Bailey laughed. "OK, let's see if we can bust out of this place. Come on." She gestured back in the direction from which she had come.

Isaac jumped down from the gurney and started walking in the direction she had indicated. "I need to take a leak, then I need a large burger and an even larger coffee, then I need a shower."

Behind him, Bailey raised her eyebrows as he marched past, smiled, and shook her head. "I can't vouch for the rest," she called after him, "but you certainly need a shower." She fell in behind Isaac.

Ten minutes later, they were in Bailey's car — Bailey driving cautiously through the early rush-hour traffic, Isaac in the passenger seat munching a large and copiously ketchuped cheeseburger with grim and carnivorous determination.

"Did you get a good look at him?" she asked.

"Who? The guy in the flat? Good enough to recognise him again, I guess. He was a mean looking brute of a guy. Imagine Ernest Borgnine's ugly brother."

"Height, weight, age, distinguishing marks?"

"Maybe six feet. A big guy — heavy set, but not fat, you know? Maybe in his forties, I'm not sure."

"Anything else?"

Isaac turned and pointed at the bruising that still held his right eye tightly shut. "He's left-handed. At least, he is with his fists. Do you think it was the same guy who shot Francesca?"

"Almost certainly. He was driving the Mazda with your plates. And he has some unfinished business at her apartment."

Isaac pondered what else might link the thug in the apartment with Francesca's killer. "Where was she shot?"

"Francesca? At Dakin Boyle's head office."

"No, no. I mean whereabouts on her body?"

"In the head. Killed instantly, I imagine."

"More specifically. Where, exactly?"

"Her left cheek, half an inch below the eye," she replied. "Why?"

That was pretty much the answer he'd been expecting. "Then your shooter was very probably left-handed too."

"What makes you say that?"

"Most people jerk the trigger when they shoot a handgun. In a left-handed person, that will send the shot low and to the right. Assuming your killer was aiming for the centre of Francesca's forehead, then hitting her left cheek — below and to the right of where the killer was aiming — is what you'd expect from a left-handed shot."

"Makes sense," she conceded with a nod. "Did the guy who attacked you have a gun?"

"Not that I saw. Just the fist — one hell of a fist, too." Isaac gently explored the bruising on his face with his free hand, winced, and thought better of it. It was not, he thought to himself, a fist he was in any hurry to meet again.

"The gun is becoming a bit of a problem," she said.

Isaac knew a hint when he heard one. The inspector had something on her mind that she wanted to talk about. All he wanted to do was eat his burger, get home, have a shower and maybe grab some sleep. Then, ideally, wake up to the news that the bad guy had been caught — and preferably beaten to a pulp while resisting arrest.

But they still had a drive ahead of them. And, beneath his bruised and grumpy exterior, Isaac's etiquette-free libido demanded that he keep on Bailey Troy's good side. He decided to indulge her.

"OK, so what's the problem with the gun? I thought you said there were two guns, anyway."

"I did. But there aren't. There are three."

"Three? How so?"

"We got the forensic report back from the scene-of-crime examination. The bullet that killed Francesca didn't come from either of the casings that we found. It wasn't even a nine mil."

"What was it?"

Bailey tilted her head to one side — making, it seemed to Isaac, an unnecessary performance of recalling the details. "According to the report, it was a jacketed hollow point projectile. It was still more or less intact, though pretty deformed. Fired from a gun with a right-hand rifling twist. Weighed between eleven point six and eleven point seven grams. And it was between nine point oh five and nine point one millimetres in diameter at the base, depending on which diameter was measured."

Isaac frowned. Nobody except forensic scientists, he thought to himself, talked in grams when it came to ammunition. "What does all that mean in proper English — grains and inches?"

"It means it almost certainly couldn't have been a nine mil. It was just a touch too wide and way too heavy. The only commonly used calibre that fits is the three fifty seven magnum. A one eighty grain hollow-point projectile — that's a pretty serious round, not just something for plinking at tin cans. And not a match for either of the cases found at the scene."

"Three fifty seven, that's a revolver round," replied Isaac. "You wouldn't expect to find any discarded cases at the scene. So that gives you cases from two different nine mil pistols, and one bullet from a revolver. Three guns in all."

"And two missing bullets," added Bailey. "We haven't found any nine mil projectiles fired at the scene. There's only one gunshot wound to Francesca's body, and there's no sign of any other bullets or bullet damage anywhere. And we've looked very, very hard for them. They aren't there. What does that tell you?"

Isaac had the sense that, just like at the café two days before, she was setting him a riddle that she had already worked out. This one wasn't exactly rocket science.

"It's part of the set up. Back in the café on Saturday afternoon we said that they should have taken away their own brass and left mine. Well they did take away their own brass — still in the revolver — and they did leave some nine mil brass. But not mine. And they left behind a bullet that was clearly not from my gun. Whatever the killers were trying to do, they weren't trying very hard to set me up."

"So where does that leave us?"

As Bailey brought the car to a stop outside his house, Isaac's mind turned to the imminent and appealing prospect of some sleep. He was finding that, unscrupulous libido notwithstanding, his interest in

Bailey's game of "twenty questions" was waning rapidly. He unclipped his seatbelt, and turned to her while simultaneously reaching for the door handle. "You're the detective, Inspector Troy. It leaves *you* with a mystery to solve. I'm just the IT guy with a black eye and a sleep deficit. So it leaves *me* going to have a shower and a nap on the sofa. Enjoy the rest of your day."

He climbed out of the car and walked towards the house without looking back. He was about half way to his front door when he heard Bailey's car whispering its way down the road. Tired as he was, Isaac still felt a faint tinge of disappointment at her leaving.

Thirty minutes later, Isaac was lying naked on his sofa, his mind drifting slowly from wakefulness to sleep as he allowed the last of the moisture from his shower to evaporate away. With an irony that only an iPod's allegedly random selection algorithm could achieve, the hypnotic lyrics of Lou Reid's "Perfect Day" started seeping quietly from his sound system.

As he dozed, images and recollections from the last 24 hours played haphazardly and unbidden across his semi-consciousness. His awareness descended from his current reality into a mosaic of Francesca's elegant kitchenware, that bone jarring fist, pupil dilation tests, sternly efficient radiographers, the powdery taste of painkillers and the succulent delight of a half-pounder with cheese.

His mind's eye segued, quite naturally it seemed to him in his sleep-disoriented state, from cheeseburgers to flirtatious and enigmatic police inspectors. As all of his encounters with Bailey replayed and collided in his head, it seemed obvious now to Isaac's semi-conscious and fantasy-enhanced senses that each one had been imbued with a profound sexuality, somehow just tantalisingly out of reach. Edging even deeper towards sleep, his dream state drifted from what had been to what must — surely, eventually — come to pass. He imagined himself with his head hovering just above Bailey's belly as he undid the button of her Levis and slowly unzipped her fly, her soft belly shifting unhurriedly beneath him in anticipation, the sweet aroma of arousal rising from her loins to linger electrifyingly in his nostrils.

A flash of sudden, unbidden and unrelated insight brought Isaac instantly wide awake. He noticed, in passing and without embarrassment, his erection becoming slowly flaccid in his hand. While his semi-conscious had been indulging his primitive carnal urges by playing out the seduction of Bailey Troy, Isaac's deepest subconscious had been solving the riddle of the half-baked false trails at the murder scene. He sat up on the sofa, reached for his cellphone on the coffee-table, and pressed the "call" button without entering a number. The phone displayed a list of recently made and received calls. He pushed the down arrow a couple of times until the unrecognised number from the previous day was highlighted, pressed the "call" button again, and held the phone to his ear.

The phone rang — once, twice. "Troy," came the answer.

"It was a contract killing. You're looking for a contract killer. Not a smart one, but one with a very smart client."

Nine

"I liked Jenny. To start with…" — *Francesca Boyle*

"Isaac?" His opening line on the phone had got her attention; she pulled the car over to the kerb to allow herself to concentrate on the conversation. "I thought you were going to sleep."

"Never mind that," he replied. "Whoever set this up was trying to frame me. And whoever they hired to do their dirty work has messed it up. You're looking for a bright guy who wanted Francesca dead, and who made the mistake of hiring a dumb thug to do the work. The dumb thug who punched my lights out at her apartment."

It made sense, she thought. But she wanted to hear his whole theory. "Take me through it, Isaac. A step at a time. Tell me what you think you've got."

"OK," he replied. "Someone wants Francesca dead. I don't know who or why, but it's someone who knows that she and I have just broken up, and that I shoot a nine mil pistol."

"Go on."

"They want to frame me for the murder, to leave a trail of evidence that points to me. That's why they get the killer to steal my plates and drive through the red-light camera. They stole the plates instead of the whole car because it was less risky — I might have heard the car being driven off or noticed that it was gone and reported it stolen. I'm guessing the car they fitted the plates to would have been stolen — you should check for stolen blue Mazda 3s last week."

She already had — basic investigative egg sucking. There were two reports of stolen blue Mazda 3s in the 5 days before the killing, only one of which had been recovered. "So far so good," she said. "Keep going."

"We talked the other day about how the plan should have been for the killer to replace the plates after the killing, so there would be nothing to suggest it was not my car in the red light photo. He was probably told to reattach the original plates to the stolen car and dump and burn it somewhere. But it looks like the killer slacked off on that part of the plan, and is still using the car to drive around in. Not very bright."

It was way beyond not very bright, Bailey thought to herself. Deliberately linking a car to a murder, then continuing to drive around in it was about as far from bright as you could get. But, in her experience, a fair percentage of violent criminals would be dumb enough to make the mistake. But nowhere near bright enough to come up with the plan in the first place. Isaac was right — it was a dumb killer working for a bright client.

"Sounds plausible," she said. "Tell me about the bullets."

"OK. So the bright client has a plan of following me to the range and collecting some of my brass after I've been practising, and leaving that behind at the scene. All the killer needs to do is kill Francesca with a nine mil pistol, pick up his own brass and leave mine it its place. If he'd done that exactly as instructed — including replacing the plates and dumping the car — then I'd still be locked up now, wouldn't I?"

"Very probably," she conceded.

"But our thug isn't one to bother with details, luckily for me. He thinks any old nine mil brass will do — doesn't even bother to match the number of cases he leaves behind with the number of shots he fires. And who will be any the wiser if he shoots his victim with a revolver, rather than going to all the trouble of acquiring a nine-mil gun just for this job?"

It all made sense, she thought. It was what the prosecutor would call a plausible narrative — a credible story that fitted the evidence. But there were still large chunks of the jigsaw missing, not the least of which were some names for the killer and his client, and a motive. Well, she had a pretty good profile of the killer, so that was the most promising line to pursue.

"OK," she said. "You've sold me. Take a few hours to catch up on your sleep, then I'll show you some photos of some of our favourite thugs. See if there's anyone you recognise. In the meantime I'm going to have a chat with your Chief Technologist friend. You said that Francesca worked for her, is that right?"

"Jenny. Yes, Francesca worked for her. I'll be at home all day. I'm not planning on going anywhere. Call me when you want me to look at mug shots."

"See you later," she said, and punched the end-call button. Then she flicked the car into drive, checked over her shoulder and eased the car out into the traffic. Ten minutes later she was walking into the reception of Dakin Boyle Pharmaceuticals.

The receptionist's identity badge gave her name as Millie. It was a deceptively cheerful name for the stern and dumpy middle-aged woman who, Bailey guessed from her chilly manner, regarded herself as Dakin Boyle's first line of defence against unwelcome intruders. And Millie looked as if she regarded Bailey as a most unwelcome intruder indeed.

Bailey was used to that. Her tomboy skater-chick look often got her a chilly and dismissive reception from those who liked to wear middle age and middle class as a badge of social superiority. Initially.

"Can I help you?" asked the receptionist with a well rehearsed frostiness that suggested that the prospect was somewhat remote.

"I'm here to speak to Jenny Watson," replied Bailey, carefully injecting just enough of an authoritarian tone into her voice to suggest that any opinions Millie might have on the matter were irrelevant.

"Do you have an appointment?"

"No. But I am investigating a murder." Bailey held out her ID for the receptionist to examine. "And generally speaking that means I don't need an appointment. Now please call Ms Watson and tell her that Detective Inspector Troy would like to speak to her."

Millie's demeanour collapsed into a flurry of apologies and hasty phone calls. Bailey had barely taken a seat in the waiting area when Jenny Watson walked uncertainly into the reception area.

Bailey stood up as the Chief Technologist approached. Jenny Watson was, Bailey guessed, in her late twenties or early thirties. Her round face was adorned by a pair of determinedly unfashionable horn-rimmed glasses. Her wavy dark brown hair tumbled to slightly below shoulder length with no obvious attempt at any kind of styling. She wore a lab coat with blue ink stains around the bottom of the breast pocket, underneath which she was clothed in jeans and t-shirt. Through the opening in the front of the lab coat, Bailey could see the words "Starfleet Academy" written on the t-shirt across what were, to Bailey's taste, quite pleasantly ample breasts. The jeans hugged a lower torso and legs that displayed just a hint of chubbiness while remaining well proportioned.

Bailey instinctively asked herself the question that always flashed unbidden across her subconscious when meeting a woman for the first time — and decided that, if the opportunity arose, she would.

"Inspector Troy, I assume?"

"Bailey Troy, yes. Please, call me Bailey. Is there somewhere we can speak?"

"Sure. My office. Come on through." Jenny turned and walked towards a set of double doors, then held one open for Bailey to walk through ahead of her. They walked side by side in silence along a brightly lit corridor for around 20 yards, before Jenny gestured through a door to the left.

The office was around 20 feet square, modern and well lit. The far corner was taken up with an L-shaped desk dominated by a large flat-screen computer monitor. Two of the four walls consisted entirely of shelving, overflowing with box files and weighty reference books. Bailey examined one of the titles: "Tumor Models in Cancer Research". The shelving continued, half height, below the large window that dominated the far wall.

In the corner opposite the desk was a circular table surrounded by four cloth-upholstered chairs. Jenny pulled out one of the chairs, sat herself down and gestured at Bailey to do the same.

"I assume you're here about Francesca. Poor girl." Jenny paused briefly and Bailey saw the merest flicker of emotion pass across her face. "Do you know what happened, why she was killed?"

Bailey shook her head. "We know she was shot. But we don't know why or by whom. That's what we need to find out. I'm hoping you can tell me a bit about her and the work she was doing here. It may help us put together a picture of what happened."

"Of course. Whatever I can do to help. What do you need to know?"

"Francesca worked for you, is that right?"

"I guess so, sort of. But basically she was just here because she was her father's daughter. He thought she needed a job, so we needed to find her something to do."

"So having her here was just an irritation?"

"Oh no. She was OK to have around. We found her stuff to do — paperwork and so on. Creating employment for the owners' offspring is part of what we do around here."

That sounded to Bailey like an invitation to open a new line of enquiry. She decided to take the bait. "Really? Tell me more."

"Sorry, I guess it's not really relevant — just a pet peeve of mine. You'll know that Bill Dakin is one of the founders. He's a really smart guy. Not like Dick, but really street-smart — sharp and mean. Anyway, Gus Dakin, his son, is on the payroll too. Someone else to make work for, but not such pleasant company."

"In what way?"

"Well, he inherited his father's mean streak, but not so much of the smarts, if you know what I mean. He draws a big salary and wanders around looking important, jetting off to Europe 'on business'" — she made quote marks in the air with her fingers as she said this — "whenever he feels like it."

But Bailey wasn't here to find out what Dakin Boyle's Chief Technologist thought about Gus Dakin. She smiled at Jenny indulgently. "I see. You were going to tell me about Francesca…"

"Oh, yes. Well as I said, she was here because her father wanted us to give her a job. So we found her stuff to do. She caused a bit of a stir with the guys, of course."

Of course, Bailey thought. But she wanted to hear Jenny's perspective, untainted by her own. "A bit of a stir? What do you mean?"

"Well, she's… she was… an attractive woman. She got quite a bit of attention that way, if you know what I mean, and dated a few of the guys here. I think she was sometimes a bit mean to them, actually. She told me that she wanted to enjoy herself before her life got too serious, before she got bogged down in her career and winning her Pulitzer Prize or whatever. And that seemed to mean dating as many guys as she could — dumping her current guy and moving on whenever a new one showed any interest."

"You didn't approve?"

"Well, as I said, it was a bit mean. But, you know, we've all done it, eh? Been young, a bit self-centred. She wasn't a bad kid; she just wanted to enjoy herself a little. The guys took it a bit to heart when they got dumped, though they were happy enough to get her to dump someone else for them."

"Sounds like the guys all got what they deserved."

"Well, Gus Dakin certainly did. He's done the same and worse to women he's dated, so any emotional trauma he suffers at the hands of women is just karma, as far as I'm concerned. I did feel a bit sorry for Isaac though — he's our IT guy. He's nice — he deserved better."

He deserves a fellow Star Trek geek to treat him right, I'm guessing, Bailey thought to herself with an inner smile. "What did Francesca do here for you, exactly?"

"Mostly she helped me with placing orders for supplies and so on. It was make-work, really — instead of me taking an hour to do it myself, I'd take an hour to explain it to her, and then she'd spend the day doing it."

"Doesn't sound very productive."

"Well no. But like I said, she was the boss's daughter, you know? And, well, she was fun to have around, I guess. Kinda bubbly, but intelligent with it. There aren't many girls around here to talk to. Just Millie the Rottweiler on reception and a few out in the factory — and you basically don't get to work out there unless your IQ is lower than your shoe size."

Bailey laughed at this, and was rewarded with a smile in acknowledgement from Jenny. They caught and held one another's gaze, just long enough to turn this into a little less of a police interview and a bit more of a girl chat.

Bailey decided to change direction — to build on this small opening of trust by getting Jenny to talk about herself for a while. "Tell me what it is you do here, Jenny. What exactly is a Chief Technologist?"

"Basically, I'm the only one who really understands what goes on here — how we manufacture the Mertusugene."

"The what?"

"The onco-viral vector. Dakin Boyle's wonder-drug. That's what it's called. Mertusugene."

"Why viral? I thought it was a cancer treatment."

"It is. But it's not a drug in the normal sense. It's a gene therapy, delivered through a virus. The disease — Merkel cell carcinoma — is caused by a virus getting in and modifying the human cell's DNA. So we send in another virus to fix it."

Bailey considered this. "I'm sure it's a lot more complicated than you make it sound."

"Well yes, of course. That's where Dick's piece of genius comes in. It's really quite clever — the therapy starts with a limited lytic infection of the striated muscle tissue that generates a much larger therapeutic dose of the secondary lysogenic virosome which..." She paused. "Sorry, I'm babbling, aren't I?" Jenny smiled apologetically, and gave a small "I just can't help myself" shrug.

"Biology wasn't really my strong subject. Sorry. Maybe you can give me the layman's version."

"OK. Merkel cell carcinoma is caused — most of the time anyway — by a virus that causes changes to your DNA. Our treatment is a different virus that seeks out cells that have the Merkel mutation and destroys those cells only."

"Sounds clever."

"It's a work of genius. It saves around a hundred thousand lives every year in Europe alone, and another seventeen thousand in Japan. All in all, we produce around a million doses a year."

"What about America, and the rest of the world?"

"Europe and Japan are our main markets. Merkel cell carcinoma is relatively rare in North America — only one or two thousand cases a year, if that. We sell Mertusugene there too obviously, but it's not a big market for us."

"And the rest of the world? Asia, Africa?"

The Chief Technologist seemed to develop a sudden and unlikely fascination with the table top immediately in front of her. "Well, it's an expensive drug, you know? Our distributors do ship it there, of course. In low volume. For those who..." Jenny's voice trailed off.

"For those who can afford it?" Bailey offered as an end to the sentence.

Jenny nodded slowly, still staring at the table. "That's how it is in this industry. Dakin Boyle is here to make a profit."

Bailey wasn't going to get anything useful to the case by debating the morality of the pharmaceutical industry, she decided. Time to change direction slightly.

"Do you have any more wonder-drugs in the pipeline," Bailey asked, "or is Dakin Boyle a one-hit-wonder?"

"We're hoping for more, of course," Jenny replied. "Dick and I — Dick, mostly — have been looking at using the same technique to treat adenocarcinomas. If we can pull that off, it'll be huge; adenocarcinomas kill millions of people every year."

"Really? I've never heard of it."

"Well no, it's a generic cancer type that shows up in various organs. Lung, prostate, pancreas, stomach. Lots of different cancers, but all with a very similar physiology. We made some really good progress in the early years, identifying a usable oncogene marker, and so on." Jenny's enthusiasm for the topic was, Bailey noted, quickly beginning to take over. "We can *create* the cancer easily enough under lab conditions, either in cloned pancreatic cells or in lab rats, depending on what we need. It's just a case of forcing the right KRAS and CDKN2A mutations in the genome, which we can do chemically. But it's been tough work constructing a useful therapeutic virosome that only targets cells with the oncogene." Suddenly, her passion waned as quickly as it had emerged. "To be honest, I'm not sure what Dick's next move is going to be. And his heart's just not going to be in it, now..."

Nothing there that will help solve Francesca's murder, thought Bailey. Time to get back to where the money is. "You said that Dakin Boyle produces a million doses a year of — what was it called again?"

"Mertusugene. Yes, around a million doses a year."

"What's a dose, exactly? How is it administered? Injection?"

"No. Tablets. The standard dose is four tablets, and the standard treatment is eight doses, each one two weeks apart. The optimum biological dose is too big to fit into one tablet once it's mixed with the required excipients, but oral administration is the easiest way to transfect the patient."

"So four million tablets a year. What's that," Bailey looked away as she did the arithmetic in her head, "about sixteen thousand tablets a day? That doesn't sound like a lot of tablets to keep a big factory like this busy."

"We warehouse the excipients for the generics here as well."

Bailey shook her head in an exaggerated display of confusion. "Sorry. Once more — in English this time, please."

"Sorry, jargon. All tablets have active ingredients — the actual drug that the patient needs — and non-active ingredients — binding agents to hold the tablets together, fillers, flavourings to stop it all tasting too foul, and so on. The non-active ingredients are what we call the excipients."

Bailey nodded slowly. "And you store those here, you said. For — what was it again?"

"The generics. We manufacture generics over at our other plant on the Wade Park industrial estate. But there isn't a lot of storage space there, so we store the excipients here and ship it over there in smaller lots."

"OK, so I get the bit about the excipients, but I'm still feeling a bit thick. What are generics, exactly?"

"You know — generic drugs. Drugs where the original patent has expired, so other manufacturers can jump in and produce the drug more cheaply. We do that for a couple of drugs. Simvastatin and Clopidogrel, to be precise."

"And you manufacture those over at Wade Park?"

"That's right. Simvastatin and Clopidogrel at Wade Park, Mertusugene here."

All very interesting, Bailey thought to herself. But she wasn't sure that any of this was getting her any closer to Francesca's killer.

"And you say that Francesca helped out with the paperwork. Would that include ordering the... sorry, what was that word again?"

"The excipients, yes. Twelve different excipient ingredients, from five different suppliers. She handled the shipments from here to Wade Park as well."

"And it kept her busy?"

"Busy enough. As I said, it was really make-work for the boss's daughter."

"Would she ever have had to take work home with her."

"No. Why?"

"There was a lot of paperwork from here at her apartment. Delivery dockets, invoices, and so on. Can you think of any reason why she would have taken stuff like that home with her?"

The Chief Technologist was staring down at the table again. "No. Sorry, I can't."

Bailey said nothing, allowing the silence to linger. Jenny Watson continued to stare at the table.

She wasn't going to get any more right now. Bailey broke the silence by standing up. "I think that's all I need for now. Thank you, you've been very helpful. I'll find my own way out."

A few minutes later, as Bailey walked across the car park towards her car, she mentally shifted Jenny Watson, Chief Technologist for Dakin Boyle Pharmaceuticals, from her "candidates for seduction" mental list to the one labelled "persons of interest".

Ten

"It's funny how guys like to act all heroic around the girls, don't you think?" — Francesca Boyle

Isaac was restless.

After his phone call to Bailey he hadn't been able to sleep — which had frustrated him, both because he was tired and because he had hoped to return to his dream seduction of the Inspector. Instead, after 20 minutes of tossing and turning on the sofa, he had given up trying to sleep. Now, dressed in yesterday's jeans and t-shirt and with coffee in hand, he was slumped back down on the sofa with the laptop resting on his abdomen.

His brain was, he recognised, too sleep-faded for him to do any useful work. Instead, he just opened the web browser on his laptop and watched as his homepage — Google — loaded. On a whim, he typed the words "contract killer" into the search engine, then, not even remotely surprised that there was such a thing, followed the link to the Wikipedia page for Contract Killing.

"In the United States, the United Kingdom, and many other countries," he read, "a contract to kill a person is void, meaning that it is not legally enforceable."

He entertained himself by letting his mind wander around the absurdity of trying to legally enforce a contract to commit a murder. A little lower down, he read that the going rate for a contract killing was $12,000. He lowered his head back onto the cushion and closed his eyes, letting the information meander in his mind. At that price a dispute with your contract killer could perhaps be handled by the Small Claims Court. Probably better, Isaac thought in quiet amusement, to find a contract killer who accepted credit cards. Then if he reneged on the deal you could just ask the credit card company to reverse the transaction. Of course, the killer might be asked by the bank to furnish proof that he had actually committed the murder in dispute, if he wanted to keep the money.

His allowed his mind to drift whimsically along this line of reasoning. Failing to perform the killing was only one way that a killer might not complete his or her contractual obligations. Francesca's killer had completed the murder, but hadn't properly performed all his other obligations — using the correct murder weapon, making sure to leave behind cases from Isaac's gun rather than just any old 9mm brass, returning the plates, dumping the stolen Mazda. Isaac suspected that, were it not for the inconvenient fact of the agreement being unenforceable, whoever had wanted Francesca dead would have been entitled to at least a partial refund. Or perhaps the killer, if he was an astute businessman with an eye for repeat business, would have offered a discount on his client's next murder to settle the matter out of court...

Isaac woke with a start at the loud thumping on the front door. "Open up! Police! Come on, time to go and look at some mug shots."

"Wha...? Bailey? Erm, yeah. Come in — it's not locked." Isaac stood and wiped his hands across his face, trying to rub away the disorientation that comes from being suddenly awoken from a deep sleep. He heard the front door creak open and thump shut, then saw Bailey Troy heading towards him down the hallway. As he looked at her, he suddenly became acutely conscious of his own unshaven, uncombed, barefooted and generally unkempt appearance.

"How did you get on with Jenny," he asked.

"Not quite as well as I might have liked," she replied — with a smile that left Isaac with the annoying feeling that, once again, he wasn't in on the joke.

Isaac raised his eyebrows, waiting for Bailey to elucidate. But she just raised her own eyebrows in return, and broadened her smile tauntingly. Whatever the joke was, it was clear that she wasn't about to explain it.

To Isaac, things that didn't add up were like an itch that he had to scratch. In his line of work, he came across many things that — on the face of it — didn't make sense. When computer systems played up, the symptoms were often contradictory and gave few clues as to the root cause of the problem. The error messages created by computer programs and operating systems were notorious for being inscrutable and just plain misleading. But Isaac was very, very good at making computers work. He had an instinctive knack for allowing seemingly unrelated and contradictory pieces of information to coalesce in his mind into a clear understanding of what was happening. It was something he did successfully day in, day out with uncooperative computer systems. And it was something that, when he turned his mind to it, he could sometimes do with people too.

With an abrupt and deflating flash of insight, Isaac suddenly realised what the joke was.

"Bailey, can I ask you a personal question?"

"No, you can't," she replied with a mock display of indignation. "You can go and put some shoes on, grab a jacket, and go and get in the car. Actually..." she made a point of conspicuously sniffing the air, "...you might want to grab a fresh t-shirt as well. Then maybe you can ask me a personal question. And maybe — if you're lucky — I might answer it."

He smiled sheepishly back at her, then pivoted around and headed to the bedroom. Once there, he grabbed an old pair of New Balance cross-trainers from under the bed and, deciding that socks were an unnecessary complication, put them on over his bare feet. He pulled off his t-shirt and grabbed a clean one from the draw — the last one, he noted. From a pile of discarded clothing beside the bed he pulled out a dark polar fleece and slipped it on. Then he went back into the lounge, where he found Bailey leafing through a copy of "Guns and Ammo" magazine with an expression that blended equal measures of distaste and fascination.

He grabbed his wallet and phone from the coffee table, caught Bailey's eye and nodded in the direction of the hallway. "OK, I'm ready. Let's go."

She dropped the magazine on the coffee table, raised her eyes in a look of "oh, so *now* you're in a rush..." and walked slowly down the hallway to the front door.

Two minutes later they were sat in the Prius, with Bailey easing the car away from the curb. "Go on then," she instructed.

"Sorry?"

"Ask your question. What is it you want to know?"

Isaac paused as he framed the question in his mind. He decided to lead with the least disappointing possibility. "OK, here it is. Are you bisexual?"

Bailey laughed. "My, that really *is* a personal question. You're a smart guy, Isaac. You'd make a good detective — you read people well. But no, I'm not bisexual."

"Oh. Sorry."

"Don't be. You were close." She turned her attention briefly from the traffic to give him an indulgent smile. "I'm all out gay, Isaac. Lesbian. A twenty-four carat dyke. A rug muncher. I'm a friend of Dorothy who dines at the Y, speaks in tongues, and tips the velvet. Now, what else can I help you with?"

"Actually, I think that just about covers it. Thanks for clarifying." It was, he reflected, the first time he'd ever asked a woman that question and, having got a brutally straight answer, he was at a loss as to where to take the conversation from here. He turned and looked at the Inspector, who was looking straight ahead but nonetheless obviously enjoying his discomfort.

"That Chief Technologist of yours is a cutie, isn't she," Bailey said after letting the silence hang for a couple of minutes.

"Jenny? I guess so, in her way," he replied. "She's a bit snooty. Thinks anyone with an IQ below 140 is some kind of lesser being."

"Yes, I noticed that," said Bailey. "But she seems to think quite highly of you. You could find yourself a bit of adventure there if you turned your mind to it, I'm guessing."

"You think so?" Isaac had never really considered the possibility before but, as he thought about it, it wasn't obvious to him why not. She was, to be sure, quite matter-of-fact about everything at the plant, and was a determinedly drab dresser. But she was not unattractive; she was shapely in what Isaac would in male-only company describe as a "built for comfort" kind of way, and — notwithstanding a not-so-mild case of intellectual snobbery — displayed flashes of the kind of understated dry wit that he enjoyed. He and Jenny were in the habit of engaging in the kind of offhand straight-faced banter that could easily, he reflected, be nudged in the direction of flirting.

But, he reminded himself, it wasn't certain that the Inspector was offering him a clear run. "I get the sense you're quite taken with her yourself," he ventured.

Bailey laughed again. "What — you want to put ten bucks on who gets to do the mattress mambo with her first? I think you've got a bit of a head start on me there, Isaac."

Isaac was quickly forming the impression that Bailey was among the alpha-males in the lesbian community. Just one of the guys. This blokeish banter with a spunky but sexually out-of-reach chick was a little weird. But, he admitted to himself, he was in no hurry for it to end.

His fascination with the Inspector notwithstanding, the more he thought about it the more he was tempted to have a crack at taking the ten bucks off her. Best, he thought, to keep his cards close to his chest on that. "We'll see," was all he offered in reply.

Isaac heard the chirping of a mobile phone rising from down by his feet. As he looked down to identify the source of the noise — Bailey's handbag — he saw in the corner of his eye Bailey reach out to the car's phone cradle, then heard her swear when she found it empty.

"Pass me my bag," she said as she pulled quickly over to the side of the road. Isaac did so, and Bailey hurriedly retrieved the phone, stabbed the answer button and held the phone to her ear.

"Troy," she announced, then — a few seconds later — "where?" Isaac could hear only a quiet and indistinct babbling from the phone in reply, but Bailey nodded urgently. "OK. Get the team there ASAP. Rendezvous four hundred metres west. That would be..." Isaac heard the phone murmur an indistinct reply. "Yep, perfect. Everyone tooled up and vested. But no lights or music on the way — let's not announce our presence. And make sure there's some uniform backup close by. Got that? Good."

Bailey tossed the phone at Isaac, flicked the car into drive and, peering quickly over her shoulder, accelerated the car away from the curb.

"What's happening?" he asked.

"We've found your plates, still attached to a blue Mazda" she replied. "I'm hoping their new owner is somewhere nearby."

Isaac had, over the last few days, formed an impression of Bailey as being rather a sedate driver. Not slow exactly, just unhurried. But she was far from unhurried now. He glanced over at the speedometer in time to see the numbers climb steadily above double the limit. Looking up at the road ahead, he saw a junction, controlled by traffic lights, approaching with unseemly haste. The lights were red, and there were two lines of cars waiting to move straight ahead across the junction. But there were no cars waiting to turn left — the left turn filter lane was empty. Bailey sped along the empty lane, braked to a crawl, then accelerated through a gap in the crossing traffic and straight across the junction — leaving a cacophony of indignant car horns behind her.

"Do they train you for this kind of driving in Police College?" he asked, discreetly trying to brace himself.

"They do," she replied calmly as she undertook a slow-moving truck by ploughing through a row of unoccupied angle parking spaces. "It was a long time ago, though. But I've got an old PlayStation, so I practise with that."

Isaac hoped she was joking. He shifted position to brace himself more tightly.

They were approaching a T-junction. Ahead of them, there was a queue of five cars waiting for a gap in the traffic. Bailey steered across the centre line to the other side of the road, causing a white Toyota Corolla that had just turned into the street to lurch uncertainly out of their way and up onto the kerb. Braking hard as she arrived at the junction, Bailey immediately turned into the flow of traffic, causing another outburst of infuriated honking.

They moved with the stream of traffic for about half a mile, moving into a run-down old style retail area. Half of the shops, Isaac noted, were boarded up, and the other half all seemed to be second hand stores selling junk that he would have sent to the tip. Bailey pulled the car over to the curb and parked next to a plain expanse of crumbling brick that Isaac assumed formed the side wall of some decrepit emporium around the corner a few yards ahead.

"Well, that was stimulating," said Isaac with what he hoped was a calm voice.

"Stay here and wait for me," replied Bailey. "With a bit of luck, I'm about to arrest a violent killer, and things could get untidy."

She undid her seatbelt, then reached across to her handbag by Isaac's feet and pulled out a small handgun — a G26 "baby Glock" — tucking it in what Isaac assumed was an "inside the waistband" holster in the small of her back. She climbed out of the car and went around to the back, opening the Prius's rear hatch.

In spite of Bailey's instructions, Isaac was in no mood for sitting quietly in the car. Bailey's driving had left him mildly hyperventilating, and he needed air. He opened the car door and stepped out onto the kerb.

Isaac remembered that he hadn't checked for approaching pedestrians at exactly the same moment that he collided with one. He swivelled out of the car straight into a face full of oncoming shirt, and felt a defensive hand pushing gently but firmly back on his shoulder.

"Hey! Careful there," came a deep and mildly indignant voice from somewhere above the shirt. Isaac straightened up to look his collision victim in the face, muttering self-conscious apologies.

Isaac was expecting to have to deal with some momentary embarrassment with a stranger. It took him a few seconds to work out exactly what it was that he was actually going to have to deal with. It started deep within his subconscious, as the instinctive reptilian part of Isaac's brain registered a visual pattern that required an urgent fight-or-flight reaction. Isaac felt the effects of the adrenaline being dumped into his system — the tightening of his stomach, the sudden thumping of his heart in his chest, the sense of time slowing down — without immediately realising why. It was exactly the same sensation that he had felt immediately before being knocked unconscious at Francesca's apartment.

Because, he slowly realised, he was looking at exactly the same man. For the second time in two days, Isaac found himself face-to-face with Francesca's killer.

Isaac wanted to call out to Bailey — to have her come and do whatever it is that cops do when dealing with brutish murdering thugs. He opened his mouth, but could make no sound. The killer gave him a puzzled look, then his eyes suddenly narrowed in recognition. He shoved Isaac hard back against the car door, then turned and ran back in the direction from which he'd come.

He travelled only about 2 metres before stumbling sideways. Isaac saw Bailey launch herself at the fleeing assassin, a Kevlar vest hanging loosely off one shoulder, her momentum forcing him off balance and against the wall.

But her weight and strength was no match for the killer's. He shrugged her off with a wave of his arm, then followed up with a sledgehammer punch to her solar plexus. Isaac heard Bailey's breath explode from her body in response to the blow, and watched her collapse to the ground — her face contorted in gasping agony. Isaac watched as the killer turned and, as Bailey lay struggling for breath on the ground, line up to land a massive kick to her head.

The adrenaline that was electrifying Isaac's body was also slowing time to a crawl. He watched as the killer, seemingly in slow-motion, shifted his weight to his right foot and brought his left leg back for the kick.

Isaac ran the scene fast-forward in his mind — picturing the heavily booted foot snapping Bailey's head back, breaking bone and dislocating vertebrae. There was no doubt in Isaac's mind that such a kick, from such a man, would cause serious, possibly permanent, damage. Without intervention from Isaac, Bailey was a fraction of a second away from almost certain permanent disability, and possible death.

In his entire life before this moment, Isaac had never — ever — been faced with the stark realities of choosing between bravery and cowardice. In the movies, brave men simply do what needs to be done, facing down mortal danger with no emotion beyond a passing disdain for those more timid than themselves, and prevailing by sheer force of willpower in the face of overwhelming odds.

Reality is not like the movies.

The reality, Isaac found, was one of near paralysing fear. He knew that if this mountain of a man turned his attentions back to Isaac, his bone crushing violence could destroy him almost as easily as it was about to obliterate Bailey. Deep down, far beyond the reach of his conscious will, Isaac's instinct for self-preservation drained his limbs of the energy for anything except flight.

Bravery, Isaac discovered in that moment, was not about being fearless. Bravery was about doing what needed to be done just when every fibre of your body was screaming at you to turn and run. Nearly drowning in his own dread and in the sure and certain knowledge that he was committing himself to pain and injury beyond his ability to imagine, Isaac pulled himself up and launched himself towards Bailey's attacker.

The force of Isaac's attack was enough to throw the killer back against the wall once more, the kick he had aimed at Bailey's head passing harmlessly a few millimetres above her face. But it was nothing more than a temporary reprieve — the killer quickly regained his balance and shoved hard against Isaac, sending him stumbling backwards.

Isaac regained his balance as best he could and looked at his opponent, waiting fearfully for the counter-attack. But the thug simply stood there, breathing heavily and staring back at Isaac with a withering malevolence. Then, after a few seconds, the killer shifted his attention to a point over Isaac's left shoulder. And, so slowly that at first Isaac thought the thug was preparing to renew the attack, he raised his hands in surrender.

Isaac turned and looked over his left shoulder. Two metres away he saw another mountain of a man, almost as thuggish as the one he had just attacked. But this one was elegantly dressed in a neatly-pressed 3-piece business suit that looked just slightly too small. And he had a handgun — a chromed Desert Eagle held in the classic two-handed Weaver stance and trained unwaveringly and unemotionally between the eyes of the killer.

Isaac heard Bailey struggling to her feet, and turned to see her stand — slowly, and clutching her abdomen in obvious pain.

"Finlayson, you idiot!" she gasped. "I told you to wear a vest!"

Eleven

"I hate violence" — Francesca Boyle

The pain was unimaginable. Her body screamed for the oxygen that had been ferociously expelled from her lungs by the punch. And yet each breath sent spasms of pain through her torso. She tried to straighten up, but her muscles simply refused to respond.

After her outburst at Finlayson, her capacity for further speech was gone. She just leaned against the wall, only vaguely aware of the police cars and uniforms beginning to swarm around the scene, of the shouted instructions at the captured killer, of him kneeling down with hands on head, him being handcuffed and led away.

She felt a hand on her shoulder. "Are you OK?"

It was, she thought, a stunningly stupid question. She used precious reserves of energy to deliver a withering look in reply. Then, after a few more laboured breaths, dug deeper to find the air to make a comment of her own.

"I told you to stay in the car. You could have got yourself killed."

As she said it, she noticed just how shaken Isaac looked. She knew from experience that his reaction would get worse over the next few minutes. She allowed herself to slide down the wall to a sitting position on the ground, and felt her breathing become more manageable. "Come and sit down, Isaac. You look like you could do with a rest." She looked up at Finlayson, who was returning his gun to its shoulder holster and carefully arranging his jacket to ensure that the pistol grip was still visible. "Why don't you go and find us all some coffees, Finlayson. Plenty of sugar."

"Sure thing, boss." The over-filled suit turned and headed down the street in search of a Starbucks.

She shrugged the Kevlar vest off her shoulder and let it drop to the ground between her knees. Then she put a hand on Isaac's shoulder. "Thanks," she said.

"Eh?"

"For jumping the guy, before he really laid into me. He wasn't being gentle, it would've hurt."

"Sure."

Bailey looked over at Isaac. His monosyllabic answers, vacant expression and almost-but-not-quite shaking hands confirmed to her that he was now fully submerged in his post-adrenaline crash. She was not, she admitted, feeling too good herself. Bailey allowed her head to rest back against the wall, and her eyes to close. She sat there, she wasn't sure how long for, as her breathing slowly returned to normal.

"Boss?"

Bailey looked up to see Finlayson crouched in front of her, holding out a small cardboard tray into which were wedged four takeaway cups. She nudged Isaac and gestured at him to take one before taking a cup herself. She took a sip, and out of the corner of her eye saw Isaac doing likewise. It was hot and sweet and strong. Finlayson must have ordered double-shots and put two tubes of sugar in each cup. Why, she wondered, couldn't he be that clued-up all the time?

"Thanks," she said, offering Finlayson a rare smile of appreciation. "Now head up the road and secure the Mazda. Then get a scene-of-crime team to go over the car. I want to know everything that car has to tell me by the end of the day. Got that?"

"No problem." Finlayson took one of the two remaining coffees from the tray, put the tray with the one remaining coffee on the ground by Isaac's feet, heaved his bulk up into a standing position and headed off up the road.

She could already feel the sugar and caffeine from the first mouthful of coffee seeping through her veins and working its restorative magic. She took another sip. The last remaining cup, still sitting in the corrugated cardboard tray by Isaac's feet, caught her eye. As she was idly wandering who it was for, Goff squatted down in front of them and took it.

"I hope you like your coffee strong and sweet," she said.

"I'm no great coffee connoisseur, boss. I like it hot and wet," Goff replied. "Everything else is just detail. Are you OK? You look like you're having a hard day."

"I think I must be getting old," she said. "I don't seem to be able to take a punch in the guts from a 200-pound gorilla like I used to." She cautiously shifted her feet under her, preparing for an attempt at standing.

"You don't practice enough. Getting to inspector makes you soft like that." Goff stood up and offered his hand to his superior officer. Bailey casually accepted it as her due and pulled herself up onto her feet. Then she turned and looked back down at Isaac, still sitting against the wall and sipping his coffee, and offered her hand in turn to him.

"Come on, before Goff here arrests you for vagrancy." Isaac looked up, smiled, accepted her hand and pulled himself up.

"I guess you won't need me to look at mug-shots any more," he said.

"I guess not," she replied. "I assume that was the guy from Francesca's apartment?"

"The very same. Not a face I'm likely to forget in a hurry. He made quite an impression." Isaac prodded gingerly at the bruising around his eye. "If you don't need me to go through mug shots, then if it's all the same to you I'd like to go home, curl up on the sofa and perhaps quietly drink a little too much Captain Morgan."

"I think we can manage that", Bailey replied. She turned back to Goff. "Get after the uniforms who took our man. I want you to process him, not them. Find out who he is. Charge him with assaulting Isaac and me here on the street this afternoon, and nothing else. Get him his lawyer and have him ready for me to interview by..." she looked at her watch, "six o'clock. Send his clothes to the lab for analysis. Have a scene-of-crime team go over his place. And get me his record and the preliminary results from the Mazda by 5:45. Got all that?"

"Suspect processed, charged with today's assault, lawyered-up and ready to chat by six. Preliminaries from the car and the guy's previous on your desk by 5:45. His clothes to the lab and SOC to turn over his place. Done." He turned and headed towards his car, a nondescript tan 2-litre Ford Focus sedan, parked across the street.

Bailey took another sip of coffee. She was still feeling winded, and breathing was still noticeably uncomfortable. But she was, she decided, able to function more-or-less normally. She turned to Isaac. "Come on," she said. "Let's get you home."

"OK," said Isaac. "But promise me you'll obey the speed limits this time," he continued, over his shoulder as he climbed into the passenger seat of the Prius.

Bailey noted the attempt at humour with relief. Isaac would, she concluded, be OK after his brush with the killer. She picked up her Kevlar vest from the ground then walked around to the back of the car, opened the hatch, threw in the vest and slammed the hatch closed again. Then she walked around the car to the driver's door, opened it, then pulled her Glock from the holster inside the waistband at the back of her jeans before lowering herself into the driver's seat — coffee in one hand, gun in the other.

Once inside the car, she passed the gun to Isaac. "Put that in my bag for me, would you. I hate the way it rubs against the small of my back when I'm driving."

"Erm... sure," he replied, and took the pistol by his thumb and forefinger at the base of the slide before reaching down uncertainly into the passenger foot well for her bag. Bailey noted how, like most men, Isaac seemed to have an irrational fear of handling women's bags — as if they might accidentally stumble upon some dreadful and secret Women's Thing within. Tampon phobia, she thought with a smile.

After watching Isaac cautiously lower the firearm into the bag, careful not to observe any of its contents, she flipped open the cup holder on the central armrest and gently placed her coffee cup in position. Then she pushed the key-fob into its slot on the dash, thumbed the start button, dropped the car into drive and eased out into the traffic.

They drove for a few minutes in reflective silence. Then, after draining the last of his coffee, Isaac said "So, you've got your killer. Is it usually that easy?"

"There is no 'usual' in homicide," she replied. "And besides, all we've got right now is a guy who assaulted us on the street. I'll need you to make a statement and formally identify him in a line-up for the assault in Francesca's apartment. We should really do that today, but we can hold off until tomorrow since you've had such a stimulating day. And then we'll need to see what we can find to link him to the murder, if anything."

"If anything? But it's got to be him, right?"

"Very probably. But proving it is another matter. We'll go over the car, his clothes, his home, his bank accounts, his known associates. Maybe we'll find enough of a link somewhere there, or maybe not. Maybe he'll talk to us, maybe he won't. If he does talk, maybe he'll give us enough to break the case, maybe not. And there's also, if your theory is correct, the small matter of who paid this guy to murder Francesca. And why. There's at least one other person out there who needs to be held to account for this, remember."

"So what happens now?"

"What happens now," she replied, "is you go home and curl up on the sofa with your bottle of Captain Morgan. And I go and do some police work."

They rode the rest of the journey to Isaac's house in silence — Bailey sipping the last of her coffee, Isaac holding his empty cup and staring wordlessly through the windscreen.

As they pulled up outside, Bailey turned to Isaac. "Take it easy with the rum tonight. I need you clear-headed for your statement and the identity line-up tomorrow."

Isaac smiled and nodded, then climbed out of the car and headed towards the house. After watching him disappear inside the house, Bailey did a U-turn and started on the short drive back to her apartment. Before she confronted Francesca's killer, she decided, she needed to take a shower. Maybe even a bath.

Twelve

"He's always been a bit of a villain." — Francesca Boyle

Detective Inspector Bailey Troy sat in the small interview room, considering the two men sitting opposite her. To her left, Detective Constable Goff sat impassively, arms crossed, a Manila folder sitting unopened on the table in front of him.

Diagonally across the table from Bailey sat Owen Walker. He was a man in his late thirties or early forties, dressed in a half-hearted, dishevelled and unironed attempt at business-casual attire — a plain white shirt open at the neck and straining against a paunch at the waist, plain charcoal grey slacks that were long overdue a visit to the dry-cleaner. He sat slumped and cross-legged in his chair, lightly drumming a pencil on an A4 pad on his lap and waiting patiently for the interview to begin. Owen, she knew, had two convictions for driving while drunk and one, long ago during a boisterous adolescence, for assaulting a police officer.

She also knew that he was being paid by the hour, having been appointed to represent her suspect at the taxpayers' expense. And she knew that his hit rate for getting acquittals for slam-dunk guilty scumbags was about 1 in 4. Although he would never number among the ranks of the dress-circle celebrity $1,000/hour criminal defence lawyers to whom the affluent guilty flocked, Owen Walker was nonetheless an advocate worthy of respect.

She turned her attention to Owen's client. Lucas Henriksen was 43 years old and had 7 convictions spread more or less evenly over the last thirty of them. Theft, assault, burglary, robbery, aggravated robbery, grievous bodily harm, obtaining money with menaces. Fairly typical for a small-time career violent criminal, although the number of convictions was not high for a man who had been in his line of work for as long as he had, suggesting that he was at least bright enough not to get caught too often.

Henriksen sat impassively in the paper dungarees that he had been given when his clothes had been taken away for forensic examination. He looked relaxed, apparently familiar with the process and unperturbed at the prospect of an eighth turn through the criminal justice system.

In spite of the caution she had expressed to Isaac, Bailey was confident that she would have the evidence to convict Henriksen of the murder of Francesca Boyle. The forensic examination of the car had found plenty of fingerprints that she was sure would provide a match. They had found jewellery that she was sure would turn out to have belonged to Francesca. Under the driver's seat they had found the gun — a Smith & Wesson 686 .357 Magnum that was currently at the lab being tested to see if it could be matched with the projectile found at the murder scene. They had the photo from the red light camera showing the car near the scene around the time of the murder. They might even strike it really lucky and get some trace evidence linking Henriksen to the scene.

And in the glove compartment, they had found an envelope containing $11,700 in crisp new fifty dollar notes. Bailey wasn't interested in using this interview to get more evidence of his guilt; she already had enough of that. She wanted to use the interview to find out where that envelope had come from.

Bailey turned and nodded to Goff, who started the tape. She recited the necessary preliminaries for the record, then turned to Henriksen.

"You've had your rights explained to you, and you understand them?"

"Yes," came the calm reply.

"Good. We both know the drill, both know how this works. So we needn't waste one another's time. You've been charged with assault following an incident this afternoon. I'd also like to talk to you in relation to a break-in at the apartment of one Francesca Boyle yesterday, and in relation to the murder of Francesca Boyle. Do you understand?"

Walker leant forward to interject. "My client acknowledges that he was at the Boyle woman's apartment yesterday, but denies breaking in." Bailey looked impassively at the lawyer. He was right, she admitted to herself; there had been no forced entry and several of the windows had been left open. "However," Walker continued, "my client does admit to the theft of some money and jewellery from the apartment. He maintains that he knows nothing about the poor girl's murder. As for the alleged assaults..."

"Let's not get ahead of ourselves," she replied. "Let me tell you what I know, and what I need from you. Then you can have a think about what you will and won't admit to. OK?"

"My client maintains..."

"Yes, yes, I heard you the first time," she interrupted. The more often Henriksen or his lawyer denied any involvement in the murder, she knew, the harder it would be to get him to tell her what she wanted to know.

She continued. "Lucas, just to get everyone on the same page here, I'm going to tell you what we already know. Some time around eight o'clock last Thursday evening, you stole a blue Mazda 3 from the Henley Heights area. Then on Friday afternoon, you stole the plates from another Mazda 3, belonging to a Mr Isaac Church, and fitted them to the stolen car. You then drove in the stolen Mazda to the offices of Dakin

Boyle, where you shot Francesca Boyle once through the head with your revolver. You dropped some nine millimetre brass at the scene, as part of an attempt to implicate Mr Church in the murder. Then on Sunday morning, you went to Francesca Boyle's apartment looking for something. We can link you to the car and the gun, we can link the car to the scene, we can link the gun to the shot that killed Ms Boyle, and we have a witness who saw you at the apartment."

"What evidence do you have linking...?"

"We're not in pre-trial discovery just yet, Mr Walker," she interrupted again. "This is my time to ask questions, not yours." She returned her attention to her suspect. "So now you know what I know, Lucas. You know what I'm going to put before a jury, and what they're going to consider for about ten minutes, max, before convicting you of murder. I'm not interested in having a discussion about it, because I know that's what happened and, as I said earlier, we both know not to waste one another's time."

She looked steadily at Henriksen. Henriksen looked steadily back, completely poker-faced. She went on. "But I'm not really after you, Lucas — you need to understand that. We both know you're just a small-time guy who got offered some easy big time money, and got caught in the middle when it all went pear shaped. These things happen, we both know that. You're not going to get off this, Lucas. I've got you nailed to the wall fair and square for the murder. But I am giving you a choice. You get to choose whether or not you're going to help me — so that I can help you by telling the judge that you cooperated with our enquiries."

Henriksen continued to stare back at her across the table. She let the silence drag on. Most people feel the urge to fill an uncomfortable silence, and she hoped that Henriksen would have the same impulse. She wanted him to ask her what it was that she wanted to know, and in so doing step across an invisible psychological line that meant he had bought into the dialogue. As soon as he asked that simple question, then he had implicitly acknowledged his guilt in the murder.

But he didn't. He had sat in that chair often enough to know when to keep his mouth shut. He wasn't relaxed or cocky, she noticed, simply expressionless. She guessed that he believed her about the weight of evidence against him. If he didn't, if her description of what had happened was too far off the mark, he would be looking more relaxed. But she could see that he wasn't relaxed, he was simply trying not to give anything away. He knew, she judged, that he was going down for murder. But he wasn't about to be bounced into deciding what to do about it.

She pressed on. "People like you and people like me understand one another, Lucas. You've made a career choice that's outside the law. I've made a career choice to hold you to account for it. That's all fair enough. But there's a big difference between a career criminal and someone who plays at being respectable but can pay money to have a promising young woman's life snuffed out. Whoever paid you to do this has no respect, do you know what I mean? They want to have it both ways. They want to have the nice law-abiding lifestyle when it suits them, and then happily drop twelve grand to get you to do their wet work for them rather than do it themselves. And they won't bat an eyelid now that you're going to get convicted for the murder that they ordered. All for a lousy twelve grand. I don't think that's fair, Lucas. I don't want you to take the heat for this on your own. You were just doing a piece of paid work. It was someone else who took the decision to have this woman murdered, not you. You shouldn't have to take the rap on this all by yourself, Lucas."

She paused for 5 seconds before continuing quietly. "Tell me who gave you the twelve grand, Lucas. I just need a name."

"My client maintains that he stole the money from the apartm..."

Henriksen held up his hand to stop his lawyer in mid-sentence. After a few seconds, he said "I'd like a few minutes alone with Mr Walker, if that's okay with you Inspector."

"You can have fifteen minutes. Interview suspended at," she looked at her watch, "6:25pm." She reached across and switched off the tape, then turned to Goff and nodded in the direction of the door. With a metallic scraping of chair legs they both got up and left the lawyer and his client to decide on their next steps.

Out in the corridor, Bailey turned to Goff. "Get me an update on any lab results, and meet me in my office in five."

"Will do, Boss." Goff turned and strode off down the corridor.

Bailey walked slowly towards her office. She had little to do there except wait for Goff to return with any news from the lab. It had been a long-shot expecting Henriksen to offer up a name. The reality was that contract killers weren't exactly at the front of the queue when it came to leniency in sentencing. Henriksen would probably have worked that out, and if not his lawyer would be telling him right now.

But then she guessed that contract killing was probably a new career move for him. There was nothing in his prior record that showed anything approaching murder, particularly not carefully planned assassinations such as this had been intended to be. She imagined his career to date had been as low cost, hired muscle — doing odd-jobs for aspiring local crime lord wannabes in the Southern Suburbs who needed pimps or dealers on their square mile of turf roughed up from time to time. An execution carefully planned to take out two people — one by death and one by being framed for the murder — was just too much of a stretch for him.

Goff knocked on the door of her office, and then walked in without waiting to be invited.

"We've got Henriksen's prints on the stolen Mazda, including on the plates, as well as on the gun and the envelope. There's also a partial print from Church's Mazda around the area of the front plate that's consistent with Henriksen's, but not conclusive. Plus there are three pieces of gravel from the shoes he was wearing that are the same as the gravel laid in front of the Dakin Boyle offices — and with about a thousand other places around town, unfortunately. No word yet on whether the gun matches the projectile recovered from the scene, or on whether they can match his prints to any found at the scene."

"Were there any prints on the nine mil cases at the scene?"

"Partials, yes. No word yet on whether they match Henriksen's."

"Any other trace evidence linking him to the scene?"

"Nothing yet, but they've got a lot to work through."

"What do we know about the gun? Have we traced it?"

"The serial number's been ground off. They may be able to work out the number through X-ray analysis of the frame, but it'll take a while."

"The ammo in the gun?"

"The gun was fully loaded. All the bullets were unfired. Federal Power-Shok one eighty grain hollow-points."

That was positive news, she thought to herself. The bullet brand matched the projectile recovered from the scene.

"What about the envelope and the notes? Are there any other prints on those, apart from Henriksen's?"

"One unmatched partial on the envelope. Not Henriksen's, not the victim's. They're still working on the notes."

"OK," she said. "I want everyone who works at Dakin Boyle fingerprinted and their prints compared with the partial on the envelope."

"I'll get onto it as soon as they open up in the morning," replied Goff.

"Did we find anything useful at his place?"

"A few more changes of clothes to send to the lab. A box of ammo that the bullets in the gun most probably came from."

"How many rounds missing from the pack?"

"Seven."

"That's six in the gun, and one used to shoot Francesca. What are our chances of finding the used case, do you think?"

"Well, it's not in the car, or at Dakin Boyle, or at his place. Short of checking every trash can and drain on every possible route between the murder scene and his place, I'd say pretty slim, Boss."

"OK," she said slowly, assessing the information. "We're pretty certain that this is our guy. But where are the evidential gaps in our narrative? What's his story going to be — consistent with our evidence, but showing him not committing the murder?"

"Well," Goff replied, "he could claim to have acquired the gun after the shooting, or that it wasn't his gun that killed Boyle. He could have stolen Church's plates just to make the car more usable. He could have just happened to have been driving through the area on Friday night and got caught by the red light camera. He could have decided to burgle the apartment having heard about the murder on the news. And he could have found the money at the apartment, just like he says. Which would mean he had no motive for the killing."

"The claim to have taken the money from the apartment is pretty weak," she said. "Francesca lived in a world of black credit cards, not cash. Best check the victim's bank records to make sure there were no large withdrawals, just in case."

"Already done," Goff replied. "There weren't. She had regular payments for rent and utility bills from her cheque account, and lived her life on her credit card, like you say. Hasn't even used an ATM for the last six months."

"Nice work. If the money didn't come from her bank account, see if you can find out where it *did* come from. Get a warrant to check the bank accounts of everyone at Dakin Boyle. And what about the envelope? Does it match any found at her apartment, or among the stationery used at Dakin Boyle, or at Henriksen's place?"

"Henriksen isn't big on stationery, but I don't know about the apartment or the office. I'll check it out."

She shook her head. "Get Finlayson to do it. Did you get any word from the lab on our chances of matching the gun to the projectile from the scene?"

"Hard to know, Boss, there's a lot of ifs. If the gun has been well used to create distinctive striations, and if the gun barrel hasn't been cleaned with a wire pull-through since the firing, then the lab guys will tell you that they'll be able to pin it down maybe seventy or eighty per cent of the time. The odds will be a little worse due to the bullet being so deformed, a little better because we know the brand of ammo and because the test shot will almost certainly be the first one fired by the gun since the killing. So more likely than not, but not certain."

Bailey raised an eyebrow. "Listen to Mr Ballistics Expert, here! Did you learn all that at Police College?"

Goff laughed. "No Boss. I learned it getting the phone number of the forensic ballistics chick at the lab this afternoon. I'll have forgotten it all by this time tomorrow."

"A nice young lady, eh?"

"Cute bod, brains, just feisty enough, and she loves guns. What could be better? Just remember I saw her first, Boss. Don't go jumping my claim."

"I wouldn't dream of it," she laughed. "Not unless she's got a truly beautiful bod, anyway. Come on, let's go and see what Mr Henriksen has to say for himself."

Two minutes later they were again sat in the interview room, looking across the table at the killer and his lawyer. Bailey restarted the tape.

"Interview restarted at 6:55pm." She looked across at Henriksen, who stared back, his face still a mask. "OK, Lucas. We all know where we stand. And you know what I want to know. So tell me, who gave you the envelope?"

Henriksen turned to face his lawyer, who took his cue to lean forward and speak.

"My client concedes that he stole the car, and that he entered Ms Boyle's apartment and stole some items of jewellery and an amount of money. But he knows nothing about the murder, and declines to be interviewed further."

Bailey closed her eyes and exhaled slowly through her nose. Then she opened her eyes and looked at her watch.

"Interview concluded at 6:56pm."

Thirteen

"It's nice to know that you've got someone watching out for you." —
Francesca Boyle

Isaac stood at the glass, looking through into the room beyond. There, in a row against the far wall, stood seven men. They all looked alike — big, hard, humourless guys, going slightly to seed in middle age. Men who had learned to get what they wanted, through intimidation and the threat of violence implied by their brawny bulk.

Isaac recognised two of them.

At the right-hand end of the line, beneath a large number "7" stencilled on the wall, stood Finlayson — the detective who had sat in on his first interview with Inspector Church, and who had made his timely appearance at yesterday's brief street brawl. He stood side on, staring along the row of men with an aggressively proprietorial look.

Isaac pointed at Finlayson. "Are you supposed to use people I already know in a line up?"

Bailey laughed. "He does fit the description quite well, doesn't he? But no, I think we can safely say that we have eliminated Constable Finlayson from our enquiries. Now tell me if you recognise any of the other six men."

Isaac remembered reading somewhere once that most suspects, when given the choice, position themselves more or less in the centre of a line-up. But the smart thing to do, if he recalled correctly, was to stand at one end. Victims paid less attention to the suspects at each end of the line, apparently, subconsciously assuming that the person they were looking for would be somewhere in the middle.

Francesca's killer had done the smart thing.

"The man on the far left, at position number one," he said. "He's the man who was in Francesca's apartment on Sunday, and who attacked me yesterday."

"Perfect," replied Bailey. She nodded at the uniformed officer standing beside the door, who then turned and stepped out of the room, appearing a few seconds later the other side of the glass to confer with Finlayson and lead the line-up participants out. "I'll get Finlayson to give you a lift home."

"Actually, I need to go to Dakin Boyle. I've got some stuff I need to do there."

"Stuff?"

"Y'know — work," Isaac answered. "I've still got to pay the bills, and the company still has to have systems that work. Just routine system support."

"Fair enough. I'll get him to drive you to Dakin Boyle."

Isaac folded his arms and looked at the back of the killer as he was led out. "Do you think you have enough to convict him?"

"Well, he's denying the murder, and he's got a good lawyer. But we've got his fingerprints in all the right places, and plenty of other circumstantial evidence, so I think we'll get a result. I'm more concerned to know who put him up to it."

"Yeah," nodded Isaac, still staring into the now empty room beyond the glass. "It's pretty creepy thinking that there's someone out there who paid to have Francesca killed. Is there any chance it was all just down to him?"

Bailey shook her head. "We found the money he was paid for the job. Someone definitely put him up to it."

Isaac was still staring absently into the adjacent room. "So what's the life of a young woman worth these days? No, wait." Isaac's mind, suddenly back in problem solving mode, had just thrown up something to check. He looked up at Bailey. "Let me guess — twelve grand?"

Bailey raised an eyebrow. "Pretty good guess. Do I need to check your fingerprints against the ones we found on the envelope containing the money?"

Isaac smiled weakly and shook his head. "Twelve grand tells you that neither your suspect nor his customer really knew what they were doing. One or other of them had to use Google to find out what the going rate is to hire an assassin. Try it yourself — go to Wikipedia and look up contract killing. It's right there."

Bailey's eyebrow was, Isaac noted, still raised in mock suspicion. "And should I," she asked, "be asking myself why you were researching the economics of contract killing on the web?"

"It just seemed topical somehow," he replied. "What are the chances of finding the guy behind all this, do you think?"

"We've still got plenty of lines of enquiry," she said, walking out of the door and gesturing with her head for him to follow. "If you promise to buy me a coffee, I'll let you know if we make any real progress."

Isaac suspected that the police were not in the habit of casually sharing details of the state of their investigations with civilians. But he took the brush-off with good grace. They walked in silence through to the front desk area.

"Finlayson will meet you outside. I'll call you if there's any progress."

"Sure." Isaac waved a casual goodbye and stepped out into the sunlight.

The front of the police station opened into a small parking area, set back from the main road. Isaac leant against the wall beside the entrance and waited for the promised ride. After a few minutes, an old third generation BMW 525i sedan swung into the parking area. Isaac noticed that, in spite of its age, the car had been well looked after. The white paintwork was flawless and scrupulously polished. He could see the bulky form of Constable Finlayson in the driver's seat, and so walked around and knocked on the passenger-side window. Finlayson looked around, then reached over and opened the passenger door.

"Jump in. The boss says to take you wherever you need to go. Where's that?"

Isaac slid into the passenger seat. The interior of the car, though worn, was as immaculately maintained as the exterior. "To Dakin Boyle. Thanks," replied Isaac. With that, Finlayson slipped the transmission into reverse and started manoeuvring out of the car park.

They drove in a stony silence that Isaac found increasingly uncomfortable. After 3 or 4 minutes, to break the silence he offered: "My name's Isaac."

Finlayson's eyes didn't waver from the road. "I know."

"Yours?"

"Finlayson."

This, Isaac decided, was going to be hard work. But he persisted. "Do you have a first name?"

"Yes. Constable."

Isaac could take a hint. He returned to silence.

Then in the periphery of his vision he noticed the detective turn and take a long appraising look at him, seemingly oblivious to what might be unfolding on the road ahead. After what seemed like ages, he appeared to make a decision, and returned his attention to the road.

"My first name's Paige. You got kids?"

"Erm, no," replied Isaac, struggling to relate the name to the bulk sitting beside him. "Why?"

"Well, if you do, if you get a boy, don't call him Paige. OK?"

"OK. Got it. What do you like to be called?"

"Anything except Paige. Only my mother gets to call me that, and I only see her twice a year." He slowly rotated his head to stare at Isaac again, as if to emphasise the point.

"Sure. Perhaps I'll just stick with Constable."

"That sounds like a good plan." The Constable returned his attention once more to the road.

As rapport went, it was slim pickings, Isaac reflected. But he felt that they had reached some kind of grudging *modus vivendi* that should at least see them through the rest of the journey. Isaac decided that he had earned the right to at least one more attempt at conversation.

"How long have you been a detective?"

"It'll be five years in September," Finlayson replied. "Four years on the highway before that. And three years general duties. Twelve years on the job all together."

"You enjoy it?"

"Detective work?" Finlayson shrugged. "It's okay. I preferred working the highway."

"So why do you do it? The detective work."

Finlayson stared ahead. "Sometimes you just gotta do what you gotta do."

There's not really anywhere to take that, Isaac thought to himself. He tried a different tack. "What do you think of Inspector Troy?"

"She's my boss."

Hard work. Isaac tried again. "She seems smart."

Finlayson turned again, assessing his passenger for several seconds. He appeared to reach a conclusion, and turned his attention slowly back to the road ahead. "She is smart. Very smart. Helluva smarter than I'll ever be. Smart takes you a long way in this job, but it's not always enough. Sometimes smart just gets you into trouble. And when it does, you need someone to get you out. And I'd hate to think of the boss getting into any trouble she couldn't get out of."

"Fair enough," Isaac responded. Fair enough, indeed.

"I stay a detective, the boss stays out of trouble. We all play to our strengths." As he said this, he eased the car into the kerb and to a gentle stop outside the imposing campus of Dakin Boyle. He turned back to Isaac, and nodded silently in the direction of the entranceway, leaving Isaac with the distinct impression that no further conversation would be tolerated. Isaac thanked the detective for the ride and, receiving just a non-committal shrug in reply, stepped out of the car and towards the foyer of Dakin Boyle.

"Good morning, Millie," he said to the receptionist as he stepped through the door.

"My Excel's still not working properly," she replied sternly without looking up. "You promised me you were going to fix that."

"You're right, I did. How about if I look at it today before I go? I need to get some database stuff sorted out for Jenny first. Is she in?"

"Of course she is," the receptionist said, still without looking up from her screen. "She's been here since seven-thirty, same as always. Works too hard, that girl, if you ask me. Mr. Boyle's here too."

Mr. Boyle. Never Dick. Isaac smiled at Millie's determinedly hierarchical view of life. In Millie's world Dick, Bill, and Gus — or "Mr. Boyle", "Mr. Dakin", and "young Mr. Dakin" as she would always call them — as owners and heirs of the Dakin Boyle empire were entitled to the formal mode of address. Dick, Isaac knew, hated it. Bill and Gus, by contrast, seemed to take it quite happily as their due.

Millie had always referred to Francesca as "Miss Boyle," too.

Isaac headed towards Dick's office, barely even aware of having decided to do so.

As befits the co-founder and co-owner of one of the most successful privately owned pharmaceutical companies in the world, Dick Boyle's office was spacious and well appointed, with floor-to-ceiling windows on two sides looking out over the well manicured lawns of the campus. And as befits a man who concerns himself more with the deeper mysteries of biochemistry than with the practicalities of running a business, the room was a mess. Even more of a mess, Isaac noticed, than usual.

So was Bill.

Bill had always had an air of the faintly forgetful about him. And, in all the time that Isaac had known him, of the faintly morose. He recalled that Jenny had once told him that he had been that way since the death of his wife, never quite fully emerging from his grief. Not incapable of a laugh or a joke when the situation required it, just a tendency to drift towards the gloomy.

As Isaac looked at the man sat behind the large and copiously papered desk, he saw that Bill had gone far beyond gloomy and was well into the realms of the thoroughly miserable. And the hint of stale sweat that he noticed as soon as he stepped into the room suggested that Bill's habitual absent mindedness had perhaps taken a step in the direction of self neglect.

Isaac quietly slid himself into a visitor's chair. After a few moments, without looking up, Bill spoke.

"They've caught him. They've caught the man who..." Isaac saw the distraught father struggle, unable to say the words "the man who killed my daughter."

"I know." There seemed to Isaac to be little more that needed to be said.

"I spoke to the police, to that Inspector Troy, just a few minutes ago. She's the one who arrested you, isn't she?" Bill looked up and attempted a smile. It didn't work.

Isaac smiled back. "Yes, that's her. She seems pretty smart. I'm sure she'll get to the bottom of it all."

"Do you think so? Do you think she'll really work it all out? Will she really find out exactly why he... did that to Francesca?"

"From what I've seen of Inspector Troy," Isaac replied, "if anyone can get to the bottom of it all, then she can."

As Isaac looked at Bill, he got a strange feeling that the older man had not found that to be as reassuring as he had intended.

Fourteen

"Guys act like it's the end of the world when you dump them; for, like, ten seconds." — Francesca Boyle

Without waiting to be invited, Isaac walked into the Chief Technologist's office and sat casually at one of the chairs around the circular meeting table.

"Are you here to speed up those reporting queries for me?" Jenny asked without looking up from her screen.

"I'll run the optimizer across the BI database, see what it comes up with. Of course," he added with a smile, "it would help if you didn't keep changing your mind about what reports you wanted to run."

Jenny's face twitched with a suppressed smile of her own, but she remained resolutely focused on the screen in front of her. "What's the point of paying for an ad-hoc report writing tool if all my ad-hoc reports are going to bring the system to its knees?"

"I keep telling you, you need a separate reporting server. Then you could run all the reports you want without affecting the production systems. What's the point of paying for my advice if you're not going to follow it?"

"I don't pay for your advice. I pay for your time to get my servers running properly. You just choose to spend the time giving me advice that I haven't asked for and that you know I'm going to ignore. I should ask for a refund."

"It's good advice. I should charge double for it."

"Sure. Try that, see how you get on."

Jenny looked up from the screen and straight at Isaac. Her expression shifted subtly from deadpan to serious, the obligatory introductory banter was over. "Have you been in to see Dick?" she asked quietly.

He nodded solemnly. "He's not in good shape."

"He hasn't been in good shape for ten years," Jenny replied. "But this has completely knocked him over. Hardly surprising, I guess. I'm still shaken about it myself when I think about it. Francesca was just... Well, you knew her, you know what she was like."

Isaac simply nodded in reply. "Why is he even here? You, Bill and Gus can run the place. He should be at home."

Jenny shook her head. "There's nothing there for him at home. Just his brother, and I don't think they really get on too well. At least if he's here Millie can keep taking him tea and biscuits."

"I guess," Isaac replied. "They caught the guy who did it, did you hear?"

A hint of a smile flickered across Jenny's face. "The way I heard it, it was *you* who caught him. It looks like he put up a bit of a fight." She raised her eyebrows enquiringly and tapped lightly just below her right eye.

Isaac gently probed the bruising around his eye. "No, not me. This black eye is about all I caught. And besides, he got away that time. He was a big guy, that's for sure."

"Well, if there were no heroics then there'll be no sympathy. You can go and get my reports working. I need to get the ISO 15378 compliance certs out today, and I want to get home in time to watch CSI."

"CSI? That's the best you've got for tonight? That's not even on until nine o'clock. Millie was right, you work too hard."

"Is that what she said?" Jenny replied with measured indifference. "Well, I appreciate her concern, of course. But I don't think Millie really understands what a wild party girl I am under this drab exterior." She returned her attention to her screen.

Remembering Bailey's comments from earlier that morning, Isaac allowed himself to reflect on what sort of girl Jenny might really be like under her self-confessed and determinedly drab exterior. He examined the contours of her t-shirt, and imagined himself slowly lifting it — easing it gently over her head to reveal what he judged were ample but firm breasts. The prospect was, he decided, not without some appeal.

"OK party girl. I'm off to fix up your reporting database. But you're going to have to work on your reputation, and you can start by skipping CSI tonight and letting me buy you a drink."

"Having a drink with you is supposed to enhance my reputation?"

"You've got to start somewhere," he said. "Eight o'clock, Top of the Tower?"

She smiled, without lifting her gaze from the screen. "If you want me to be there by eight o'clock then you'd better get those reports running right now."

"I'm on to it. See you there." With a parting smile, he jumped up and left.

Dakin Boyle's server room was little more than a cupboard. It contained one rack of computer and network equipment, a small table and an old office swivel chair. A noisy and absurdly overpowered air conditioning unit kept the air temperature oscillating between 15 and 18 degrees Celsius, averaging eight degrees below the temperature that Isaac had specified to the HVAC engineer on several occasions. Isaac zipped up his sweater, pulled out his laptop and plugged in the network cable that had been left lying across the table.

Isaac didn't really need to sit in the server room to work on the servers, he could connect to them from any network connection across the campus. But he liked to be able to concentrate undisturbed when he was working, and if he shut himself in here then he wouldn't be interrupted. He fired up his laptop and logged on.

It took him about forty five minutes to find and fix the source of Jenny's slow reports — one of Jenny's new report definitions was causing multiple full-table scans when it ran. He added a new index, allowed it to build, and ran the report. It completed almost instantaneously. Job done, money earned.

Isaac leaned back in the chair and looked at the rack of equipment. It wasn't just Jenny that didn't follow his advice; the rack was a mess. Every piece of equipment was out of warranty. And there was, Isaac knew, no redundancy built into the systems. One fried motherboard could see Dakin Boyle grind to a halt for days. A fire, or a burglary, or a disgruntled ex-employee with a sledgehammer could leave them unable to operate for weeks.

Isaac had on many occasions suggested to Bill and Dick that they needed to upgrade the equipment, to replace it with something with some built-in redundancy, preferably with a duplicate set-up across the campus in the plant building. Dick, though co-owner, rarely concerned himself with the details of the commercial side of the organisation — he would usually just agree with Isaac's recommendations with a hand-waving dismissal of the detail, an acknowledgement that Isaac knew best, and a suggestion to take it to Bill. But Bill Dakin, like many business owners with no shareholders or external directors to hold them to account for their risk management, was a hard man to part from his money on the strength of a "what if".

Isaac tapped on the keyboard, started up the backup console program and examined the information it showed him on the screen. The backup had run successfully last night, and the system had a fresh tape in the drive ready for tonight. At least Jenny was diligent in changing the tapes and taking them off-site. Keeping them at her home was not the most secure of off-site storage facilities, but it was better than nothing.

Before leaving — or at least, before attempting to leave via the main reception — he would, he knew, need to fix Millie's Excel problem. He knew exactly what the root cause of Millie's problem was — Millie. She was the only person in the company whose computer was still using the 2003 version, which she refused to allow to be upgraded on the basis that she had neither the time nor inclination to learn how to use the newer software. As a consequence, Millie increasingly found herself unable to open spreadsheets that others emailed her. All of which was, according to Millie, Isaac's fault.

It would be easy enough to fix. He established a remote-connection to Millie's desktop across the network — he knew better than to ask her to yield the keyboard, even for five minutes, to let him work directly on her machine — and installed the add-on software that would allow Excel 2003 to open files from later versions of the program.

There was more that he had to do. There were new virtual servers to be set up for the testing of Pharmazeutika v12. But that would take several hours, and he was not in the mood to tackle it today. It could wait. He spent thirty minutes checking the logs, free disk space and other signs of health on each of the servers, then shut down his laptop, packed it up and headed towards the reception.

He stopped as he passed Dick Boyle's office, and looked in. Dick was still sat at his desk, staring at his screen. One hand on was the mouse, the other beside the keyboard, neither was moving.

"I'm just about to call a cab and head off, Dick," he called through the door. "Give me a call if you need anything, OK?"

Dick looked up, vaguely startled. "Eh? Oh, sure. Thanks for coming in." There was a pause as the two men looked at one another, Isaac conscious that more should be said, but not knowing what to say. Then he noticed Dick frown in puzzlement. "Why a cab?" he asked.

"Sorry?" Isaac replied.

"You said you were getting a cab. Is there something wrong with your car?"

"No, not really. But it's evidence, apparently. The plates in particular. I can't drive it until the police have finished with it."

"Oh, right. Of course. Well, erm..." After a moment of apparent indecision, Dick got up and walked across to the low cabinet that stretched half way along the far wall. A cardboard box sat on the papers strewn over its top. He reached into the box and pulled out a small pale coloured Gucci shoulder bag, which Isaac recognised as Francesca's. Dick fumbled with the bag's unfamiliar fastening before opening it, reaching in, and pulling out a set of keys. He weighed the keys in his hand for a few seconds, then looked up and tossed them at Isaac.

"You should use Francesca's car," Dick said as Isaac scrabbled to catch the keys. "She won't... well, I think she would have wanted you to use it. It's in the car park. It's just been sitting there since Friday. And to be honest I'd really rather it was... not there. You understand, I'm sure. You will take it, won't you?"

"I... erm... yeah. Of course. That's very kind, Dick. Thank you. I'll take good care of it."

Isaac left Dick to his grief and headed out to the car park. He wasn't entirely sure whether he had just been lent a car or given one. But in any case it would be good to have a means of transport again. And Francesca's late model Audi A3 would certainly be a step up from his Mazda.

It was a strange feeling getting into Francesca's car. Isaac could smell a hint of her perfume still lingering in the car interior. It was, he recalled, some expensive Christian Dior type — she had told him once that it was her "summer" fragrance. It left Isaac with the uneasy sense of her being there in the car with him. He stabbed at the controls in the door armrest to wind down all the windows before dropping the car into drive, manoeuvring carefully out of the car park, and heading for home.

Fifteen minutes later he pulled into his driveway. He had enjoyed the drive. He had only ever been a passenger in the car before, but he found the two-litre engine just powerful enough, and the suspension firm enough, to make driving it fun. It was a long way from being a sports car, but quite nimble. If it did turn out to be a gift rather than just a loaner, he wouldn't complain. But even though the drive had blown away the last remains of the Christian Dior, he suspected he would be feeling the ghost of Francesca Boyle in the car for some time to come.

He climbed out of the car and walked up the driveway to his front door. As he opened the door and stepped in, and with a mental agility that comes naturally to young men everywhere, he left behind his tangle of emotions over his dead ex-girlfriend and turned his thoughts instead to the prospect of getting laid that night.

Isaac knew from experience that turning the prospect into reality would require some preparation. There was laundry to be done — both clothing and bed linen. The place would need to be tidied, the liquor cabinet re-stocked. Did Jenny drink wine? Red or white? He didn't know. Best to get both — a Sauvignon Blanc and a Merlot. Isaac knew enough about wine to successfully navigate a wine list, without really caring enough about the subject to be a wine snob. For dating, he stuck to basic varieties and chose labels that avoided obviously pretentious pricing but could be relied upon to deliver a pleasant drinking experience. It was a formula that had served him, and his libido, adequately well over the years. To cover all the bases, he added a bottle of Baileys to his mental shopping list. Then he walked into the bedroom and started picking up dirty laundry from the floor.

At precisely 7:55 that evening, Isaac stepped from the cab at the foot of the Plaza Tower and paid off the driver. He had foregone the luxury of driving into town, having decided that the use of a dead ex-girlfriend's car was not conducive to a successful outcome on a first date.

Although he didn't regard himself as a vain man, Isaac did like to take care over his appearance at times such as this. He had dressed in a freshly laundered and immaculately ironed indigo chambray shirt over a plain white crew neck T-shirt. The sleeves were rolled to just below the elbow, and the shirt hung untucked over black tailored trousers. Although he hadn't shaved — he had decided that a day's worth of stubble enhanced the image he was aiming for — he had nonetheless applied just a hint of Burberry Touch after-shave. He walked into the lobby of the Plaza Tower and over to the elevators, then pressed the elevator call button. A set of elevator doors immediately slid open. He stepped in and punched the button for the top floor.

The Top of the Tower was one of those rare bars that had discovered the secret of always being popular while at the same time never appearing to be crowded. Being on the top floor of one of the tallest commercial buildings in the central business district, it was popular with those office workers who were affluent and discerning enough not to flinch at its moderately absurd prices. The ambience was subdued without being gloomy, the background music pleasant without being obtrusive, the service prompt without being rushed.

Jenny Watson sat at the bar, nursing a long pale drink over ice. Slightly to Isaac's surprise, she looked absolutely stunning.

The horn rimmed glasses were gone. Her hair had been curled and blow-dried into the sort of tastefully casual look that took hours to create. Her face had been discreetly and expertly made-up to create a hint of arousal without any obvious sign of having been painted. She wore a charcoal coloured knee-length evening dress with elegantly simply lines, topped with a hypnotically plunging neckline that Isaac's eyes found impossible to ignore.

This was Dakin Boyle's Chief Technologist as Isaac had never seen her before.

Isaac slid into the barstool beside her and gestured to attract the barman's attention. "Hi," he offered.

Jenny turned to him with half a smile. "Is that the best you've got? I was hoping for 'wow, you look beautiful,' at least."

"Wow, you look beautiful," he replied.

"Gee, thanks." Jenny took a sip of her drink.

"Actually, no. You do. I'm, er... I mean it's not..." Isaac made a conscious decision to stop and engage brain before proceeding further. "Really, you do look quite amazing. I'm glad you came."

"OK, good recovery. You're off the hook." She looked up at him and smiled. A genuine, warm smile. "But you'd better order your drink before the barman here dies of old age."

Isaac ordered a Heineken, no glass, from the patiently waiting barman, who returned with the bottle a few seconds later. Isaac slid his credit card across the bar. "Run a tab on that for me, will you?"

"Sure thing." The barman picked up the credit card and placed it alongside 3 others behind the cash register.

"Let's go and find a table," he suggested. They both slid off their barstools and headed to a vacant table in the far corner.

"Tell me about the black eye," Jenny said as soon as they were seated. "I want to hear all about it."

"OK. Dick called on Saturday and asked me to help clear out Francesca's apartment. I went round there on Sunday, let myself in. He was already in there. The guy who killed Francesca, I mean. He must've been looking for something. A big ugly guy, he was. Anyway, as soon he saw me he punched my lights out. Just one blow, and it was all over. The next thing I know he's gone and I'm lying on the floor surrounded by police and paramedics."

"Ouch! Are you OK? Not concussed or anything?"

"Well, I spent the rest of Sunday hanging around at the hospital waiting for a doctor to tell me something useful. But in the end I gave up and left. So I could possibly be about to drop dead from a brain haemorrhage at any moment. But I doubt it. The headache has gone, and the swelling around my eye has gone down enough that I can kinda halfway see out of it again. So I think the official diagnosis has to be: black eye, go home and stay out of trouble."

"Sounds like good advice. But from what I hear, you didn't follow it."

Isaac smiled and shook his head in acknowledgement. "Well I tried to. I thought I was just going to go through some mug shots at the police station with Bailey," Isaac replied. "But they found him before we even got to the station. I was there when they arrested him. There was a bit of pushing and shoving," he said with what he hoped was heroic understatement, "but basically they just handcuffed him and took him away."

But it wasn't Isaac's heroics that had caught Jenny's attention. "Bailey? You mean the inspector? I've met her. She seems... nice."

Isaac chuckled. He knew exactly what that meant. "Maybe. But I don't think I'm really her type."

"Oh? Why's that?" Jenny asked, raising her drink to drain the last of it. Her voice was just a smidgeon louder than it needed to be. Isaac suspected that the drink wasn't her first.

"Well... I think... Actually, it's because *you're* more her type."

Jenny slammed the glass down on the table as she tried to laugh and swallow at the same time. "Really? Oh my god! She's a cherry picker? Are you sure? How do you know?"

Cherry picker. Isaac reflected that he had learned more euphemisms for lesbianism in the last two days than in his previous 28 years. "Yes, I'm sure. She told me. I think she quite fancied you, actually."

Jenny laughed again. "What *were* you talking about, that got her to tell you that? No, on second thoughts, I don't want to know." She laughed and waved her hands in mock denial, before leaning towards Isaac and continuing in a conspirational stage whisper: "You know, I don't think I've ever had another woman get the hots for me before. She seemed very calm and professional when she interviewed me."

"What did she want to know about?" A part of the problem-solving area of Isaac's cortex, the small portion of it not currently given over to the task of getting this beautiful woman naked and moaning ecstatically beneath him, was still puzzling over the many loose ends that surrounded Francesca's murder.

"Oh," Jenny gave a dismissive nothing-really shrug. "She wanted to know about the kind of work that Francesca did. Then she asked about how the Mertusugene was made. She didn't know that it was actually a virus, rather than a drug as such, so we went through that. And she asked about the generics we make over at Wade Park. It just sounded like general background stuff, rather than any particular line of enquiry. She got a bit frosty when I told her that we didn't ship much product to Africa because too few people there could afford it."

"I imagine she would," Isaac answered non-committally. "It's not my favourite aspect of this industry either, to tell you the truth," he continued. "But I guess nobody would invest in drugs if they couldn't make money from them."

Isaac signalled a passing waitress, raising his eyebrows and pointing at Jenny's empty glass and his drained bottle. The waitress nodded and disappeared, reappearing a few moments later with fresh drinks.

"Cheers!" Jenny picked up her drink and took a long sip. Isaac wondered exactly how many drinks Jenny had drunk before he arrived. She was not drunk exactly, he judged, but certainly more chatty than usual.

"Oh, I don't know," she said. "I think Dick would."

"Sorry? Dick would what?" Deep in his thoughts, Isaac had lost track of the conversation.

"He would do his drug work even if there was no money in it," she replied. "He always disliked the money side of things."

"But not Bill..." Isaac mused, almost to himself.

"Hell no! He's the reason... oh, never mind." The intensity of Jenny's response took Isaac by surprise. She looked down at the glass in her hand, suddenly morose. After a few seconds, she raised the glass to her lips and took a long swig.

Isaac leant forward. "He's the reason for what, Jenny?" he said quietly.

Jenny was still staring down at the glass in her hand. Isaac watched as she took a deep breath in, then out, through her nose. Then she looked up at him, and appeared to come to a decision. She gave him a small conspirational smile that, it seemed to Isaac, maybe wasn't entirely genuine.

"OK. You know that Mertusugene is basically a virus, right?"

"Well I'm a bit vague on the details, but yes."

"And what," she prompted, "Do you know about viruses? What do they have in common — influenza, strep, HIV, hep-B, hep-C — what's true of all of these viruses, of all viruses?"

Isaac shook his head slowly. "It's not really my area of expertise," he replied. "You might need to help me out."

"They're all infectious! Viruses have to be. They don't have any independent life of their own outside of the host organism. So they have to be infectious in order to continue to exist."

"OK, so they're all infectious," he said, uncertainly. Isaac instinctively sensed that there was some significance to this, but it was still just slightly out of his reach.

Jenny paused and took another long drink before continuing.

"But Mertusugene isn't. It's a virus that isn't infectious."

"So what?" Asked Isaac. As he said it, he realised the implication of Jenny's revelation, just a fraction of a second before Jenny started spelling it out for him.

"If it was infectious, the Mertusugene virus would spread naturally among humans, giving those who were infected a natural immunity to Merkel cell carcinoma. It would dramatically reduce the market for the product. It's the non-infectiousness of the drug that makes Mertusugene such a money spinner."

In spite of not being entirely sure whether he really wanted to know the answer, Isaac felt compelled to ask his next question.

"How did the Mertusugene virus come to be non-infectious?"

Jenny drained the rest of her drink. "After we had the therapeutic dynamics of the virus worked out, Dick and I — Dick doing the brain work and me doing the donkey work — spent a year finding a way to make it incapable of replicating beyond the host. We could have just released the original virus into the wild and pretty much eliminated Merkel cell carcinoma overnight. But instead now people need to pay Dakin Boyle to be cured. I guess that's the nature of the business we're in. Gus calls it 'legitimate value capture from innovation' — I guess having an MBA *and* a father like Bill will make you think like that."

"Jesus!" Isaac drained his Heineken and put the empty bottle on the table. The waitress reappeared, picked up the empties and held them enquiringly at an angle. Isaac nodded without even thinking about it, and she left to fetch more drinks. "How many people know about this?"

"Well, it's not exactly a secret," she replied. "It's not something we emphasise in our marketing material of course. But all the regulatory agencies — FDA, EDQM, MHRA, BfarM — know how Mertusugene works, what it does and why. And there's no reason for those guys to rock the boat. It's an effective treatment for a dangerous cancer, so it's all boxes ticked and smiles all round as far as they're concerned. Dick and Bill get rich, we all get paid, those who get the disease and can afford the treatment get to live, and those who can't afford it and die are none the wiser."

"Jesus!" Isaac repeated. The waitress returned with fresh drinks; Isaac picked his up and took a long drink from the bottle. "I can believe Bill would be up for something like this, but what made Dick go along with it? Why would he agree to do this, to do the work to make the virus non-infectious? He was always the scientist, the 'in it for the public good' guy."

"I don't know," she replied; with a degree of emphasis that caught Isaac by surprise. "It was not long after his wife died. He was pretty messed up over that. In the early days, when we first started working on the therapeutic dynamics of the virus, he was a fun guy to work with. He had a passion for what he was doing. We were curing cancer, why wouldn't you have a passion for the job? But later, he was just — I don't know, determined. Poor Dick. After his wife died, Francesca was the only bright spot in his life. And now..."

They sat silently, each lost in their own thoughts, while they slowly finished their drinks. Then Jenny put her glass down on the table, leant over and slapped Isaac playfully on the thigh.

"Come on," she said decisively. "You can walk me home, it's only three blocks from here. Then, if you've no objection, you can spend the rest of the evening fucking me senseless. I think I rather need that tonight."

Fifteen

"He tried to get me to call him 'Uncle' when I was a kid. Fat chance."
— Francesca Boyle

Bailey Troy pressed the "end" button on her phone, and watched as Isaac Church's number disappeared off the screen.

Although it was only 8:30am, she had already been at her desk for an hour, and breakfast was a distant memory. Since getting to her office, she had been reading through forensic and scene-of-crime reports, trying in vain to divine a promising line of enquiry. Piled up beside her desk were the boxes of Dakin Boyle documents from Francesca's home study. Bailey had been contemplating opening the topmost box and looking there for inspiration when the call from Isaac had come.

And now, after a five-minute phone conversation, she had her line of enquiry. She pressed "4" on the phone keypad to speed-dial Goff's mobile, and raised the phone to her ear. Goff answered on the third ring.

"Boss?"

"Where are you?"

"Just across the road grabbing a coffee."

"OK. Get me one as well and meet me out front in five minutes. We're going to have a chat with Bill Dakin." She ended the call without waiting for an answer.

Exactly seven minutes later, Bailey drove her car around from the back of the station and eased into the kerb by the main entrance. Goff was waiting, a large disposable coffee cup in each hand. Bailey reached over and opened the passenger door, and Goff slid into the passenger seat, placed one coffee in the cup holder between the seats and took a sip from the other. As soon as he had closed the door, Bailey accelerated away into a gap in the traffic.

"What's the plan, boss?" asked Goff as he manoeuvred his seat belt into position. "Haven't we already spoken to Bill Dakin?"

"Well Finlayson has, which I'm not sure really counts," she said, vaguely aware — as she was every time she did it — that it was slightly unprofessional to be denigrating one subordinate in front of another. "But we might just have the possibility of a motive. It may be that Dakin Boyle has a few dark secrets that it would prefer to keep under wraps."

"What secrets?" Goff held his coffee away from his face as his boss took a sweeping left turn, then resumed drinking once the car was again cruising at the limit.

"Our friend Isaac has had the benefit of a little pillow talk with Jenny Watson — the chief technologist at Dakin Boyle. Apparently the company went to great lengths to make sure that only people who could pay for the drug got the benefit of it. So Dakin and Boyle got rich, and lots of people died who didn't need to. That could be something that someone might go to some lengths to keep under wraps."

"But Boss, I don't get it. Isn't that how the drug market works? Drug companies sell drugs, people take the drugs, hopefully the drugs work and the people get well. You don't take the drug, you don't get well. Doesn't sound like much of a crime."

"But their drug isn't just a drug, it's a virus. If they'd released it as it was originally developed, then it would have spread naturally, curing the cancer as it went. But instead, they spent a year working on making sure that it *wouldn't* spread naturally."

"I dunno, Boss. It sounds a bit weak. Not a good look for the company perhaps. But it's not as if their customers are going to go elsewhere for their cancer cure. Is it something to go all homicidal over?"

Bailey wondered about that herself. As theories went, it wasn't the strongest one she'd ever had. She picked up her coffee from the cup holder and took a sip. "I guess we'll find out," she said — as much to herself as to the constable. "We need to talk to Bill Dakin again anyway, Finlayson may have missed something. And I want you there to give me a second opinion on him. But while we're driving, tell me what else you came up with yesterday."

"Well, the ballistics lab came back with a 'probable' match between Henriksen's gun and the projectile recovered from the scene. The markings are consistent with being fired from that gun, but not sufficiently distinctive to eliminate the possibility of it having been fired from a different one. The projectile was pretty deformed, so we were lucky to get even that."

"Doesn't sound like it's going to get us beyond reasonable doubt," she observed. "Carry on. What else have you got."

"We've identified the partial print on the envelope containing the money. Amelia Barr, the receptionist at Dakin Boyle."

"Millie the Rottweiler."

"Sorry Boss?"

"Millie the Rottweiler, that's what Jenny Watson calls the receptionist."

"Yeah, well, that figures. She wasn't very happy about being fingerprinted. And she was even less happy when I went to talk to her about the envelope. Started acting up as if I was accusing her of the murder. I was tempted to arrest her for unlawful possession of an attitude."

Bailey smiled at the thought of that. Although he had the build and the accent of a working class street brawler, Goff was as easy going and as by-the-book as any cop she knew. Millie the Rottweiler would, Bailey knew, have been calmly indulged her indignation. "OK, so you discovered a Rottweiler in possession of an unlicensed attitude. What else did you find?" she asked.

"The envelope came from Dakin Boyle's stock of stationery. The receptionist looks after the stationery cupboard, restocks it and so on."

"Who has access to the stationery?"

"Everyone who works there, apparently. She was quite clear on that. When she first started there, she told me, she used to keep the cupboard locked. People needed to ask her for anything they wanted. But after a while one of the boss guys there — Boyle, I think — told her she had to allow everyone to help themselves. If people were going to take home a hundred grand a year or so plus a few pencils, then so be it, he told her. I got the sense she wasn't happy with the arrangement, but she made it pretty clear that she was not accountable for what happened to the envelopes."

"OK, so once she'd finished covering her butt about not being responsible for all the stolen stationery, did she remember anyone in particular taking an envelope recently?"

"Nope," Goff replied. "Nobody much uses envelopes these days, according to her. Everything's done by email. Even some invoices come and go electronically somehow, apparently. She reckons that she hasn't had to replenish the envelopes for months. Which just means that, if she's telling the truth, someone took it while she wasn't there."

"Security cameras?"

Goff shook his head. "They don't have them, remember?"

They were on Edmund Road now, approaching the junction where the red-light camera had snapped Henriksen on his way to the murder just five days before. The morning traffic was heavy with light trucks and vans on their way to and from the many workshops and warehouses that made up the area.

Bailey downed the last of her coffee. The filter light turned green just as she started to slow for the junction. There were no other vehicles in the turn lane, so she turned into Strand Avenue with a broad sweep and gently accelerated back up to the limit. "What else have you got?"

"The computer forensics guys have put a read-only copy of the contents of the victim's home computer on the shared drive for you to look at when you're ready. I've had a look. Mostly it's the usual stuff — old college assignments and so on. But there are a lot of big spreadsheets in there. They look like extracts from an accounting system. The column headings are pretty cryptic, but they look like they're full of account codes and so on. Hard to tell exactly what they mean unless you know what you're looking for, I guess."

"Something for me to look at on a rainy day. Anything else?"

"One more from the computer guys. They said that someone had been trying to log onto the computer. Five consecutive attempts, all failed — most probably because they were using the wrong password."

Bailey recalled seeing the failed login message on the screen when she had been in the apartment after the attack on Isaac. The most obvious explanation was that the killer had been trying to access the computer — the computer which, it now appeared, contained information extracted from Dakin Boyle's systems. So his brief was not just to kill Francesca, she speculated, but to tidy away some incriminating data as well. Delete the contents of the computer's hard drive, and remove the paper documents from the flat. But he was disturbed by Isaac before he could do either, so now all that potentially incriminating data was in her possession. Another small win for her from Henriksen's amateurism — anyone who knew what they were doing wouldn't have wasted any time trying in vain to guess a password, they would've just smashed the computer case open and ripped the hard drive out.

She glanced across at Goff, and got the sense that there was something more — that he was maybe saving the best for last. "You got anything else for me?"

Goff smiled, staring straight ahead. "Just that the forensic ballistics chick I told you about — Doris, her name is — has got one helluva lot of energy, and a cute little angel tattoo on her left buttock."

Bailey threw her head back with laughter. "My god, you mean to tell me you're screwing a woman named Doris? Have you any idea how sad that sounds? Was her father a Doris Day fan, or something?"

"Hey! Don't be name-ist, Boss. Doris is everything you or I could want from a naked woman on a sheepskin rug, and more. If you'd got there first, you'd have done the same, trust me."

"So how did she get lumbered with that name?"

"Apparently her mother was into Greek Mythology, and Doris was the name of some mythical sea nymph."

"A sea nymph, eh. Can she swim?"

"I don't know, Boss," Goff replied. "But I'll bet she can dive."

Bailey laughed again, and twisted round and slapped Goff on the arm with the back of her hand. "Behave, constable. And be sure to give me her number once you've got bored with her. Sea nymph indeed."

Bailey flicked the indicator stalk and brought the car to a stop by the centre line, opposite the entrance to the Dakin Boyle administration building. The indicator ticked loudly six times before there was enough of a gap in the oncoming traffic for Bailey to take the turn. She eased the Prius into the parking area in front of the building, and glided silently into the visitor's park nearest the entrance. Then, with a flurry of seatbelts being removed and car doors opening and closing, the inspector and her constable got out of the car and walked into the foyer.

"Inspector Troy, Constable Goff — what a pleasure to see you both again." Millie's deadpan but humourless face left them both in no doubt that this was her attempt at irony. "Who would you like to see today?"

"Bill Dakin, please," Bailey replied.

Millie turned and examined her computer screen with a frown, then looked back at Bailey. "Do you have an appointment?" Bailey simply raised her eyebrows in reply. "Not that it matters, I suppose," continued the receptionist, with slightly overdone resignation. "I'll see if I can find him for you. Take a seat."

The waiting area comprised two plain two-seater sofas in the far corner, facing onto a low table with two neat stacks of magazines. Goff and Bailey took one sofa each, and Bailey started leafing through the magazines. Newsweek, National Geographic, Scientific American, Fortune. One of the two stacks was taken up entirely with copies of a magazine named Pharma, which Bailey had never heard of but which described itself on its masthead as "the global magazine for the pharmaceutical and biopharmaceutical industry." She picked up a Scientific American. Goff, she noticed, simply sat and stared patiently into space.

A man whom Bailey guessed could only be Bill Dakin walked into the reception area at a fast march. He was a small man — maybe five feet five — and immaculately presented. His dark suit was perfectly pressed, the single-breasted jacket held together at the front with a single button. The cuffs of the white cotton shirt, complete with cuff-links, extended elegantly beyond the jacket sleeves. His dark and tightly curled hair was cut short and was devoid of grey — unfeasibly so, in Bailey's mind, for a man who appeared to be in his mid fifties.

Dakin approached Goff with a broad smile and hand outstretched. "Inspector Troy, I assume."

Goff looked impassively at the hand, then up at the face of its owner, and tilted his head silently in the direction of the Inspector.

"Eh? Oh, yes, of course. Sorry. I had a fifty percent chance of getting it right, I suppose." Bailey took the hand that was now being thrust in her direction and held it as she brought herself to her feet.

"Do come on through," Dakin continued. "You will have some tea, won't you? Millie, could you organise us some tea? Thank you so much. Or coffee. Would you prefer coffee, perhaps?"

"Tea will be fine," Bailey responded.

Dakin turned and headed down the corridor at the same high speed with which he arrived. Bailey followed him, having to lengthen her stride to keep up. Goff hung behind, turned to Millie and mouthed a silent "coffee" while tapping himself on the chest, before following.

Dakin's office was like Dakin — exquisitely well presented. The desk was large and made of an expensive looking dark red wood. There was a 22-inch flat screen monitor wired to a laptop computer barely 12 inches across, the Apple logo conspicuously emblazoned across the closed carbon-fibre lid. Except for the screen and the laptop, the desk was empty. The wall opposite Dakin's desk was adorned with a single simply-framed painting, roughly sixteen inches by twelve — a *plein-air* impressionist representation of a young girl standing in long grass and staring through a rough-hewn fence at a bull. It was clearly an original. Bailey got the impression it was an expensive one.

Like father, like son, Bailey thought to herself. A taste for owning fine art seemed to run in the family.

Instead of going to the desk, Dakin sat at one of two leather sofas that framed a circular coffee table in the middle of the room. "Please," he said, gesturing at the two officers to sit. They each took a place at opposite ends of the remaining sofa.

Bailey started. "As you will have guessed by now, I'm Detective Inspector Bailey Troy. This," she gestured at Goff, "is one of my officers, Detective Constable Goff. We need to ask you some questions in relation to the murder of Francesca Boyle."

Dakin sat forward, forearms on his thighs. His reply came in a high energy rapid fire of syllables. "Yes, yes. Of course. Dreadful business.

Poor Dick. Absolutely horrible for him. Anything I can do to help, anything at all."

Bailey pulled a notebook from her handbag. "You gave a statement to one of my other constables. According to that, you left here at twelve thirty on Friday, spent the afternoon playing golf, then spent the evening drinking in the clubroom. Is that right? Do you have anything you want to add to your statement?"

"No, that's about the size of it. Took a cab home from the club around eleven. Took another cab back to the club Saturday morning to pick up the car. Got home to find your man waiting on the doorstep. Hell of a shock, I can tell you. I've known Francesca since she was a kid. It was — well, I'm sure you can imagine. Plenty of alibis, by the way. At the golf club, I mean. In case I'm a suspect." He smiled at the joke.

"Yes, I know. They check out fine. That's not a problem. We've arrested someone for the murder, as you may have heard. We're more interested in why they did it. That's what I want to talk to you about."

"Well yes, I had heard. I guess that's the main thing now — that the person who did it gets held to account. Just some local thug, is the rumour. Is that right?"

"A local man, yes. But we are continuing to investigate. To make sure we have the full picture, you understand. I was hoping there were some things you could tell me about Francesca."

"Francesca? Of course, if it will help. What would you like to know?"

"I understand she had studied journalism, and was looking for work in that field, is that right?"

"Yes. She'd just finished her degree. Did quite well, in fact. But getting that first job is always hard for youngsters these days. That's why she was here. Work experience, you see — looks good on the CV."

"But," Bailey pressed the point again, "she was definitely looking for journalism work?"

"Oh yes. She was forever emailing off her résumé to different places. Very diligent. Not a lot of interest, though, I gather."

Bailey made a point of holding Dakin's gaze as she asked her next question. "Did she have any sample pieces of work, do you know? Any articles that she'd written to illustrate her capability? Maybe something about Dakin Boyle?"

Dakin seemed briefly lost for an answer. He reached up and pinched his nose between thumb and forefinger, looking away as he did so. Then he lowered his arm back to its original position resting on his thigh and, after a brief sideways glance at Goff, returned his gaze to the Inspector.

"You know, I don't know!" he exclaimed. "It would have been a good idea, obviously. I don't know why I didn't suggest it. Her writing really was very good. Maybe she had. Jenny might know, you should ask her."

"Yes, we will," replied Bailey.

Millie the Rottweiler bustled in at that moment, carrying a tray. She set it on the table with a smile that she shared between Dakin and Bailey. The tray contained an elegant tea pot with two bone china cups, each one set on its own saucer and with a quarter of an inch of milk in the bottom. To one side, was a large chunky mug of milky coffee — instant, with undissolved powder still slowly circulating on the surface. Dakin returned Millie's smile, then reached forward to pour the tea.

"There's a lot of great stuff goes on here, you know," he continued. "Plenty to write about. Not just the Mertusugene. It's still a great story, of course. But it's a bit old now."

"But if she really wanted to show her journalistic credentials, a puff-piece about her father's company might not cut it." She made a point again of locking eye contact with Dakin before continuing. "I'm thinking more along the lines of a fearless investigative journalist throwing light on the dark secrets of Dakin Boyle."

Again, the pinch of the nose. "I'm sorry, Inspector. I don't really think we've got much in the way of dark secrets here." He smiled, then pulled a face to make a point of considering the question more carefully. "Trade secrets, certainly — some of the details of our manufacturing processes. Commercial secrets too, I suppose. Distribution deals and so on. But no really dark secrets, as far as I know." He smiled as he finished speaking, and held his hands out in a gesture of mock apology.

Bailey didn't return the smile. "The drug — remind me, what is it called?"

"Mertusugene," Dakin replied. "Not very memorable, I agree. Unless you're an oncologist, that is."

"Mertusugene," Bailey repeated. "But I'm told it's a virus, rather than a drug exactly. Is that right?"

"Pretty much, yes. The Mertusugene actually infects the patients muscles and then uses the muscle cells to create a massive dose of the therapeutic virus — what we call the virusome — to attack the tumour. The virusome interacts destructively with the cancer-causing DNA in the tumour cells — the oncogenes, in the lingo — and kills the cell.

Goff tilted his head, looking puzzled. "How does the cancer DNA, this oncogene you mentioned, get into people in the first place?" Aren't people's genes fixed? Do we carry genes for cancer?" Bailey turned and raised an eyebrow at the constable. "Sorry, Boss," he said sheepishly. "Just curious."

Dakin smiled and nodded indulgently at the question. "Some people, for some cancers, yes. There is a genetic origin for some cancers — certain types of breast cancer, for example. But not for Merkel cell carcinoma — that's the only cancer that Mertusugene treats, by the way. No, Merkel cell carcinoma is caused by a virus, Merkel cell polyomavirus. We're not very original in naming these things, are we? Anyway, the MCV virus causes changes in the cell DNA, which then leads to the cancer. We just send another virus in after it to kill off the cell." Dakin finished with a you-see-it's-all-quite-simple-really smile that left Bailey feeling slightly patronised.

"But," she responded, "if your drug is really a virus, why doesn't it spread naturally?"

A flash of understanding crossed Dakin's face, quickly replaced by a broad smile. "Ah, now I understand. You've been talking to our Chief Technologist. Well, I'm sorry to disappoint, but there are no dark secrets there, much as Jenny might like there to be." Dakin lent back in the sofa, as if making himself comfortable to tell a story. "The early research versions of the therapy were communicable, that's true. And we had to put an enormous amount of effort into preventing it from passing from person to person. It really was quite difficult to achieve — pushed poor Dick to his limits. And he's a very, very bright guy."

"Why was it so important to prevent it spreading naturally?" In spite of Bailey's best effort, it sounded more like an accusation than a question.

Dakin bounced back up into his leant forward, forearms on thighs posture. "Because there are *rules*, Inspector!" He turned his palms up and spread his fingers to emphasise the point. "You can't go releasing new viruses into the wild. There would be an absolute uproar, no matter what good it did. The authorities would simply never allow it. There are good scientific reasons too, of course. We know what the virus does in humans — it will cure MCC in people who have it, and it does nothing in people who don't. But we don't know what it will do in a dog, or a goldfish, or an *Escherichia coli* bacillus. If we allowed the communicable form to circulate in the wild, there's no telling what would happen. It could be 'I Am Legend' for real." He became noticeably less animated as he reflected on the reference. "Did you ever see that movie? I preferred the English original '28 Days Later' myself."

She had seen both movies, and what Dakin said made sense. Certainly it made more sense than killing a young not-quite journalist just to stop a story about a drug company wanting to get paid for its product. But she wasn't quite ready to give it up yet.

"Journalists are not always the sort of people who would let the truth get in the way of a good story," she said. "I'm sure a good one could put the sort of spin on it that would make Dakin Boyle look bad. Cause a bit of a dip in the share price, perhaps?"

"There is no share price, Inspector. Dick and I are the only shareholders, and we're not selling. And let's not forget that this mischievous journalist that we're talking about is Bill's daughter. Whom I've known for ten years, and who understands — who understood," Dakin paused and looked down at the floor, his hands falling limp, before continuing. "Francesca was an intelligent woman who understood what her father had done to bring Mertusugene to market, and why."

"I'm sure you're right," Bailey responded. "Thank you for your time." She stood up, Goff and Dakin both doing the same a second later.

Dakin held out his hand to Bailey. "You know," he said with a smile, "Jenny knows all this stuff. I think she just likes to sound a bit melodramatic when she's had a few drinks. We all have them, eh, our tall tales, told to impress."

And that, thought Bailey, was probably the closest they had got to the truth during the entire interview. They completed the parting courtesies and left.

Outside, Goff and Bailey looked at one another across the top of the car. "What do you think?" she asked.

"I think your theory, which was pretty weak to start with, just got blown completely out of the water." Goff replied.

"I think so too. Back to the drawing board, I guess."

"But I'll tell you what else I think. Dakin is hiding something, and he thought for a while there that we were on to him. But we weren't. Whatever it is, we're still a million miles away from working it out."

Sixteen

"Russell was just, ugh! But, you've gotta do what you've gotta do..."
— *Francesca Boyle*

The early morning daylight slowly woke Isaac from a deep sleep. As he came to, he found his face nestled in Jenny's hair, and his right hand draped gently across her breast. Before he was even fully conscious, and without thinking about it, he started to caress lightly around her nipple. In response, Jenny sighed languorously, rolled away from him onto her left side and pushed her buttocks back, slowly but firmly, into his groin. Isaac's loins responded as they should. He gently bit her neck and less gently tweaked her nipple as he shifted into position — causing a sensuous half gasp, half squeal from Jenny in response.

This would be the sixth time they'd had sex over the thirty six hours since Jenny had first invited him back to her apartment. During their first night of coupling they had happily explored and devoured every contradiction that the sex act can offer new lovers — they had been intimate and self-absorbed, boisterous and gentle, considerate and demanding, vigorous and tranquil. Their second night had differed from the first only in that they had actually got as far as the bedroom, eventually.

They lay beside one another now, spooning; the two of them moving to a single steady rhythm, locked together at the hips. Their pace was slow and sleepy, as if this time it could last forever. But eventually Isaac felt the inevitable sense of urgency slowly replacing the timeless gentle pleasure of the act. He started moving more quickly, his caresses replaced with a more demanding kneading of her flesh. The urgency became an all-consuming immediacy, the warmth became white heat. He gripped her hips uncompromisingly and drove himself hard inside her to expel what must surely be the last of his seminal fluid deep within her belly. He felt her tighten around him, and heard her strangled gasp as her orgasm coincided with his. And then they were done — limbs entwined, breathing heavily, profoundly content simply to lie together, drifting peacefully back to sleep.

Isaac snapped awake, unsure how long he had dozed after their early morning love making. He looked at his watch — 7:15 am. "Come on," he said firmly, slapping the fleshy rise of Jenny's buttock just hard enough to get her attention. "It's a school day. Time to get moving."

Jenny came suddenly awake, yelping in surprise at the sudden sting on her rump. She turned to Isaac to deliver a look of mock indignation before grabbing the duvet and pulling it up over herself. "You might be able to function for two days running on three hours sleep, but I can't. I'm working from home today." She nestled her head determinedly into the pillow, pulled the duvet up further around herself and defiantly closed her eyes.

Isaac shrugged, grabbed his overnight bag and his pile of abandoned clothes off the floor, and walked around the bed and through into the en-suite to shower and prepare for the day. He emerged fifteen minutes later, looked down at Jenny's sleeping form, smiled, and left.

Twenty minutes later he pulled into his driveway. His reticence about using Francesca's car on a date with Jenny had been abandoned the previous evening in favour of the simple convenience of being able to drive to his destination. He let himself in to the house, walked through to the kitchen, grabbed two slices of bread from the half consumed white loaf in the breadbox, dropped them in to the toaster, and started preparing his first coffee of the day.

His mobile chirped. He pulled it from his pocket and checked the callerID. The display read "INSP. TROY". He pressed the answer button and held the phone to his ear.

"Hello."

"Isaac? Bailey. Good morning. I hope you slept well?" Isaac could sense the Inspector's smirk across the phone connection.

"It was a very relaxing night. Thank you for asking," he replied. "How can I help you?"

"I've been checking out your new lover's story about Dakin Boyle covering up the work they did to stop the virus being infectious."

"What did you find. Anything useful?"

"Not really. It's true the virus isn't infectious, and that they made it that way deliberately. But there are rules about releasing new infectious viruses, apparently, which more or less amount to you're not allowed to do it."

"Who told you that? Bill Dakin?" Isaac couldn't help allowing an obvious note of scepticism to creep into his voice.

"That's what he told us, yes," she confirmed, with a hint of irritation. "But I'm not a complete idiot, Isaac. We have checked it out. We pulled the paperwork overnight. The FDA, European Medicines Agency, the PMDA — they all required that the virus be non-communicable. It's an agreed worldwide standard, apparently."

"So, back to square one looking for a motive, then."

"Not quite," Bailey replied. "Right now, I think there was something going on at Dakin Boyle. Something that gave someone a motive to kill Francesca. I don't think we're looking for a jealous ex-lover, or any kind of family feud gone sour. There's something very wrong going on somewhere in that company, and Francesca Boyle was killed because of it."

Isaac recalled Dick Boyle's oddly ambivalent reaction to his assurance that the police would get to the bottom of Francesca's murder. He pondered the possibility of Dick being involved in anything that might lead to the death of his daughter. It was almost inconceivable.

"How do you know?" he asked. "What could possibly be happening at the company that was worth killing for?"

"I don't know. But I've got a dead wannabe journalist with piles of the company's paperwork in her apartment, and a bunch of people at Dakin Boyle who give me the feeling that they're not telling me everything they know. My gut says that Francesca had uncovered something. Something that got her killed."

"And your gut is always right?"

"No," she admitted calmly. "My gut is often wrong. But it's right often enough to be worth following up."

"Fair enough. But why are you telling me all this? You're the detective, remember? I'm just the computer geek."

"You're the computer geek who's currently getting Dakin Boyle's Chief Technologist all weak at the knees and loose at the mouth. You know all the main players there. You know how the place runs — at least, how its computer systems run. And you seem to have a talent for problem solving. My gut tells me that you're not a part of whatever's going on; so I'm asking you to keep your eyes and ears open, to keep your brain in gear, and to call me if you come across anything that strikes you as odd."

"Is that all you've got? Your main line of enquiry is hoping that I'll notice something odd?"

"Not at all," Bailey protested. "We've got Henriksen, he has known associates, and his known associates have their own known associates. We may be able to join the dots between Henriksen and whoever paid him. Or he may decide that he doesn't want to take the fall alone after all, and tell us everything we need to know. But I'm not leaving any stone unturned, so I'd like you looking out for anything unusual as well."

"OK. If I see or hear anything suspicious, you'll be the first to know."

"That's all I ask. Thanks. I'll leave you to your day." The phone went dead before Isaac had the chance to formulate a reply. The toaster popped up his toast, slightly overdone, as he put the phone back in his pocket.

He buttered the toast and poured himself a coffee, then swung up onto a kitchen stool to consume his breakfast. He replayed his conversation with the Inspector in his mind. She had made a comment about him knowing how the place ran. As he pondered this he realised that, actually, he didn't. He knew what the computer systems did, of course. He knew what functionality the business needed from its computers — the standard business needs of accounts receivable and payable, general ledger, payroll, plus the systems to support the demanding audit, quality control and verifiability requirements of pharmaceutical manufacturing. But he had never really ventured out into the offices and the plant to see how it was all being used. He had mentally pencilled in today as being the day he would — after many days of procrastination — finally set up the new Pharmazeutika servers. But that could wait one more day, he decided. This morning he had discovered an itch that needed scratching, he wanted to discover more about how the plant at Dakin Boyle actually worked.

The obvious person to show him around the plant would have been Jenny. But today she was "working from home" and, in all probability, still in a deep post-coital slumber. That left Russell Bridgeman, the plant manager and the man for whom Isaac had been dumped by Francesca — the man she was dating when she was murdered. Isaac had never had cause to work particularly closely with Bridgeman, and had not felt any great urge to seek him out to socialise with — an indifference that he suspected was fully reciprocated. But, he decided, neither of them had any real reason to be positively hostile to one another, so he would ask Bridgeman to give him the guided tour.

He picked up the phone and made the call. Two minutes later it was all arranged. Russell Bridgeman, though sounding slightly puzzled, would be happy to show him around the plant after lunch. That left him the morning to fill. It had been a week and a half since he had been at the range — too long. He headed to the study to grab his Glock and a couple of packs of ammo.

Five hours later, at exactly 1:30pm, Isaac pulled into the parking area at Dakin Boyle. He climbed out of the car — he still wasn't sure whether the Audi was his or just on loan — and headed to the production plant. There was a small office area grafted onto the side of the large brick building, seemingly as an afterthought. Through its windows, Isaac could see Russell Bridgeman talking to a young warehouseman. There was a nondescript door on the office wall nearest to Isaac, wedged open to — Isaac assumed — allow the outside air in to cool the office. As he approached the door, he saw a small sign affixed to the door near the handle: "fire door, keep closed."

Isaac walked in and called across to Bridgeman to attract his attention.

"Hi Isaac, come on over. I'll be two minutes finishing up here, then we can go."

Russell Bridgeman was somewhere in his mid thirties, Isaac guessed. He was slightly shorter than Isaac and had a large and faintly portly build, as if he spent his spare time devoted to beer and brawling in more or less equal measure. He wore his long black hair tied back into a pony tail. Beneath his lab coat, he was wearing black jeans and a black t-shirt — the t-shirt emblazoned with a large Harley Davidson logo. Near the door, Isaac passed a black leather motorcycle jacket with a cut down denim over it, hanging on a hook. The denim also had the Harley logo on it. It was, Isaac recognised, the jacket that Bridgeman wore when he rode to work each day on his 400cc Yamaha Virago.

Bridgeman and the warehouseman finished their conversation; the warehouseman nodding as he turned away and disappeared through a door into what Isaac assumed was the main area of the plant.

"Is there anything in particular you'd like to see?" Bridgeman asked Isaac.

"I'd just like to understand a little better how it all hangs together," he replied. "I know what all the IT systems do, but I think it would help if I saw a little of the manufacturing process itself, a little of what the systems are supposed to support."

"Fair enough. You can have the grand tour. After you." Bridgeman gestured to the door through which the warehouseman had departed a few seconds before.

The door led to a large and high ceilinged area, brightly illuminated with glaring blue-tinged fluorescent lighting. It was filled with a bewildering tangle of futuristic glass and steel industrial machinery, all uncannily clean and polished. Isaac had expected it to be noisy, but there was just a quiet mains-frequency hum and the faint distant clatter and swish of equipment moving to a regular rhythm. From where he stood, Isaac could see maybe three or four people tending the equipment with a quiet, monastic devotion.

Bridgeman followed Isaac through the door. His biker-going-to-seed appearance contrasted incongruously with the sterile hi-tech environment of the plant, but he nonetheless managed to project a casually self-assured sense of being The Man In Charge.

"We run two completely separate manufacturing lines here," he said. "I'll walk you through the main one."

"Why have two?" Isaac asked. "Why not just one?"

"You'd have to ask Jenny for the detail, but it's something to do with quality control. If one line gets contaminated or goes out of spec, we can continue to manufacture on the other line. Most of the work on the second line goes on at Wade Park, we just create the API here and do the initial mixing, then truck everything over to Wade Park for them to complete the tableting."

Isaac furrowed his brow. "API? What's that?"

"Sorry," replied Bridgeman. "Jargon. It stands for Active Pharmaceutical Ingredient. The actual virus itself. In the old days, before acronyms caught on, we used to call it the pharmacon — just as cryptic but perhaps a bit more, I dunno, artistic. That's progress, I guess," he said with a theatrical shrug and a smile. "Come on," he continued, "I'll show you where it all begins." Bridgeman started off along an access way between the outer wall of the building and the quietly humming machinery. Isaac hurried after him.

After a few seconds, they came to what appeared, to Isaac's eyes, to be a large and futuristic glass-house. The lighting inside was even brighter than in the main area of the plant. Through the full-height windows Isaac could see people in hooded white coveralls, wearing face masks and protective eye-wear, studiously tending to benches full of complex looking apparatus.

"Here it is," said Bridgeman, "the clean room. This is where it's made — the secret sauce, the Mertusugene virus. I can't take you in, I'm afraid. Can't even tell you exactly what happens, really. Trade secret."

This was not quite what Isaac had been expecting. "Aren't viruses grown in chicken eggs?" he asked.

"You're thinking of the 'flu virus," replied Bridgeman. "Mertusugene is different. It's an entirely synthetic virus, created from scratch through a chemical process. Even if we wanted to, we couldn't grow it in chicken eggs. It's not self-replicating."

Isaac nodded. He remembered Jenny's tale of the efforts made to make sure that the virus wouldn't replicate in the wild.

Bridgeman continued. "The Mertusugene virus doesn't reproduce itself. When it infects human cells it forces them to create secondary virosomes, which then attack the cancer. If we tried to grow the Mertusugene virus in vitro, we'd just get one generation of the secondary virosome, then nothing."

Nothing indeed, Isaac reflected. All because of Dick's determined efforts to ensure that the virus couldn't spread.

"Anyway," Bridgeman continued, "The virus is blended inside the clean room with a small amount of cellulose filler. Once the virus is bound to the filler then the whole mix can come out of the clean room and into the tableting process. Here, I'll show you." With that, he turned and started walking round to the far side of the clean room. Isaac followed.

Built into the far corner of the clean room was a small wire chute, roughly four inches in diameter, leading from a trapdoor the size of a cat-flap in the Perspex window. At the other end, where the chute curved up to end the descent of its contents, was a cylindrical plastic container with a screw-top lid, around eight inches long and three inches wide. Bridgeman picked up the container and handed it to Isaac.

"Here you go. That's eight thousand tablets' worth of Mertusugene right there — about half a day's production for this line. You've got almost exactly one million dollars' worth of cancer cure in your hand."

Isaac stared at the container for a while, reflecting on the fact that this was the first, and very probably last, time that he had ever had a million bucks worth of anything in his possession. He handed it carefully back to Bridgeman.

"Half a days' production, you say. So all the money generated by the company comes down to two of those little containers a day?"

"Four, actually," replied Bridgeman. "Two from this clean room and two from the other. These get tableted here, the ones from the other clean room go over to Wade Park to be tableted on the line there."

Isaac nodded. "What happens on the rest of the line here?"

Bridgeman started walking down an access-way leading away from the clean rooms. Isaac fell in beside him. Bridgeman narrated as they walked, with what was clearly a well-rehearsed routine. "The API needs to be mixed with various other inactive ingredients — the excipients, as we call them. We use a combination of polyethylene glycol and polyvinylpyrrolidone as our binding agent — the stuff that makes it all stick together as a tablet. We use a dry binding process to mix the API with the binders, here." He gestured towards a large steel vat to their left. "We can't use wet binding, of course," he continued, as if that was the obvious observation, "because it starts to activate the virus." Isaac found himself nodding knowingly in response to Bridgeman's monologue, subconsciously trying to create the impression that he was making sense of what he was being told.

"The polyvinylpyrrolidone also acts as a disintegrant, It forces the tablets to disintegrate in the gut. Once they're swallowed, you understand," Bridgeman continued — switching from the impenetrably arcane to the blindingly obvious with no discernible change of tone or pace. "Then we add magnesium silicate, that's talcum powder to you and me, to act as a dry lubricant, add cellulose as a filler, mix it all up and stamp it into tablets."

They walked towards the rear of the plant as Bridgeman continued his recital. "The mixing and tableting is actually the simple part. About half of the floor space — everything in front of us here," Bridgeman held out his arms and waved his hands to indicate the large expanse of quietly clattering machinery in front of them, "is where the packaging is done. It's a complex business — the tablets are sealed four at a time into bubble-packs the size of your palm, each bubble pack is put into its own small cardboard box, and these are then put into larger boxes of twenty doses. All highly automated, of course, there's only half a dozen of us here to oversee the whole process."

They finished Bridgeman's tour close to a small loading dock at the rear of the plant. Bridgeman walked over and pointed into a sturdy box roughly two feet square at the base and rising about three feet from the floor. It was approximately two-thirds full of the twenty-dose boxes.

"This will be our day's work, once it's full," he said. "Sixteen thousand tablets, Four thousand doses, enough to save about five hundred lives. The courier comes to pick it up and take it to the airport at the end of each day. Of course," he added with a smile, "we don't tell him it's worth two million bucks."

Isaac smiled back. "I expect it would only make him nervous," he replied.

"I expect so," Bridgeman agreed, jumping down off the loading dock and walking out into the open air. Isaac followed, landing more heavily than he expected and having to put one hand out to balance himself on the ground. When he regained his balance, he saw Bridgeman standing with an unlit cigarette in his mouth, and holding a pack of Marlboro, the lid open and one cigarette slightly extended, in his direction.

"Not for me thanks," Isaac said, waving his slightly grazed hand in polite refusal.

"No, I didn't think you smoked," said Bridgeman. "But I do like to offer. Back when cigarettes first started getting expensive, but everyone still smoked, I couldn't afford to offer them around. But now that virtually nobody does, I can afford to offer again. Just as long as nobody accepts." He gave the now familiar smile before bringing a disposable lighter from his pocket to his face and, shielding the flame from the breeze with his left hand, lighting his cigarette.

After taking a deep draw of smoke into his lungs, Bridgeman held the cigarette up between his fingers. "They'll kill me eventually, I know," he said. "But I'm kinda hoping that Mr Boyle will have done whatever it is he does to work out a cure for lung cancer before then." He shrugged and turned his attention back to Isaac. "So what else can I show you?" He followed the question with another deep and apparently satisfying draw, and Isaac saw his attention dilute just slightly as he savoured the nicotine hit.

"Actually," Isaac replied, "I think that's all I need. It's been most helpful. Thank you for making the time to show me around."

"No problem, any time."

With that and a minimalist wave from each of them, Isaac turned and started walking back around the plant building to where he had parked the Audi.

There was, he reflected as he walked, certainly plenty of money at stake in the business of Dakin Boyle. He had sort of known that all along, of course — the more than half billion dollar annual turnover of the company was regularly reported on in glowing terms by the financial press. It was one thing to read about it, but holding a million dollars' worth of life-saving drug in his hand gave a somewhat different perspective.

More than that, though, Isaac had the feeling that he had learned something important this afternoon. But for now it remained just out of reach. He knew from experience not to rush these things, in time the significance would come to him.

He rounded the corner of the plant and saw the Audi, parked where he had left it. And next to the Audi, leaning against a nondescript Ford Focus, he saw Detective Constable Goff. As he saw Isaac, Goff stood up and started walking towards him.

"Good afternoon Mr Church," Goff said as he got to within speaking distance. "I wondered whether I would find you here."

"Not a bad guess," Isaac replied. "How can I help you?"

"I've been talking to Ms Watson's colleagues. I believe she's a, ah, friend of yours?"

Isaac smiled at the euphemism. "A friend, yes. What about her?"

"She hasn't been at work at all today. That's quite unusual, people were concerned."

Isaac smiled again. "I don't think it's anything to worry about. She had a bit of a restless night. I think she may have decided to take the day off."

Goff wasn't smiling. "I don't know what she had decided to do with her day, Mr Church. But whatever it was, she didn't do it. She's dead."

Seventeen

"There's no dignity in death." — Francesca Boyle

Bailey Troy stepped aside from the doorway, allowing the two scene-of-crime officers to bustle out of the bedroom and prepare for their methodical examination of the lounge. Then she walked in, stood by the foot of the bed and looked on as the medical examiner completed his inspection of the naked body of Jenny Watson. He was kneeling down by the side of the bed to Bailey's left, squeezed uncomfortably into the small gap — barely eighteen inches wide, she estimated — between the bed and an old wooden chest of drawers against the wall.

Medical examiners were not, she reflected, the sort of people who were easily distracted by the obvious. In spite of the belt looped around her neck and untidily knotted to the bedstead, the examiner seemed absorbed in scrutinising the corpse's left hand.

"Care to speculate on a cause of death," Bailey asked in a deadpan tone.

"Eh? Hmm? Oh, sorry yes," replied the examiner, looking up from his analysis of the dead technologist's fingernails. "Well, erm, I'll need to do the full examination, of course. But from what I've found so far," he continued, nodding at the lolling head of Jenny Watson, "what you see is what you get. Venous congestion caused by moderate pressure from the ligature, leading to cerebral anoxia and death. The head is quite congested, you see. Enough pressure to constrict the veins, but not the arteries. Death occurred here, of course, as you can see from the, um..." He pointed to the belt, then turned and circled his finger in the general direction of the urine stain on the sheets, beneath the dead woman's legs.

Bailey looked again at the naked corpse that had, until a few hours ago, been the understated but undeniably sexy Jenny Watson. But whatever she might have been in life, there was absolutely nothing sexy about her death. The dead woman's face was, as the examiner had pointed out, dark purple everywhere above the belt around her neck. Her eyes were open and bulging, as if the pressure of the blood built up inside her head was trying to push them out. Her tongue protruded grotesquely between her lips. Below her neck, the rest of her body had the waxy blue pallor common to most Caucasian corpses.

"Suicide or murder, do you think?" she asked the examiner.

"Well that's for you to find out, of course," he replied. "But my initial guess would be neither."

"What then?"

"Erotic asphyxiation gone wrong, would be what I'd put my money on right now," he replied. "It's quite common, you know. Restrict the blood supply to the brain somehow, which causes a reduction in available oxygen and a build-up of carbon dioxide, leading in turn to a pleasant giddiness and light-headedness. Which makes masturbation considerably more enjoyable, so I'm told. Terribly dangerous, of course, people die from it all the time. Almost all men though. I've never seen a female case before myself. First time for everything, I guess."

"So you think she was masturbating?"

"Quite possibly. Although she seems to have had the benefit of the real thing quite recently," the examiner replied, pointing casually between the corpse's legs, where a tiny trickle of pale viscous liquid could be seen emerging from her vagina and progressing down her perineum.

"Perhaps her partner had, erm — well, you know — not quite taken her the full distance, and she wanted to finish up properly, as it were. Again, quite common, so I'm told." The examiner looked up at Bailey, as if he were about to add a further comment. But then he appeared to think better of it, and returned to his examination of the corpse. He had, Bailey thought to herself, probably made the right choice.

"Time of death?"

"Well, we have extensive pallor mortis, except for the head, of course, so at least thirty minutes before I arrived. The corpse's rectal temperature was," he paused to examine his notes, "thirty four point two degrees Celsius, which would put time of death maybe two or three hours ago. No sign of rigor mortis yet, so certainly no more than three hours ago. So most likely between eleven thirty and twelve thirty this morning."

"Any sign of a struggle?"

"Nothing obvious," the examiner replied. "No recent bruising. No scratches around the neck or broken fingernails to indicate that the victim was clawing at the ligature. There is some biological material under the fingernails here," he said, holding up the hand he was studying, "which I'll test. But at first glance it just looks like epithelium — no blood, so nothing to indicate any kind of frenzied scratching of an attacker. We can get DNA from it, of course, and from the semen. And I'll do a sperm motility count on the semen as well, to estimate the time when it was, um... deposited."

"OK. When can I see an initial report?" Bailey asked.

The examiner looked at his watch as he considered the question. "Probably late this evening," he replied. "By eight thirty tomorrow morning at the latest."

Bailey nodded and scanned the room. It was small — typical of modern shoe-box inner city apartments. The bed looked cheap and old, about the same vintage as the chest of drawers. Bought second-hand, she guessed. It was a basic double rather than a queen-sized, the kind of bed used by someone who typically slept alone but wanted to be prepared for the odd occasions when they didn't. To her left, just beside the old chest of drawers, was a door into what Bailey guessed was an en-suite bathroom. By the head of the bed to her right was a small bedside table. Bailey walked around to get a good look at the scattering of items on it — Jenny's glasses, a watch, a glass half full of water, a paperback novel lying open face-down. "Sarah's Education" by Madeline Moore — being read for the umpteenth time, if the battered state of the cover was any guide.

From where she stood next to the bedside table, Bailey looked across at the corpse lying on the other side of the bed. She wasn't, she decided, immediately convinced by the examiner's erotic asphyxiation theory. Jenny would have slept on the side of the bed where she had the bedside table. Why would she move over to the other side of the bed just to masturbate?

Bailey stepped out of the bedroom, through the adjoining lounge area where the scene-of-crime officers were scrupulously noting down and photographing every aspect of the room. Directly opposite her was a kitchen alcove, spotlessly clean and tidy. Apart from two coffee cups upended on the drainer, nothing was out of place.

Two cups.

She turned and laid a hand on the shoulder of the nearest scene-of-crime officer. "I want the kitchen fingerprinted. Those two coffee mugs, the refrigerator, any milk inside the refrigerator, the teaspoons, any coffee jars, anything that you might touch while making a hot beverage. Got it?"

The officer shrugged and gave her a resigned nod in acknowledgement.

Her survey of the scene complete, Bailey walked out of the apartment's front door to the elevator lobby. There she found Finlayson, exactly where she had left him ten minutes previously. And in exactly the same position — feet planted firmly eighteen inches apart on the carpet, shoulders square and broad, hands clasped loosely together in front of his groin, suit jacket held together at the front with a single button and bulging conspicuously under his left arm around his absurdly impractical Desert Eagle pistol. His head turned to watch her, with no obvious sign of inquisitiveness, as she walked back out of the apartment.

"Where's Goff?" she asked.

"He's just picked up Church and is taking him in. Should be there by now."

"And the cleaner? And Gus Dakin?" The two who had found the body.

"Both taken back to the station by some general duties guys."

"OK. Call and tell Goff to wait at the station until I get there to interview Church. And tell him to hold the other two as well. I'm on my way now. You stay here until the scene-of-crime guys have finished going over the place, and the uniforms have completed their door-knock. If either of them finds anything interesting, call me and let me know." She left Finlayson rummaging in his pocket for his mobile phone and headed out of the apartment.

Twenty minutes later she was sitting, with Goff at her side, staring across the table at Isaac Church. It was the same interview room where she had interviewed him after the discovery of Francesca Boyle's body, and Isaac appeared to be in a very similar state — shaken, confused, and radiating that frightened "this just can't be happening" sense of denial.

If this were an ordinary case, a straightforward in-home sex crime with no forced entry, then the boyfriend would be the obvious initial suspect. And, more often than not, would turn out to be the perpetrator. Which would mean that she'd be starting by warning him that he was under investigation and reminding him of his rights.

But this was not an ordinary case. Someone had already gone to some lengths to frame Isaac for one murder, and Bailey's gut was telling her that this was another attempt at misdirection. A murder made to look like an accidental death. Her investigation into Francesca's death was being helped by an overcomplicated plan, incompetently executed. Bailey suspected that she would find the same factors at play in the death of Jenny Watson.

She turned and nodded at Goff, who switched on the recorder and recited the interview preliminaries. She then directed her attention back to Isaac.

"You understand that we're investigating the suspicious death of Jennifer Watson?"

Isaac nodded distractedly. Bailey raised her eyebrows and tilted her head in the direction of the tape recorder. Isaac sighed, then said "Yes, I understand."

"You're not under any suspicion at this stage, Isaac. But we do need to know everything you can tell us about Jenny's movements over the last twenty four hours, OK?"

"Sure."

"Good. Let's start with when you last saw her."

"That would have been around seven thirty this morning. I stayed over last night. I got up at seven fifteen — I remember checking the time — showered, and left about fifteen minutes later. Jenny was still in bed. She looked asleep."

"Shouldn't she have been going to work? She was normally an earlier starter, wasn't she?"

"She was tired. Neither of us had got a lot of sleep. We'd been... y'know."

"Fooling around?"

Isaac nodded, staring into space. Then he glanced at the tape recorder. "Yes. Fooling around. Having sex. She was, well... we didn't rush, you know? We found plenty to do, and took our time over it."

Bailey found her attention wandering as she contemplated the idea of finding plenty to do with Jenny Watson in bed. With a conscious effort of willpower, she returned her focus on the interview.

"Did you engage in any sado-masochistic activity with her?"

Isaac smiled thinly and shook his head, still staring into space. "No, she was pretty vanilla in that sense. Not prudish, far from it. But no riding crops, ball gags, or lederhosen, you know? Nothing like that."

"Nothing that might have been dangerous, that might have caused injury, if it had gone wrong?"

"No. Just the stuff, y'know, the stuff that people do. Nothing outside of the square." Bailey saw the hint of another wistful smile form briefly on Isaac's face as he recalled the memory.

In Bailey's experience, people's views on what was inside and what was outside of the sexual square varied quite considerably. But she decided to let it pass. "When did you last have vaginal intercourse together?"

"This morning, just before I got up."

"So, around seven?"

"I guess, thereabouts."

"Did you use a condom?"

"No. Jenny said she had that taken care of. The pill, maybe, I guess. I don't know. But no, we didn't use a condom."

"OK," Bailey nodded. "Now tell me, what side of the bed did you sleep on?"

"On the right. Jenny always sleeps... always slept, on the left, apparently. So do I, but — y'know — her bed, her rules."

"Did she tell you that? That she always sleeps on the left?"

"Yes. We had a bit of a play-fight over it, when we got to the bedroom. Just messing around — pushing, tickling, rolling about."

"And she won, in the end?"

"Well yes. Like I said — her bed, her rules. It was just a bit of fun."

"And that's where she was when you left — asleep on the left-hand side of the bed?"

"Yes."

"Just to be clear, that's the left side of the bed as you are lying in it. That would be the right-hand side as you were looking from the foot of the bed?"

Isaac paused; staring upwards as he appeared to unpick the question, picturing the scene and checking his left and right before answering. "Left-hand side of the bed as you're lying in it, right-hand side as you look at it from the foot of the bed. That's right. That's where she was sleeping. Correct."

"OK. That's helpful. Thank you. What did you do after you left the apartment?"

"I went home, had breakfast. I was having breakfast when you rang. After your call I finished breakfast and went to the range for a few hours, then went in to Dakin Boyle."

"Did you go straight from your place to the range?"

"Yes."

"And from the range straight to Dakin Boyle."

"No. I went via home to put the gun back in the safe. That just took a minute or two, then on to Dakin Boyle."

"What time did you get there?"

"To Dakin Boyle? One thirty. I had arranged to meet Russell Bridgeman. He showed me around the plant — I'd never seen the manufacturing side of the operation before, though it might be interesting. And maybe useful."

Bailey decided to ignore that teaser for now. "And the range, what time did you get there?"

"Oh, maybe nine o'clock. Some time around then. I did some practice drills — some triple-nickels, El Presidentes, clock-draws, that sort of thing. I took my time, I had the whole morning to kill. I mean..."

"It's OK. Was there anyone else there?"

"Like an alibi, you mean? I thought I wasn't under suspicion."

"You're not. But if Jenny's death was murder, and we prosecute someone for it, then you're the obvious guy that the defending attorney is going to try to pin this on. So I need to be able to eliminate any possibility that you were involved." It was a good interview line — one that she used regularly, whether it was true or not. In this case, it was.

Isaac looked questioningly at her, then shrugged. "There were people coming and going. They would all have had to sign the attendance register. You'll find my signature in there too. I guess you could go through that and question the other people who signed in. Someone would have seen me — I was on Range Five for most of the morning, it's directly across from the club house."

Bailey decided to change tack. "Tell me about Jenny. What kind of mood was she in, last night and this morning?"

"This morning she was just sleepy. Last night she was fine. I took over a bottle of wine and a pizza. She'd recorded a couple of the new episodes of the Big Bang Theory, so we watched those. We laughed and messed around. She was taking Penny's side, I was taking Leonard's. We had fun."

"Did you talk about work at all? About Dakin Boyle?"

"Not really. She might have had a bit of a downer going on about work, now that you ask. She got quite moody when we at the Top of the Tower on Tuesday night, telling me about how they'd had to work on the virus to make sure it wouldn't spread naturally. But last night she would just say 'no shop talk' and change the subject whenever I started talking about anything remotely work related. I didn't read anything into it at the time."

If Bailey had been talking to someone she suspected of being involved in the killing, she would have had many more questions to ask. Going by the book, she should have asked them anyway — instinct and hunches are not to be trusted. But Bailey wasn't big on going by the book. And there was someone else she had a whole load of questions she wanted to ask.

"OK Isaac. That's been helpful, thank you. Interview terminated at," she looked at her watch, "four thirteen pm." She leant over and stopped the tape recorder. "Wait here, and I'll organise someone to take you home. This has been tough on you, I know." Isaac just nodded, still starting into space.

Bailey caught Goff's eye and tilted her head in the direction of the door. They both got up, Goff opened the door and held it as Bailey walked through, then followed her and closed the door behind him.

"Find a uniform to take him home," she angled her head back towards the door they'd just passed through. "Once you've done that, get back over to the victim's apartment. Check for the wine bottle and the pizza box, and look around for any contraceptive pills — bathroom or kitchen, probably. Get the TV recorder pulled in for forensic examination, what's on there and what was played last night. Then find Finlayson — he's probably still standing in the lobby outside the apartment — and get him to check out the attendance register at the Pistol Club. He needs to contact everyone who was there this morning to find out if and when they saw Isaac at the club. Now, where's Gus Dakin?"

"Interview room 4, Boss." Goff nodded down the corridor.

"Has he been waiting there long?"

"At least a couple of hours, I'd say. There's a uniform in there with him — Rayner, I think his name is. He was first to attend the scene."

Rayner, Bailey recognised the name. After a second of reflection, she remembered — he was one of the cops who had attended Francesca's apartment when Isaac had been attacked.

"Good," she replied, emphatically. Good that Rayner was there; she needed a second officer in the interview, and Rayner seemed like a good cop. And good that Dakin had been waiting for so long. That would be getting him annoyed, and annoyed people made mistakes.

Bailey turned and walked in the direction of interview room 4.

Eighteen

"It's uncanny, how he works thing out." — Francesca Boyle

Isaac sat in the passenger seat of the patrol car as the officer drove. He had asked to be dropped back at Dakin Boyle; that's where he had left his car — or Francesca's car, he still wasn't sure which — after receiving the news of Jenny's death from Detective Goff.

It was his first time in a police patrol car. In the back of his mind he was aware that, under normal circumstances, he would have been full of questions — about the comms, the data terminal, the licence plate recognition system. But not today. Today, sitting in the patrol car confronted by its normally intriguing array of technology, he was almost completely absorbed in his own numbness. The real world impinged only peripherally on his consciousness, as if it were playing on a distant television screen to which he was paying no attention. His awareness clung, unbidden but nonetheless determinedly, to a grey and empty nothingness.

Emerging briefly to observe his own mental state, he supposed that this must be what grief felt like. Grief for Jenny. Grief for Francesca. And guilt at having selfishly failed, he now realised, to give Francesca's memory the grieving it was due in the hours and days immediately after her death. But his introspection lasted no more than a few seconds. Anything that approached consciously thinking about the lives and deaths of the two young women simply repelled his mind back into the greyness, just as one magnetic north repels another. The greyness was cold, and it made his body feel metallic, weak, and empty. But nonetheless he clung to it — it was the least painful place for his mind to be.

But somewhere, down in the deepest part of his brain where his conscious thoughts held no sway and from where insight — welcome or otherwise — would occasionally spring unbidden, was the nagging feeling that something from today just didn't add up.

"Are you sure you're going to be OK from here?"

"Eh? Sorry, what?" Isaac snapped back to the here and now. The patrol car was stopped, and the officer was looking at him expectantly.

"Dakin Boyle," the officer announced. "This is where you wanted to be dropped off. Are you sure you're OK? Because I can take you home if you want. It'll be no trouble."

"No. No, thank you. I'll be fine," Isaac assured the officer. He unclipped his seat belt, opened the car door, and climbed out onto the kerb. Then, aware that the officer was still watching him and making no attempt to pull away, Isaac started walking towards the main door into reception.

He got to within six feet of the door when it swung open and Millie bustled out.

"Oh hello," she said, looking at him in surprise. "You're late. I was just about to lock up."

Isaac glanced at his watch. 5:30.

"Ah, yes. Sorry. I just need to, um." Isaac didn't, he realised, have any idea why he was here. "Look, why don't I just go in, and you can lock up behind me. I'll let myself out through the fire escape when I'm finished."

"I suppose that will be all right," Millie replied. She started fumbling through the keys in her hand, then stopped and looked up at Isaac. "Terrible business, today," she said, barely audible. "Poor Jenny. On top of…" She stopped, screwed up her eyes, shook her head, and made feeble shooing gestures at Isaac.

Isaac placed one hand on Millie's shoulder and squeezed it gently. Millie's demonstration of grief suddenly made his own more manageable. The grey fog lifted; he found himself back in the world. Isaac patted Millie's shoulder before dropping his hand to his side, smiled at her in acknowledgement of a shared pain, then turned and went through the door into the reception.

As he stopped and wondered what to do next, he suddenly realised what it was that didn't add up.

He strode quickly over to the reception desk, sat down in Millie's chair, and switched on her computer. As he waited for the machine to boot, he ran over the numbers in his head.

A login prompt appeared on the screen. Isaac paused, he was about to do something that every IT professional knew they should never do. He was about to go nosing around in his client's data. He took a deep breath, and typed in his login credentials.

Isaac was usually pretty confident in his own mental arithmetic, but this was simply too strange to be true. Either he was fumbling the sums in his head, or the data he was basing them on were incorrect. He needed to double-check both. Because if his arithmetic was right, and his facts were right, then there was something very strange going on.

After a few minutes, the computer finished wheezing its way through the login process. He moved the mouse over to the screen icon labelled "accts" and double-clicked. He waited for a few seconds while the software loaded, then clicked on the menu item "accounts receivable".

Isaac knew that all of Dakin Boyle's distribution was handled by a German company with some tongue-twistingly Germanic name that he could never remember. He clicked on a drop-down list of customers; there was only one — Therapeutische Logistik. That was it. He selected the company, and clicked on a menu item at the top of the screen labelled "invoices". The screen filled with a list of items.

A few minutes of examining invoice details revealed a simple pattern. Dakin Boyle sent three invoices every month to Therapeutische Logistik: one for Mertusugene, the cancer drug; and one for each of Simvastatin and Clopidogrel, the generics. The invoices for the generics averaged about $300,000 each, but the amounts being billed for the Mertusugene dwarfed this, each invoice demanding between thirty eight and forty three million dollars.

Isaac grabbed a pencil and started scribbling numbers on Millie's blotter. He had known that the company made most of its money from the Mertusugene, but this seemed simply too out of balance. The answers he had calculated on the blotter stared back at him. He went back and double-checked that he had got the right number of significant digits everywhere. He had. The blotter scribblings did not lie.

Nearly five hundred million dollars in revenue from Mertusugene. Around seven million dollars from the generics — less than 1.5% of the total. Isaac looked up from the screen and asked the question out loud to the empty reception.

"Why would you bother?"

After a few seconds, he slowly shook his head and returned his attention to the computer. With one of the Mertusugene invoices open on the screen, he opened up Excel in a window over the top. He smiled as he noticed that it was the old 2003 version — thanks to Millie's intransigence the only computer in the company that hadn't been brought up to date. He adjusted the Excel window to allow him to see the invoice line details in the application window beneath. Eighty four thousand doses billed at $41,874,000. He tapped the numbers into Excel, calculating the charge for each dose as $498.50. A few more keystrokes pulled up the number that Isaac wanted to verify: nine hundred and ninety seven thousand dollars for the two thousand doses, or eight thousand tablets, that came from each container like the one that he had held in his hand that morning. Russell had been right, very nearly a million dollars for half a day's output from one line.

Isaac didn't need either Excel or the blotter to check any more arithmetic, he knew exactly what was wrong. If half a day's output from one line was worth a million dollars, then a month's output from one line would be worth around forty million dollars. More or less the same amount that was being invoiced to the distributor.

But there wasn't just one manufacturing line. There were two, one here, and one at Wade Park. Isaac again lifted his gaze from the computer, stared at the empty space in the middle of the reception, and asked the room the second of the two questions that were now troubling him.

"What's happening to the other half of the Mertusugene?"

Nineteen

"He was bound to mess it up." — Francesca Boyle

Bailey settled herself into the chair next to Officer Rainer, then looked silently across the table at her interview subject.

Gus Dakin's tousled hair and two days-worth of stubble looked exactly as it had when she had last seen him at his apartment four days ago, reinforcing Bailey's opinion that the look was a carefully manicured projection of stylish unkemptness, rather than the real thing. His plaid Tattersall shirt — open at the neck and radiating a price tag of, Bailey guessed, around $500 — managed to discreetly showcase his Adonis physique without clinging to it.

But for all his expensive elegance, Gus Dakin looked like he needed a cigarette. Badly. He had The Look. That look of fear and confusion, the look she had last seen on the face of Isaac Church as he had sat in the interview room along the corridor five days previously. The look of those who find themselves in the unfamiliar position of being either the collateral damage or the perpetrator of murder.

Now Bailey had to discover which category Gus Dakin fell into.

As Bailey watched, Dakin's gaze flitted in her direction to make eye contact. But less than a second later it was gone, redirected to the fingernails of his left hand, where he scratched at an invisible blemish with his right.

Bailey waited patiently for him to break the silence. She didn't have to wait long.

"I'm sorry, but I'm not really used to this," he said, giving up on his fingernails and staring at the bare wall. "Just part of the daily grind for you I expect, Inspector. But..." his voice tapered off, and his attention returned to his fingernails.

Bailey counted silently to five, then leant over, started the tape recorder, and recited the formal preliminaries of the interview. Then she sat back in her chair and stared calmly at Gus Dakin.

"Gus," she said, tilting her head in a conspicuous attempt to make eye contact again. After a second or two of determined fingernail grooming, Dakin lifted his head and reluctantly returned her gaze. "Tell me about this morning," she continued.

"Well, I, erm... I was working from home, and..."

"What were you working on, exactly?"

"It was a paper. For an upcoming conference. The European Conference of Oncology Pharmacy, this coming September. Not my paper, of course. Jenny's. She was going to present there, in Budapest." He used the city's Hungarian pronunciation, Budap*esht*. "It was about trends in the spread of Merkel's since Mertusugene was introduced. I was checking the epidemiology data."

Plausible, Bailey thought. But a lot to check. She scribbled in her notebook. "Why did you go to Ms. Watson's apartment?"

Dakin's eyes fell back down to his hands as he started to answer. "Well, to start with I just wanted to talk to her." He paused and raised his eyes slowly to resume eye contact, each eyeball seeming to weigh a ton as he did so. His face was composed, expressionless, as it rose. "I rang her cellphone, but got no answer. Just went to voice-mail. So I rang the office. Millie told me that Jenny hadn't been in."

Bailey pondered the significance of Dakin's eye aversion and fidgeting. It was a popular belief, even among some of her colleagues, that this was a sure sign of lying. But Bailey knew that life was never that simple. People fidgeted and avoided eye contact for all sorts of reasons, including simple nervousness. And police interviews made most people nervous.

But when people forced themselves, against their instinct, to make eye contact — that was a different matter.

She continued her questioning. "What time was this? What time did you make the call?"

"It was around twelve thirty." The answer came straight away. As if, Bailey reflected, he had committed the answer to memory. Most people didn't memorise the times of their phone calls, Bailey reflected. An honest answer would have been more vague and uncertain.

"Which phone did you use to make the call? Your cellphone, or a land-line?"

"My cellphone, I used my cellphone," he replied emphatically.

Bailey considered taking his phone of him there and then, claiming it as evidence. But there was nothing useful she could learn from the phone itself that she couldn't learn from the phone company records. Gus Dakin struck her as the kind of guy who would suffer separation anxiety without his phone, and she didn't want to cause him any unnecessary stress. Not yet.

"So Millie told you she hadn't come in to work. Tell me what happened then," she prompted.

"Well, that's when I decided I should go round to her place, to see if she was OK. So I tidied up what I was doing and drove to her apartment. I found her in the bedroom, lying on the bed. She was..." He shook his head, and looked back down at his hands, which were now fumbling around one another in his lap.

Bailey decided to push the point. "She was what, Gus?"

"She was... dead. Lying there, with that thing around her neck. Her face all dark. It was terrible." There was a flash of emotion across Dakin's face, halfway between fear and disgust. But then it was gone, and as he lifted his face to again meet her eyes, it was again expressionless. "Why would she do that to herself?"

The sight of Jenny's dead body had definitely shaken him, Bailey decided. But he had been rehearsing that last comment, waiting for an opportunity to use it. And he had made a point of making eye contact again. Even though Bailey didn't believe that avoiding eye contact was a sign of lying, it appeared that Gus Dakin certainly did.

Bailey was, she concluded, looking at Jenny Watson's killer.

"How do you know she was dead? Did you check her pulse?"

"No," he replied. "Nothing like that. I didn't touch her. She just looked... I didn't need to check, I could see just from looking that she definitely wasn't alive."

"Have you seen a lot of corpses in your time, Gus? Enough to know for sure whether someone was dead or not."

"What? No, I haven't seen a lot of dead bodies. None really, until today." Dakin's eyes lost focus and his gaze shifted off to the left as he reflected on the question. "Muriel Boyle at her funeral, I suppose, but that was ages ago. And the undertakers do what they do, of course, to make the body look OK. I remember Muriel looked as if she was just sleeping. But today, Jenny, she was... I don't know. I've just never seen anyone look so completely lifeless." He shook his head slowly, and the corners of his lips twitched downwards briefly. Then he returned his gaze to Bailey. "She was dead when I found her, I'm sure of it."

Time, Bailey decided, to change tack. "How did you get into the apartment?"

"What?" Dakin seemed taken aback by the change of direction, just as Bailey had intended. "Well, through the front door. I went up in the elevator, and went in through the front door."

"Was it open or closed when you arrived?"

"Open. I mean, no. Closed. It was closed, but it wasn't locked. I knocked, and then I opened it and walked in when I got no answer."

"You're sure?" Bailey wanted a firm commitment from him on this. "It wasn't just a little ajar? It was definitely closed?"

"Yes, definitely. Closed, but not locked."

"And you drove over there, you said. Is that right?"

"Yes, that's right."

"What time did you arrive?"

"It would have been around one o'clock, I guess. Yes, around one o'clock."

"Where did you park your car?"

"In the angle-parking outside the apartment building. It's still there. It will have a ticket by now, I suppose."

And it could make for interesting reading, Bailey thought to herself. "Tell me exactly what you did when you arrived at the apartment."

"Well, as I said, I knocked at the front door. When I didn't get an answer, I went in. The lounge area was empty, so I went and looked in the bedroom. That's when I found her."

"You didn't do anything else first? Didn't help yourself to a drink of water, anything like that?"

"No, of course not. Why would I? I was looking for Jenny. She wasn't in the lounge, so I immediately went and looked in the bedroom."

"Was there anybody there when you arrived?"

"No. Just Jenny. Her body, I mean."

Interesting, Bailey thought, that he should feel the urge to clarify that. "What did you do after discovering the body?"

"Just as I found her, the cleaner arrived. She saw the body too, of course, and got quite upset. A little hysterical, actually. I took her into the lounge and sat her down, then called the police. They arrived very shortly after that."

"You just sat her down, didn't get her a drink or anything?"

"No, just sat her down. Spoke to her a little to help her calm down, that was all."

"OK. There's just one more thing I need you to do for me. Would you stand up, please."

Dakin shrugged and stood, letting the chair slide back as his legs straightened. "Now raise your shirt a little for me please, just enough so that I can see the top of your jeans."

Dakin hesitated, and Bailey saw a flash of emotion cross his face — too quickly for her to be sure what it was — as he realised what she was asking. He gripped the hem of his shirt with both hands, and raised it until Bailey could see two inches of lean and muscled abdomen above the waistline of his jeans.

"I see you're not wearing a belt."

"No," he replied. A flat, unemotional monosyllable.

"That's all I need for now. Thank you for your assistance, you're free to go. Interview terminated at," Bailey looked at her watch, "seventeen forty six."

Twenty

"I never understood how he could live in such a mess." — Francesca Boyle

---

Isaac came fully awake at 6:00am, just as the daylight started to lighten his bedroom. As soon as he became conscious, he was immediately anxious to push on with what he wanted to do today, and was impatient for 8:00am to come around so that he could get started.

He threw the bed covers back, swivelled out of bed, and strode naked into the en-suite bathroom. He emerged 15 minutes later — showered and shaved — pulled some clean underwear and a shirt from the wardrobe, retrieved his Levis and Reeboks from the pile of yesterday's discarded clothing, got dressed, and headed out to the kitchen.

Isaac prepared his breakfast on auto-pilot — toast, muesli, plunger coffee — powering up the laptop on the breakfast bar as he clattered cups, bowls, and plates around in his well-rehearsed morning routine. Within 5 minutes he was sipping coffee and browsing the news on the local paper's website.

Isaac skimmed over the main headlines — taken up with the loud and ineffective posturing of the World's politicians over some unpromising development in the Middle East — and scrolled down to the local news. Jenny's death was the second item.

Tragedy Strikes Dakin Boyle Again

Friday, 01:30am

Police are investigating a second untimely death at Dakin Boyle Pharmaceuticals.

Dr Jennifer Watson, Dakin Boyle's Chief Technologist, was found dead at her home in the central city yesterday afternoon, after failing to arrive at work as expected. Police are refusing to speculate on the cause of death, or to comment on whether foul play is suspected.

Dr Watson was one of the researchers behind Dakin Boyle's flagship lifesaving anti-cancer drug Mertusugene, credited with saving over a million lives since its introduction nearly 10 years ago.

The death of Dr Watson follows the murder of Francesca Boyle, daughter of company co-founder Richard Boyle, last week. Police are refusing to comment on whether the two deaths might be connected. However, there has been an arrest in relation to the Boyle murder, and a 43-year-old man has been remanded in custody.

Staff at the pharmaceutical company are said to be devastated by the tragic deaths of the two women in less than a week.

— Staff

Isaac scrolled through the rest of the news, spent thirty seconds trying, and failing, to create some spark of interest in the game reviews in the site's Technology section, then gave up. He slammed the laptop's lid down impatiently and downed the last of his coffee.

He looked at his watch — 06:35am. Just under an hour and a half before he could make the phone call.

There were plenty of things he could be doing, plenty of worthwhile paid work piling up for Dakin Boyle and other clients. But these would all require him to engage his brain to a degree that, he felt, was beyond him today. So instead he turned his mind to his last resort when it came to keeping busy without having to think too hard — housework.

Isaac's attitude to housework was, as was that of most affluent and single young men, that (a) it generally didn't need doing, (b) to the extent that it did need doing, it was best to pay someone else to do it, and (c) whatever you couldn't pay someone else to do, it was best to do it as infrequently as possible, and then as quickly as possible. To this end, he employed a rather stout and menopausal force of nature by the name of Mrs Murphy to take care of his housework. More specifically, the terms of Mrs Murphy's employment obligated her to bustle into Isaac's apartment at around midday each Friday, spend as many hours as she deemed necessary to do whatever housework she deemed necessary, write a list of all the things she had done and an indignant commentary on how unreasonable it was of him to expect her to do them in a small notebook on the breakfast bar dedicated to the purpose, and leave an invoice for her time calculated at an hourly rate that most cleaners wouldn't dare to even dream of. Isaac's obligation, in return, was to promptly and uncomplainingly pay the demanded monies by electronic funds transfer into Mrs Murphy's account, to write regular small missives of humble thanks and apology in the notebook, and to leave out a gift-wrapped bottle of Jameson Irish Whiskey for her each Christmas. It was an arrangement that had been in place for several years, and which suited them both nicely.

But, for some reason known only to her, Mrs Murphy deemed laundry to be a task above her rather generous pay grade. She was prepared to gather up discarded clothing and pile it all in the blue basket, and to pull laundered items from the white basket, iron them if required, and store them in the appropriate drawers or on the appropriate racks. But the task of transforming dirty clothing in the blue basket into clean clothing in the white one was, apparently, a task to be performed by Isaac himself.

Isaac swivelled round and stepped off the stool at the breakfast bar, took the six steps into the laundry, and surveyed the empty white basket and the somewhat overflowing blue one. Failure to attend to laundry for a whole week was an offence that Mrs Murphy would feel compelled to write about at some length, he knew from experience. So he knelt down, upended the contents of the blue basket onto the laundry floor, and started separating the whites from the coloureds.

An hour later the first load of washing had been deposited in the white basket while the second load was starting its turn through the drier. Still another twenty minutes before he could make the call. He went back into the kitchen, made himself another coffee, then sat back at the breakfast bar, slowly sipping and reflecting.

Two clean rooms at the main plant, each producing enough active ingredient for 16,000 tablets of Mertusugene every day. That's 32,000 tablets, or 8,000 4-tab doses, every day. In an average month, that would add up to 168,000 doses. Which is exactly double the number of doses that the company had been billing to its distributor. It looked like the distributor was only being sent, or at least only being billed for, half the Mertusugene.

Isaac had learned from experience that, when something didn't seem to add up, there was usually some simple explanation — most often a mistake in the arithmetic. He ran the numbers through his head a dozen times, even pulled out a scrap of paper and wrote them down. There was no mistake. Only half as much Mertusugene was being invoiced as was being produced — at least, if the numbers Russell Bridgeman gave him were correct.

It was time to check the numbers from another angle. He swivelled round to his laptop, loaded Google's homepage into his browser, and started typing. Ten seconds later he was looking at Dakin Boyle's official prescribing information sheet. Thirty seconds after that he had the first piece of information that he needed — a standard treatment was a course of eight doses, each dose administered two weeks apart. One dose was four tablets. Ninety three per cent of patients went into full remission after a single treatment, and a further five per cent after a second treatment. There was no evidence that further rounds of treatment had any effect for the unlucky two per cent.

Back to Google, looking for new articles this time. A search for "Mertusugene" and "lives saved" gave him a page full of articles from financial and medical journals. A check of the first four gave him the same answer to his question: slightly over one hundred thousand lives saved a year.

One hundred thousand lives a year, eight doses, four tablets per dose. That's three million two hundred thousand tablets. The news articles all talked about "over one hundred thousand", and there were the few who needed two treatments, and the unlucky two per cent who weren't going to be among the hundred thousand lives saved, so round up the number of tablets to maybe four million. One million doses a year, just over 80,000 doses a month. Pretty much exactly the number the distributor is being billed for.

And half the amount that, according to Russell Bridgeman, was actually being produced.

Isaac was prepared to take a punt that the distributor was being sent the Mertusugene being produced at the main plant. He had seen the package on the loading dock with his own eyes, after all. So what was happening to the Mertusugene being produced at Wade Park?

He looked at his watch — 8:00am exactly. He pulled out his mobile phone, pulled up his contact list, and scrolled through to the name he was looking for. Then he thumbed "call" and lifted the phone to his ear.

The phone rang three times, then was answered with a business-like "hello".

"Russell, hi. It's Isaac."

There was a pause before the response came. "What can I do for you, Isaac?" The reply sounded distinctly unenthusiastic. But then, Isaac reflected, Russell was not the most animated of people.

"A couple of things. Firstly, I wanted to say thanks for the tour round the plant yesterday. It gave me exactly the information I needed."

"OK." Again, no enthusiasm. No "you're welcome" or "it was no trouble." Isaac pressed on.

"Secondly, I was wondering if you could suggest someone I could talk to about getting a tour of Wade Park. Maybe even make a call for me, to set it up."

"Ah. Yeah. Look, erm... The thing is, I'm not really going to be able to help. Sorry."

"Oh," Isaac replied, momentarily at a loss for what else to say. He had been halfway wondering whether Russell might be a little lukewarm, having been imposed upon once. But he hadn't been expecting an outright rejection. "Why's that? I can make the call myself if you can give me a name. I don't want to be any trouble."

"Yeah, it's not that," Russell replied. "It's just that, well, it looks like the company's starting to take security more seriously now. What with — you know — Francesca and Jenny. Truth is, I got into a bit of trouble for showing you around yesterday. Old Man Dakin was pretty livid about it. So no more tours, nobody in the plant unless they're on the plant payroll."

Isaac took a couple of heartbeats to assimilate this information. Tightening up security in the plant was hardly the most rational response to the two murders. But then most companies' alleged "security" practices were pretty irrational at the best of times — what real security practitioners called "security theatre". In any case, Russell sounded genuine; he'd obviously had the hard word.

"Hey, look, sorry about getting you into trouble," Isaac replied. "Just forget about Wade Park, if I'm not allowed in there, then I'm not allowed in. I'll leave you to get on with your day."

"Sure. See you." The phone went dead.

Isaac Looked at his phone, closed the contacts list and thumbed his speed dials into view on the screen. Then he pressed on the icon in the top left of the screen and put the phone back to his ear.

"Good morning. Welcome to Dakin Boyle Pharmaceuticals. How may I help you?" As ever, Millie managed to recite the warm and welcoming phrase without any trace of either warmth or welcome.

"Hi Millie. It's Isaac."

"And what can I do for you?" In the gap left where the warmth and welcome should be, Millie now managed to add a sense of tired resignation towards an imminent imposition that would undoubtedly add to her already unreasonable workload.

But Isaac had, through years of exposure, grown immune to Millie's habitual frostiness. "I just need some information," he replied. "Tell me, who's in charge over at Wade Park?"

"That would be Sharon," Millie replied. "Sharon Goldman. I suppose you want her phone number," she continued, finishing on a rising note to let it be known that such a supplementary question was really one imposition too many.

"No, not at all. All I needed was the name. You've been very helpful," Isaac responded, secure in the knowledge that being very helpful was the last thing that Millie wanted. "I'll probably see you later. Bye." He thumbed the "end call" icon on his phone without waiting for a reply, grabbed his keys, swivelled round on his stool and headed to the door.

Twenty One

"We really didn't plan on him doing something this dumb." —
Francesca Boyle

Bailey sat at her desk, sipping gingerly at her first coffee of the day and looking across her desk at Goff. He was standing just inside the doorway and holding a loose-leaf folder, which was open revealing an untidy pile of papers. He looked bleary-eyed and dishevelled, as if he had been up all night. Which, Bailey guessed, he had.

"What have we got?" she asked.

"From the apartment, we have..." Goff paused and shuffled through the papers, "...one large Pizza Hut box retrieved from the refuse can under the sink. The cash register receipt was still attached to the box with sticky tape. It was ordered on-line at eighteen seventeen hours last night and picked up from their central city store. We've checked with the staff there, but nobody remembers handling the pick-up. I guess having someone pick up a pizza from a pizza store is not a very memorable event. Plenty of prints on the box. Then we have an empty wine bottle, also out of the refuse can, and also with plenty of good prints. *Château Reynon Bordeaux White En Primeur* — an averagely good vintage with a flash name and a flashier price, if you ask me. Bought by someone who was trying to impress, would be my guess."

"OK, so you're a wine snob. What else have we got?"

"There were no wine glasses, plates or cutlery in the lounge or on any of the kitchen surfaces," Goff continued. "So they'd washed up and put everything away after eating the pizza and drinking the wine. There were two coffee mugs on the drainer; both clean, and absolutely no prints."

"Spoons?"

"One teaspoon," he replied. "In the sink."

"Anything else?"

"Lots. The PVR is seventy-five per cent full, and has every episode of the Big Bang Theory, seasons one to eleven. They've all been watched, but it's impossible to tell if any were watched last night. There are no contraceptive pills anywhere in the apartment."

"So she wasn't on the pill."

Goff looked up briefly from the papers in his hand. "We'll come back to that, if that's OK with you, Boss."

Bailey smiled indulgently. "Sure. In your own time…"

"The front door is secured with a Yale night-latch. Unless the lock is deliberately latched open — which it wasn't during our examination — the door is always locked when it is closed. There's no handle on the outside; the only way to open it is with a key."

"So Dakin was lying about the door being unlocked."

"It could have been latched open when he arrived, and then someone unlatched it between then and when we arrived. But otherwise he was lying, yes."

"Get scene-of-crime to check the latch for prints."

Goff smiled and held the folder up a little higher. "There's plenty in here about prints, when I get to it Boss."

Bailey smiled her indulgent smile again. "Sorry. You're telling the story. Do carry on."

"We have preliminary post-mortem results back. As far as immediate cause of death is concerned, it was very much what you see is what you get. A moderate amount of pressure from the belt causing venous congestion, cerebral anoxia and death. The belt wasn't tight enough to stop the blood flow into the brain, just enough to stop it leaving again. Consistent with accidental death arising from erotic asphyxiation. Quite popular, apparently; gives you quite a buzz, when it doesn't kill you."

"Hmm. So self-inflicted, then? No sign of a struggle?"

Goff shook his head, then smiled. "Except for one thing. There was Benzodiazepine in her blood, and in her stomach contents."

"Roofies?"

"Yep. Flunitrazepam, seventy micrograms per litre of blood. Enough to make her pretty dopey pretty quickly. And we found it somewhere else too."

"Where?"

"On the spoon in the sink. The spoon hadn't been washed. It was encrusted with partially dissolved coffee powder, with traces of Flunitrazepam. She took the roofies in her coffee."

"So now we're back to murder?"

"Maybe," Goff replied. "It's possible she deliberately took the roofies for the high, then decided to go for some icing on the cake with some breath-play. But that doesn't explain the belt."

"What about the belt?"

"Patience, Boss. There's more from the post-mortem."

But Bailey's patience was wearing thin. "Just tell me what you've got," she said, with a deliberate hint of sharpness.

But Goff had no intention of speeding up his performance. He ran his finger down his notes, as if to remind himself of some detail. "You remember I said there were no contraceptive pills in the apartment? She wouldn't have needed them." He looked up at Bailey, waiting for her reaction.

"Because...?"

"Because she had a..." he looked back at his notes again — this time, it seemed to Bailey, genuinely hunting for the right phrase. "Here it is, a subdermal contraceptive implant. Two, actually, in her upper arm." He tapped on his right bicep to emphasise his point, without taking his eyes from his notes. "Two implants of levonorgestrel," he sounded out each syllable carefully. "That's how it's usually done, apparently — two implants at a time."

"All very interesting," Bailey observed drily. "But can we get back to something more relevant to the actual murder?"

Goff looked up, eyebrows raised in a hint of mock indignation. "I thought perhaps it might be relevant. Y'know — motive?"

"We already know she was sexually active — with Isaac. So what?"

"Not just Church, Boss. The post-mortem report says the implants have been there for at least twelve months, judging by the state of the scarring. So I checked with her GP — and she's been using contraceptive implants constantly for the last ten years."

"You think she might have been sexually involved with Dakin? She seemed to have a pretty low opinion of him."

"It's not unknown for people to have a low opinion of their ex-partners, Boss. I can vouch for that." He grinned at his own joke, but Bailey just responded with an unsmiling 'get on with it' look. "Anyway," he continued, "it's maybe worth looking into."

"OK. She was sexually active, and it wasn't Isaac who popped her cherry. Duly noted. Now tell me about the belt."

"The belt, right." Goff went back to examining his notes. "Well, the victim's waist measurement was seventy one centimetres. But the hole in the belt that showed stretching — the one that was used — was at eighty six centimetres. It wasn't her belt."

"And Gus Dakin wasn't wearing a belt when we brought him in. Tell me, do guys wear jeans without a belt?"

"Not dress jeans, Boss. Not unless they've had a complete style bypass. Not the likes of Gus Dakin."

"So all this makes Gus Dakin our main person of interest, for now. But we're going to need more to pin this on him for certain."

Goff smiled again. "There is more, Boss."

Bailey forced herself to relax the stern-boss routine a little. "You are enjoying this, aren't you. Come on then, let's hear it."

"I took the liberty of getting the fingerprint guys to pull an all-nighter, matching the prints that scene-of-crime pulled from the apartment. Separating out all the noise, there are three interesting sets of prints — described as A, B, and C in their preliminary report."

Goff paused — purely, yet again, for dramatic effect, it seemed to Bailey. "Go on," she said, trying to keep the impatience out of her voice.

"Set A have been matched with the victim. They're found nearly everywhere, as you'd expect. On the wine bottle, the pizza box, the refrigerator door, the milk bottle, the front door latch. But not on the belt, and not on the coffee spoon. Set B is also on the wine bottle and the pizza box, but not on the refrigerator, the belt or the coffee spoon. If set B matches Church's prints, then that would be consistent with his story. Set C is the only set of prints found on the belt. They're also on the refrigerator door, the milk bottle, and the spoon, but not on the pizza box or the wine bottle. And not on the door latch, or anywhere on the outside of the door."

Bailey drummed her fingers lightly on the desk as she mentally collated all the pieces of the jigsaw. "So all we need to do is match set C with Gus Dakin and we've got him nailed, no?"

"Already done, Boss. They're his prints all right."

Bailey ran it all through in her mind, speaking out loud. "He lied about the door being open when he arrived, so the victim must have let him in to the apartment. He made the coffee that drugged her. He is the only one who handled the belt that strangled her. I'll bet good money that if we check his previous girlfriends we'll find that he knew all about breath play, and I'll bet more money that the belt is exactly his size. He went round there, drugged her, strangled her, and was disturbed by the cleaner before he could clean up and get out. It's about as slam-dunk as it gets, don't you think?"

"Pretty much, Boss." Goff paused before continuing. "Do you want more?"

Bailey rolled her head back and laughed out loud. "There's more?" She held her hands out towards Goff and made a mock beckoning gesture. "OK, give me the rest."

Goff smiled, closed the folder and dropped it on Bailey's desk. "Dakin's car was parked in the angle-parking outside the apartment, as he said in his interview with you. And it did get a ticket, as he guessed it would. But the ticket was issued at ten forty eight that morning. That's over two hours before he said he got there."

"Nice."

"And there's a nice big cherry on top. When we searched the car, we found half a dozen spent nine-mil ammunition cases in the glove box. And there were at least three different types of strike mark on the primers, as if they'd been grabbed at random from the brass bin at a shooting range."

" So he's in the frame for killing Francesca as well. Has he left the building?"

"Yep," Goff replied. "He was out of here like a scalded cat as soon as you finished interviewing him. Took a cab back to his apartment."

"Go and fetch him back, under caution. I think we need another chat."

Twenty Two

"I think Sharon felt that life had passed her by. She loved to live vicariously through the adventures of others." — Francesca Boyle

---

Isaac waited by the centre line for a gap in the oncoming traffic, the Audi's indicator ticking patiently. Across the road, a large sign mounted behind and above a chain link fence announced the entrance to Dakin Boyle's Wade Park manufacturing plant.

It had been a pleasant 20-minute drive through unusually light morning traffic. He had enjoyed the trip — where driving the Mazda had been nothing more than something that needed to be done to get from point A to point B, driving Francesca's Audi was somehow a simple pleasure in itself. And he was no longer haunted by the residual smell of Francesca's perfume — either it was gone, or he simply no longer noticed it.

Isaac picked his gap and made the turn. The entranceway opened into a staff car parking area. There were no designated visitor parks, no reception; just a plain rectangular quarter acre of asphalt marked out into parking slots over most of its area, with the rightmost quarter sternly stencilled with bright yellow lines and 'No Parking' lettering. Around two-thirds of the parking spots were filled — perhaps twenty cars in all, mostly old or low-end models. Behind the asphalt area was a long, low brick building with a corrugated steel roof. The building looked relatively new and well-kept — the brickwork was clean, the roofing iron unblemished and rust-free. A continuous row of windows ran the length of the building just below the roof, revealing harsh neon lighting within. To the right of the building, behind the zone of yellow lines, was a large loading bay — its roller door raised to slightly above head height. About 10 yards to the left of the loading bay, a simple aluminium framed door of frosted glass was the only other visible way into the building.

Isaac parked the Audi and climbed out. There was no obvious sign of life around the loading bay, so he decided to try the door. He swung the car door closed and thumbed the key-fob as he walked away; the car responded with the heavy clunk of locks being servo'd into place and the *chirp-chirp* of a car computer advising that its orders had been carried out. Isaac pressed the key-fob again, just for the pleasure of hearing the car's response a second time — the remote locking on the Mazda had stopped working long ago.

Isaac grasped the spherical aluminium door handle and opened the door. Beyond was a dim room of maybe 300 square feet. There was another door, slightly ajar, directly opposite. The rest of the opposite wall was given over to a bank of lockers.

"Hello," he called out from the doorway. "Anybody here?"

"Hi," a female voice responded, from somewhere the other side of the far door. "I'll be with you in just a second."

Isaac stepped into the room and looked around him. It was some kind of staff room, clean but drab. To his left a bench-top ran along the wall, punctuated by a sink midway along its length. Along the bench were mugs, coffee jars, a few lunch boxes, and an old microwave oven. Under the bench, a refrigerator hummed quietly. There were two plain wood-veneer tables in the centre of the room, each with a scattering of stackable chairs around them.

"Can I help you?"

Isaac turned to face the woman who now stood in the far doorway. She was dressed in a white lab coat, beneath which protruded jeans-covered legs that ended in a pair of unbranded cross-trainers. She appeared to be in her mid-fifties and had, Isaac assessed, once — perhaps a couple of decades ago, before the sagging and stretching of child rearing and hard living had taken its toll — had a pleasantly hour-glassed body. Similarly, her face had the look of having once been beautiful, before life had worn it down to a no-nonsense flintiness.

"I'm looking for Sharon Goldman," he said.

"You've found her," she replied. "And you are...?"

"Isaac Church. I'm the..."

"Oh yes, of course," she interrupted. "You look after the computers, don't you? Jenny's told me all about you. About you and her." She broke into a smile as she spoke, briefly dissolving the decades of accumulated harshness.

Isaac glanced away, across the room. Today's newspaper was lying on the nearest table, neatly folded and obviously unread.

She didn't know.

But Isaac wasn't here to deliver death notices. "Ah, yes, well... I, erm... I didn't know you two were friends."

"Well, not exactly friends," Sharon replied. "But you know how us girls like to gossip."

That was a bit of gender stereotyping that Isaac would have hesitated to say out loud. But, he decided, Sharon was female and so entitled to say it. And in any case the subtext was clear — 'I know that you and she are an item'.

That, and 'I don't know that she's dead.'

"Yes, well..." Isaac muttered, as his mind worked overtime on how to get the conversation away from dangerous territory and back on track. "You're expecting me, I hope. She told you I was coming over?"

"No, I had no idea, sorry," Sharon responded. "I haven't spoken to her for a day or so, I'm afraid. But that's okay. Tell me what you need, and I'll see what I can do."

So much for tightened plant security, thought Isaac. As was the case for most employees in most workplaces, company policy seemed to come a distant second to personal relationships — even when it came to friends of friends — in Sharon Goldman's list of priorities. Or maybe she just hadn't got the memo yet.

"You'll have heard that we're installing a new version of the Pharmazeutika software. I just wanted to get a better understanding of how things worked out here, so that we can configure the system to work properly for you. I was hoping you could show me around, explain a bit about what goes on here."

Sharon looked sceptical. "A new version, eh? Well I hope it's going to be easier to use than what we have now. I seem to spend my whole day just entering CGMP audit data sometimes. Those screens are a real pain in the rear, if you don't mind me saying so."

"Well, I'll be sure to look at that," Isaac replied. "But would you have some time to show me around now? I can come back later if it's not convenient, but..."

"No, no. Now's fine, of course. Come on." Sharon beckoned him towards the inner door, then turned to lead the way. "What would you like to see?"

"Maybe we could start with a quick tour of the Mertusugene production process," Isaac responded, with what he hoped was a convincingly indifferent shrug.

Sharon chuckled and smiled indulgently over her shoulder at Isaac, pausing halfway through the door. "Nothing that fancy here, I'm afraid. Just the generics, Simvastatin and Clopidogrel, that's all we manufacture. All the Mertusugene comes from the main plant."

"Are you…?" Isaac stopped himself. Of course she was sure. She ran the place. He started again. "Sorry, I just assumed that you produced Mertusugene here as well. My mistake." His mind raced, assimilating the new information and deciding what his next step should be. "Maybe we should just start at the beginning, then. Where the raw materials arrive."

"Goods Inward it is, then. Come on." Sharon resumed her way through the door, turned to her right, and disappeared from view.

Isaac followed, and found himself in a windowless corridor. He turned right to follow Sharon. The corridor led to a small series of steps about twenty feet away, that rose up about three feet then opened out into a larger naturally lit area that, he assumed, was the interior of the loading bay. He walked quickly to the steps, then went up them two at a time, emerging from the corridor to see that his assumption was correct — he was on the loading dock.

The loading bay was empty, and unusually clean. Well, Isaac reflected, unusually clean for a loading bay, perhaps not so unusual for a loading bay in a pharmaceutical plant. Sharon was standing in the middle of the loading dock, looking around in a contentedly proprietorial manner. "Starting at the beginning, this is where stuff arrives. And where it leaves, for that matter. We don't have much storage room here, so the excipients get shipped over here daily from the main plant."

"Sorry," Isaac interjected. "Excipients? Remind me, what are they?"

"They're the inactive stuff in the tablets — the tableting agents and so on."

"Right, got it," Isaac responded. "As distinct from the Pharmacon, the Active Pharmaceutical Ingredient. Do I have that right?"

"The API, yes. Someone's been giving you lessons, obviously." Sharon gave him a knowing smile.

But Isaac had no intention of indulging Sharon's obvious desire to bring the conversation back to the topic of Jenny. "Well, I pick up things, you know. And the API, you manufacture that here?"

"The Simvastatin and Clopidogrel, yes. Just basic biochemistry cookery, really. Not even very exciting to look at. Then we blend the API with the excipients, press it into tablets, package it up and ship it out." She gestured towards the roller door of the loading bay with a flourish, as if imagining the departure of the finished drugs. "What would you like to see first?"

"Maybe you can show me where you store the excipients before they're used," Isaac replied.

"Why not," she said. "Let's start with the mind-numbingly boring and work our way up to the not very exciting. Our storage room, such as it is, is round here." She turned and strode across the loading deck, then turned left through a large opening at the far end.

Isaac followed, and found himself on the edge of a storage area about half the size of a tennis court. The room was noticeably even cleaner than the loading bay — the walls spotless matt white and the floor covered in plain and polished linoleum. As he stepped into the room, he felt a slight stickiness as he lifted each foot, and looked down to see a three feet wide strip of adhesive dust trap around the doorway.

About half of the floor space was taken up with stacked cartons and plastic containers of various shapes and sizes, each product in its own area. "How long would all this last you?" Isaac asked with a sweeping gesture around the room

"There's enough of most inputs here to last us two or three days," Sharon replied. "But we get deliveries most days, so it's just buffer stock, really."

Isaac cast his eyes around the room, and saw what he was looking for in the corner immediately to his right. A small cluster of half a dozen small cylindrical plastic containers, each one around eight inches long and three inches wide. He walked over and picked one up. It felt just the same in his hand as it had the last time he had held one, when it had been handed to him by Russell Bridgeman during his tour of the main plant the previous day.

But unlike the one he had held yesterday, this one was labelled — the words "Butyl parahydroxybenzoate" dominated the top of the label, followed by a mass of impenetrable tabular text below. "What's this?" he asked.

"Butylparaben," Sharon replied. "We use it as a low-dose prophylactic antimicrobial during the tableting process. Or if you prefer plain English, it's to make sure there are no bugs in the tablets. The whole manufacturing line is about as sterile as you can get, so I'm not sure why we bother, to be honest. Just a precaution, I guess." She glanced discreetly at her watch before treating him to a wide smile. "Shall we continue your tour?"

Isaac got the sense that Sharon was torn between hurrying him along and pressing him for the inside story of his relationship with Jenny. But he had, he decided, seen what he needed to see. And nothing good could come of indulging his host on the topic of Jenny Watson.

"Actually, thinking about it, I really need to come to grips with the Mertusugene manufacturing process before I start to think about the generics. I should probably do that before taking up any more of your time. But thank you, you've been very helpful. I can get out this way, I take it?" He said, pointing back towards the loading bay.

Sharon looked perplexed. "Erm, okay. Yeah, sure. Go out through the roller doors and you'll see the parking area on your right. Feel free to come back for the rest of your tour any time. And give my love to Jenny."

Isaac smiled, said nothing. Then he turned and walked out to the loading deck, jumped down to the ground level and headed out under the roller doors.

Twenty Three

"People are not always what they seem at first glance." — Francesca Boyle

---

Bailey Troy stood waiting patiently. She could go no further until the guard behind the security window had satisfied himself that her ID was legitimate, that she was who she said she was, and that she should be admitted beyond the "sterile" area where she now stood. A dissonant jumble of indistinct but harsh sounds drifted in from the distance — of hard footsteps on hard floors, of iron doors slamming open and closed, of walkie-talkie squelch tones, of angry voices.

Prisons, Bailey thought to herself, needed more soft furnishings.

The guard slid her ID back through the slot at the bottom of the bullet-proof security window — a slot, Bailey noted in passing, that was easily large enough to accommodate the barrel of a gun. Someone really didn't think that through, she reflected. "The officer will escort you to your interview room," he said, gesturing at the inner door with what seemed to be disappointment at having failed to find any reason to refuse her entry.

Another prison guard had appeared beyond the iron-barred door that had prevented her from progressing any further. The door made a loud metallic *tock* and swung open towards her. The guard beyond the door turned and walked away, seemingly indifferent as to whether she followed or not, his hard-soles shoes clacking noisily on the hard floor.

She followed, her Reebok cross-trainers making barely discernible squeaking sounds as she walked.

Thirty seconds later, they were standing in front of a stern steel door adorned only with a door handle and a covered peep-hole. The guard slid the cover away from the peep-hole, looked in, then opened the door and stood to one side. "Sound the buzzer when you want to leave," he said, making no attempt at eye contact.

Bailey stepped through the door, which then clanged noisily shut behind her. She turned and looked back at the door, which looked much the same on this side as it had on the other, only without a door handle. At shoulder height slightly to the left of the door was a large plastic push-button, which she took to be the buzzer that she was to use to signal her wish to leave.

She returned her attention to the room. The centre of the room was dominated by an old wooden table, with two chairs on either side. One of the chairs on the far side was occupied. In the opposite wall was a door identical to the one she had just entered by — no door handle, buzzer to one side. On each side of the door stood a prison guard. The guard on the left stood, unmoving but relaxed, in the formal military "at ease" position — hands behind his back, feet eighteen inches apart, staring disinterestedly into space. He looked lean and fit, like he took regular exercise, but without the conspicuous muscling of a narcissistic gym bunny. Bailey judged him to be around thirty. Just a regular guy doing a boring job, letting his mind go blank until it was time to move.

The guard to the right was older, maybe mid fifties. He was leaning back against the wall with his arms crossed above his ample belly. In spite of his overweight torso, he had the spindly arms and legs, and the pallid complexion, of the life-long heavy smoker. He was staring disdainfully at Bailey — an expression that, she reflected, was common to those old-time social inadequates that still clung on here and there in the Corrections Service. Those who had taken the job for the power it gave them over others, and who resented finding people in their prison over whom that power did not apply.

Bailey turned her attention to the man she had come to see — the occupant of the chair on the far side of the table. He was a big man, powerful but not lean — as if his strength came from genes and hard work, rather than from pumping iron. He sat calmly, hands resting together on the table, fingers loosely interlaced. His clean prison overalls fitted his powerful frame comfortably, creating an impression of a well presented craftsman rather than a violent criminal.

"Hello Lucas," she said.

Lucas Henriksen looked up and smiled. "Good afternoon, Inspector. A pleasure to see you again."

She sat down opposite Francesca Boyle's killer. Time for what the textbooks call some 'psycho-social preamble'. She smiled at the killer across the table. "I hope you're well. How are they treating you in here?"

"The level of service is much as it's always been, Inspector. Three squares a day, which is nice. Not exactly *cordon bleu*, but adequate for my tastes. And the company is, of course, always..." he paused and glanced over his left shoulder at the pot-bellied guard slouching against the wall behind him, "...entertaining." He leaned forward and continued in a stage whisper: "Though Mr Lawrence there does have a bit of a halitosis problem, I'm sorry to say."

Bailey turned and looked at the guard in time to see his jaw muscles clench. To his right, she could see his younger colleague biting his lip to suppress a smile. Henriksen was, she reflected, considerably more urbane than the average small-time thug, once he got talking. And getting him talking was exactly what she needed to do. She smiled as if to indulge his small but sophisticated act of defiance. "Well, I'm sure Mr Lawrence appreciates your concern for his oral hygiene." She paused and allowed the smile to fade from her face before continuing — a verbal paragraph mark to separate the social niceties from the business talk. "I see you've no lawyer with you today. You understand that you're entitled to have one with you during the interview. Don't you?"

Henriksen waived a hand dismissively. "Yes, yes. Of course. But I don't think we need to bother Mr Walker with this, Inspector. I think we both know where we stand."

"I know where you stand, Lucas. You're going down for the murder of Francesca Boyle. I've got enough evidence to convict you a dozen times over."

Henriksen paused then slowly shrugged, as if weighing up her statement and not finding it entirely convincing. "We will have to wait and see about that, Inspector. But as I said, we both know where we stand. I'm not particularly inclined to discuss the matter."

"And as I told you last time we spoke, my main interest is in finding who paid you to kill Francesca. I thought you ought to know that we're getting close. So if you do want to cooperate, you should understand that time is running out."

Henriksen smiled again, a look of almost avuncular kindness on his face. "I appreciate your concern, Inspector. But, as I've just said, I'm not particularly inclined to discuss the matter." He paused before continuing. "But just out of curiosity, do you actually have a suspect? I assume that young man, the computer guy, is no longer in any trouble."

Rule number one of forensic interviewing: the detective asks the questions, the suspect answers them. Not the other way around. Stay in control of the dialogue. But this was exactly the direction she had wanted to take the interview, so she chose to indulge him.

"Mr. Church is no longer a person of interest, no. I'm afraid your attempts to put him in the frame were a little too clumsy. But as I said, we're getting close. Very close. Now, tell me what you know about Gus Dakin."

"Gus Dakin?" Henriksen slowly shook his head. "Is he your suspect?"

"Just tell me what you know about him?"

"Well... nothing, Inspector. From the name, I assume he's something to do with the company — you know, Dakin Boyle. Is he related to Bill Dakin? He's the guy who runs the company, isn't he?"

Henriksen was, she noted, making a determined attempt to turn the interview round — to get her answering his questions. He was clearly no fool, in spite of his chosen profession. Well she may have given an inch, Bailey reflected, but she wasn't going to let him take a mile. She ignored his question. "Did Gus Dakin pay you to murder Francesca Boyle?"

He chuckled and shook his head. "I told you, Inspector; I don't know any Gus Dakin. And we're not going to discuss Francesca's death, remember?"

Francesca. He used her name. Not 'the girl' or 'that woman' or any one of a dozen other phrases that Bailey might have expected from a hired killer, but her first name. She filed the fact away to ponder later, then pushed on with the interview.

"Lucas, I need a name. Who paid you to murder Francesca Boyle?"

The killer shook his head again. "I'm sorry, Inspector, but I've said all that I'm going to say. And probably more than I should." He placed his palms face down on the table and pushed himself slowly into a standing position. "But I have enjoyed our chat. Do drop by again some time."

He started to turn towards the door, then stopped, and turned back towards Bailey. "Just out of interest, have you ever met my wife, Henrietta? A slightly unfortunate name for someone married to a Henriksen, eh? But she's a lovely lady. You'd like her. Still love her to bits, of course; even though we couldn't make it work, in the end. She was never entirely happy about my chosen profession. Even so, she'll be quite upset about..." He paused, and waved around him at nothing in particular. "Well, about all this, you know."

He stopped and stared into space for a few seconds before continuing. "One last thing. I just wanted to say sorry for the, erm, you know." He formed a fist with his left hand and mimed a punch into the abdomen of an imaginary opponent. "That was uncalled-for. I expected it caused you some considerable discomfort. I do apologise."

He stood motionless for a few seconds, then appeared to decide he had said enough. He turned and took two steps toward the far door. The younger of the two guards looked at Bailey and raised one eyebrow. She nodded at him and closed her eyes, letting her head fall back. She heard the sound of a buzzer, and of the door clanking open, then closed again. When she reopened her eyes, she was alone.

Twenty Four

"It is a terrible, terrible thing." — Francesca Boyle

Isaac opened his front door and headed straight for the kitchen. He needed to think straight, and he needed to think deep. Which meant that he needed coffee.

His laptop was open on the breakfast bar, and he thumbed its power button on his way to the espresso machine. Once at the machine, he operated it on auto-pilot — pre-ground coffee from the overhead cupboard, water into the jug from the tap then into the machine from the jug, the jug placed on the machine's hot plate ready to receive the hot liquid when the machine was ready to dispense it. The beans were Arabica, Ethiopian Harar. A true coffee connoisseur would have regarded it as sacrilege to pre-grind the beans, he knew. But Isaac didn't regard himself as a connoisseur, he just knew what he liked. And he liked Harar coffee, which — to Isaac's palate — tasted pleasantly like a hot, caffeinated Merlot.

Five minutes later, Isaac was sitting at his breakfast bar, his right hand wrapped around a large ceramic coffee mug containing what the machine makers had intended to be a dozen shots of espresso, and his left resting gently on the keyboard of his laptop. He could feel the first sips of the coffee already starting to revitalise his mind.

He stared at the laptop screen, at the list of hits Google had given him for his query "Mertusugene".

"About 283,000 results (0.41 seconds)" started the page, as if the search engine was in some kind of race, before going on to list what it regarded as the most promising web pages: Wikipedia, National Institute of Health, WebMD, drugs.com, MedicineNet, and others invisible below the bottom of the browser window.

Isaac opened the suggested pages in turn. Wikipedia offered its information under headings that he didn't entirely understand — Pharmacology, Pharmacokinetics, Pharmacogenetics. The National Institute of Health went to the other extreme, seemingly aimed at a reading age in single figures: "Why is this medication prescribed?", "How should this medicine be used?", and so on in the same intellectually pre-digested style. The other sites fell somewhere between these two extremes. None of them told him anything helpful. Not, he admitted to himself, that he knew what he was looking for. But even though he didn't know what it was, he knew, without consciously understanding why, that he wasn't seeing it.

He clicked on the browser back button to return to the Google results page, and typed "Merkel cell carcinoma" in the search field. 353,000 results, 0.38 seconds. Wikipedia again, The Mayo Clinic, the National Cancer Institute, The Skin Cancer Foundation, MedScape. He started with the Wikipedia page and scrolled down to the section entitled "Epidemiology", which he guessed — correctly — was medical science jargon for "how many people get this disease, where and how". He started reading:

> *This type of cancer occurs most commonly in Western Europe and Far East Asia (most commonly Japan), where there are around 150,000 new cases a year. In those regions, it typically affects males aged between 40 and 60 years of age. It is highly correlated with the occurrence of hypercholesterolemia (high*

levels of blood cholesterol) and other hyperlipidemias, coronary artery disease, peripheral vascular disease, and cerebrovascular disease. In the United States, where the incidence is much lower (around 1,500 new cases a year), it is seen to occur mostly in patients aged over 60 and does not display the same correlations with circulatory diseases.

The disparity in incidence levels between Europe and East Asia on the one hand, and the rest of the world on the other, is not well understood, although lifestyle and environmental factors are suspected [citation needed]. Reliable historical data on incidence levels of the disease are not available, which has impeded research in this area. In the past, Merkel Cell Carcinoma was often mistaken for other histological types of cancer, including basal cell carcinoma, squamous cell carcinoma, malignant melanoma, lymphoma, and small cell carcinoma, or as a benign cyst. However, anecdotally, it is widely believed that the incidence of the disease in Europe in particular has risen markedly in recent years [citation needed].

Isaac went back and read these paragraphs a second time, then a third. Then he closed his eyes and slowly tipped his head back, letting his mouth fall slightly ajar as he did so.

There was a piece of the puzzle somewhere in those paragraphs, his caffeine charged instinct told him. He had no idea where it fitted, or how, or even why it was relevant. But there was definitely something lurking in that text. He left it lying unfiled in his subconscious, reopened his eyes, lent forward and continued his investigation.

To the right of his laptop was an A5-sized notepad, open at a page with just two words written on it, in Isaac's own handwriting — the names of the two generic drugs produced by Dakin Boyle. In the address bar of his browser window he quickly typed "wiki", then pressed the tab key to allow it to auto-complete wikipedia.org.

The Wikipedia home page loaded, and he typed in the first of the two words written in his notepad.

"Simvastatin"

> *Simvastatin is a hypolipidemic drug used with exercise, diet, and weight-loss to control elevated cholesterol, or hypercholesterolemia. It is a member of the statin class of pharmaceuticals. Simvastatin is a synthetic derivative of a fermentation product of Aspergillus terreus.*
>
> *The primary uses of simvastatin are for the treatment of dyslipidemia and the prevention of cardiovascular disease. It is recommended to be used only after other measures such as diet, exercise, and weight reduction have not improved cholesterol levels sufficiently.*

Isaac noticed as he finished reading that he suddenly felt slightly cold and shivery. His hands shook almost imperceptibly as he moved the cursor up to the search box on the Wikipedia page and typed the second of the two words written in his notepad.

"Clopidogrel"

> *Clopidogrel is an oral, thienopyridine-class antiplatelet agent used to inhibit blood clots in coronary artery disease, peripheral vascular disease, and cerebrovascular disease. The drug works by irreversibly inhibiting a receptor called P2Y12, an adenosine diphosphate (ADP) chemoreceptor on platelet cell membranes. Adverse effects include haemorrhage, severe neutropenia, and thrombotic thrombocytopenic purpura.*

Isaac read the paragraph a second time, feeling noticeably colder and more shivery as he did so. Then he clicked on the browser's back-button and re-read the entry for simvastatin Then he navigated back to the page for Merkel cell carcinoma and read the epidemiology section again. Then he let his hands fall into his lap, slowly raised his head and stared without focussing at the far wall of the kitchen.

"Jesus H. fucking Christ!"

He sat unmoving for a few seconds, then suddenly leapt up from the barstool, ran down the hallway and into the bathroom, collapsed over the toilet bowl and was violently sick.

Twenty Five

"I was devastated at first. But then, it's funny, you just kinda get used to the idea." — Francesca Boyle

---

As Bailey turned the corner of the corridor on the way to her office, she saw Goff walking towards her. As he saw her, he smiled and raised the folder he had in his hand and waved it.

"Hey, boss. I think you're going to like this."

"Let's hope so," she replied. She pointed at the door midway along the corridor between them. "In my office."

Goff got to the doorway ahead of her, then stopped and waited for Bailey to pass through first. Bailey went through the door, walked around to the far side of her desk, and eased herself into her seat; a comfortably padded, *faux* leather office swivel chair, with a high-rise back and armrests — precisely as dictated for officers of inspector rank by police specifications. In the open space in front of the desk there was a visitor's chair — plain, unpadded, stackable, and clearly intended for those of a lower rank.

Goff remained standing. He held the folder casually at groin level, and maintained an almost totally impassive expression — just the merest hint of *I-know-something-you-don't-know*.

"OK, what have you got?"

"A couple of things," he replied. "An interesting snippet from the autopsy of the victim."

"Which one?" Bailey asked pointedly. "We've had a bit of a run, remember."

"The first one, the Boyle woman."

"Francesca. What about her?"

"Well, I'm not sure how relevant it is, but the autopsy shows that she was dying anyway. Pancreatic cancer." Goff opened the folder and flicked through the sheets within until he found what he was looking for. "Ductal adenocarcinoma of the pancreas, it says here. Extensively metastasised but possibly still largely asymptomatic." He ran his finger over the page as he read the words, then looked up. "In English, I think it means that the cancer had spread throughout her body, but wasn't actually causing her too much of a problem yet. But still only about six months to live, so the pathologist reckons — twelve at the outside. And not a very nice way to go, apparently. I checked with her GP, too; he confirmed it's all true. She knew about it, diagnosed a few weeks ago after she went to the doctor concerned about dark coloured urine. Very odd to see it in someone so young, according to the GP. More a thing you see in people in their sixties and seventies."

Something in Goff's news resonated with an elusive snippet buried deep and, for now, out of reach in Bailey's memory. She frowned. "Go over the stuff about the cancer again," she said.

Goff referred back to the report. "Ductal adenocarcinoma of the pancreas. Extensively metas..."

"Adenocarcinoma," Bailey repeated. That was the word that was ringing bells. But she couldn't quite remember where she had heard it. She filed it away to reflect on later. "OK, enough about that. You said you had a couple of things. What else?"

"Erm, yes. Three, actually. Thing two is this, we've found the connection between Henriksen and Dakin Boyle. It's his wife — I've just interviewed her after you mentioned that odd comment Henriksen made to you. They've been separated for years, apparently. But it turns out that she has Dakin Boyle to thank for being alive."

"She got treated by the cancer drug?"

"More than just that. She was on the first clinical trial. The cancer was quite advanced when the trial started. She would've been a goner for sure without it, but made a complete recovery in record time. It made her a minor celebrity among everyone at the company. She was on first name terms with Dakin, Boyle, Watson, all of them. Even the Rottweiler. She even remembers Francesca as a kid."

"As a kid that her husband has now murdered," Bailey observed drily.

"Well, yes. She did get a bit emotional about that."

"And thing three?"

"Oh right, the last thing, yes." Goff couldn't suppress a smile. "Well, I think we might've found her killer."

Bailey raised her eyebrows and stared sceptically at the constable. "We know we've found her killer, Goff. I arrested him, remember? Lucas Henriksen. The man with the cancer-survivor wife we were talking about ten seconds ago? We've got him on remand right now."

Goff smiled again and shook his head. "I don't mean the trigger man. I mean the guy who paid for the job. Checking the accounts of the Dakin Boyle staff paid off; we've found where the money came from. Two separate withdrawals of six grand each — cash advances against the same credit card. The first exactly two weeks ago, the second the following Monday. Two different branches, opposite sides of town."

"The name," Bailey demanded impatiently.

"Dakin," Goff replied.

Bailey considered this, and nodded to herself. "So he killed them both. Makes some kind of sense, I suppose, although they're two very different MOs, and he made a complete hash of it second time around."

"Eh? No boss, not him. Wrong Dakin. The money came off the Old Man's credit card. Bill Dakin. It was him who paid for the hit on the Boyle woman."

"Let's not jump to conclusions," Bailey countered. "The money came — or probably came — from his credit card. It could have been him. It could have been the son. Or it could have been someone else. There's still a lot to piece together here."

"You're right, boss. Sorry."

"So let's start piecing it together. The money we recovered was all in new notes, right? So let's see if we can link the serial numbers to the cash advances. And get someone to go to each of those two bank branches, pull the security videos and interview the staff — see if we can get a positive ID on the person who made the withdrawals. Then get someone to go and pull in Old Man Dakin; let's see what he's got to say. Have him cautioned and lawyered up if that's what he wants, too."

"The videos and staff interviews are already in hand, Finlayson is dealing with that," Goff responded. Bailey made a conscious effort not to roll her eyes as she heard that. He continued: "I've given the bank twenty of the banknote serial numbers, to see what they can tell me about those. The numbers weren't sequential, unfortunately. I'll go and pull in Dakin." He leant forward and dropped the folder on Bailey's desk, then turned to leave.

"One more thing before you go," Bailey called out. "How are you getting on with that chick from ballistics? What was her name?"

"Doris." Goff shook his head and gave a self-deprecating smile. "I guess I must've done something wrong. Or maybe she's strictly a one-night stand kinda girl. Either way, she's not taking my calls." He shrugged. "Still, onwards and upwards, eh boss? Onwards and upwards." He paused briefly before continuing. "You should feel free to have a go yourself, if you're so inclined; I'm sure you'll enjoy the experience if you manage to pull it off. You have my blessing." He held his hands outstretched, palms upwards, and made a slight bow. "Just don't fall in love." Then he turned and left.

Bailey stared into space for a few moments, then picked up the phone and dialled the Custody Desk. The phone rang three times, then was answered with a gruff "Custody".

"Troy," Bailey announced herself with equal gruffness. "Have Gus Dakin taken to an interview room for me. I'll be there in five minutes."

She reached forward and pressed the phone's handset rocker to cut off the call, and stared into space for a few moments. She looked at the time displayed on the bottom right of her computer screen — 3:45pm. Still time, she thought. Worth a try.

She held the phone handset to her ear and dialled the number for the ballistic forensic lab. The phone chirped three times before a voice answered with a simple "forensics".

"Inspector Troy here. I need to talk to the person who did the ballistics report on a case I'm handling. I believe her name is Doris..."

Twenty Six

"It had to come out eventually." — Francesca Boyle

Isaac was not in the habit of parking in the visitor spaces at Dakin Boyle. He had learned long ago, by way of a stern lecture on the topic from Millie, that the term "visitor" was applied only to people who were going to pay money *to* the company, not to people who were being paid *by* the company.

But today Isaac was in no mood for the subtle courtesies of commerce. He swung the Audi into the visitor's parking space nearest the entrance, then opened the door and stepped out of the car in one movement. He glanced at his watch — 4:00pm. Dick will still be here, Isaac thought to himself. He took the four steps up to the doorway in two bounds and walked through the automatic doors, which had barely opened wide enough for him to fit through.

"Is Dick in?" he asked Millie without slowing as he walked across the reception area.

"Well, yes. But I don't think..."

But Isaac didn't care what Millie thought. "Thanks Millie. That's all I need." He kept on walking, leaving the receptionist to fluster away in impotent indignation.

Twenty seconds later, Isaac opened the door of Dick Boyle's office and walked in. Dick was sitting behind his desk — looking, if anything, even more dishevelled than when Isaac had last seen him, on Tuesday. He was wearing an old beige pullover that was going visibly thin at the elbows, underneath which was visible an old white t-shirt that had grown stretched and baggy at the neck. He looked like he had just walked in from doing some gardening, and he hadn't shaved in at least couple of days.

In all the time that Isaac had known Dick, he had never known him not to shave.

"Mind if I come in?" Isaac asked. It was a rhetorical question, he was already standing in the middle of the office.

Dick looked up and, with what was obviously some effort, smiled weakly. "Of course. Come in, Isaac. Sit down." He gestured at a visitor's chair next to the desk.

Isaac walked to within 10 feet of the desk, and remained standing. He closed his eyes, and slowly took in a deep breath. Then he reopened his eyes and slowly exhaled, considering the wretched Dick Boyle as he did so. "Dick, if I ask you a straight question, will you give me a straight answer?"

Dick sat slowly back in his chair and looked at Isaac. He said nothing. After a few seconds his eyes flicked downwards as, it appeared to Isaac, he reflected on the request. As he looked at Dick, Isaac thought that he had never seen a man look so… empty. His face was expressionless. There was no sign of grief, or of pain. No anger. No sadness. Dick was, it seemed to Isaac, drained of all emotion except tiredness. No, more than just tiredness, he thought, more of a profound exhaustion.

After several seconds, Dick appeared to make up his mind. Still looking down at his desk, he nodded slowly. "I guess so, Isaac. I guess so. It can't make much difference now. Go ahead, ask your question."

"What are you putting in the generics?"

Dick let out a deep sigh, slowly rested his forearms on the desk in front of him and stared at his hands, once more nodding slowly.

Then he looked up, staring Isaac directly in the eye. "Please, Isaac. Take a seat."

Twenty Seven

"He's never, really, had to do anything for himself; never learned how to think things through properly." — *Francesca Boyle*

Bailey stared across the table at Gus Dakin. As with her last interview with him a few hours ago, Officer Rainer was sat next to her, the obligatory second officer. Gus Dakin looked much as before. The same Tattersall shirt, the same belt-less jeans. The same scared look of being completely out of his depth. The same Gus, the same Bailey, the same Rainer. The same harsh, claustrophobic interview room.

But this time Gus was not alone on his side of the table.

Pierre LaFontaine was the most high-priced, though in Bailey's opinion far from the best, criminal defence lawyer in the city. Rather like a Rolex watch, people who could afford it bought LaFontaine's services not because he was better at his job than the alternatives, but simply because he was — and looked — more expensive. He sat impassively next to his client in an immaculately pressed dark grey bespoke three-piece suit, looking considerably older and more experienced than his forty three years of age and eleven years in practice as a criminal barrister really justified. He was, Bailey reflected, the only person she knew who dyed his hair grey. There was a slim leather portfolio case open in front of him on the table, revealing a ruled A4 pad within. The lawyer held a Mont Blanc pen in his hand — it's iconic six-pointed star top advertising, to Bailey's mind, its owner's willingness to pay a thousand dollars for what everyone else took for free from the stationery cupboard.

Bailey leant forward, started the tape recorder and recited the interview preliminaries for the benefit of the recording. She looked up to speak to Gus, but was greeted with the sight of LaFontaine raising his pen to signify his intention to speak.

"We need to make it clear, I think, that my client has not been arrested and is here of his own free will. Is that your understanding, Inspector?"

"That's correct," Bailey replied. "But Mr. Dakin is a person of interest to our investigation into the death of Jennifer Watson. And he is under caution."

"And why exactly is my client of interest?"

"You understand perfectly well, Pierre..." she used his first name, knowing how much he disliked her doing so "...that this is where I ask the questions, and your client answers them."

"Or not, Ms. Troy. Or not," he replied, replacing his earlier use of the title "Inspector" with "Ms". Quite a demotion in his old-school view of the world, Bailey surmised. "Unless," he continued, "we have suspended the right to silence?"

"I believe the correct technical term is 'privilege against self-incrimination', Pierre. And no, I don't believe we'll be relying on Mr. Dakin incriminating himself. Shall we begin?"

LaFontaine nodded silently and barely perceptibly in acquiescence.

Bailey shifted her attention to her suspect. "When we spoke earlier today, you said that you tried to ring Ms. Watson from your apartment at around 12:30, is that right?"

LaFontaine scribbled hurriedly on his notepad, then looked up and said evenly "my client declines to answer".

"And why is that?"

"You know better than that, Inspector. Next question."

"OK. Let's talk about when you got to Jenny's apartment. What time was that?"

More scribbling. "My client declines to answer."

Bailey turned her head to facer the lawyer, raising her eyebrows. But he never lifted his gaze from his pad. She continued. "Let's try this then. Talk me through again what happened when you got to the apartment."

"My client declines to answer."

Bailey looked up at LaFontaine and frowned. "Is your client going to answer any of my questions, or are we all wasting our time here?"

"Well, Ms. Troy, I guess you're going to have to ask your questions, then we'll find out, won't we?"

It was an old trick — Defence Lawyering 101. Let the police ask as many questions as they want, each one revealing a little more information on the case they are building — what they know, and what they just suspect. Hence all the hurried note-taking. LaFontaine would be using all the information inferred from the questions she asked to start building his defence — a narrative that allowed his client to plausibly claim innocence in the face of the evidence. It was a well-rehearsed game of cat-and-mouse — if she had had questions that she really wanted answers to, she would have mixed them in with ones that she already knew the answers to and other ones that were completely irrelevant, just to muddy the picture.

But there was only one question that she really wanted to ask.

Bailey leant forward and rested her elbows on the table, leaning across to get close to Gus Dakin. "OK Gus, just one more question, and then we can wrap this up." She paused before continuing, counting slowly to 5 in her head.

"Why did you have Francesca Boyle murdered?"

Dakin shot upright in his chair, his face swivelling back and forth in wide-eyed confusion between his lawyer and the two police officers.

"What?" he exclaimed, his voice loud and quavering. "Francesca? No! Not Francesca! I never…"

"Shut up Gus!" his lawyer interjected, before turning to face Bailey. "Ms Troy, this interview is over," he announced haughtily. "We're leaving, now. Come on, Gus." LaFontaine stood up and held his hand out to beckon his client to his feet.

Bailey also stood, and held her hand out, palm forward in a gesture of restraint towards the lawyer. "Before you go, gentlemen, I think Officer Rainer has something he would like to say to Mr. Dakin." she turned and nodded at the officer, then manoeuvred around the table towards the door leading out of the interview room.

"Angus Dakin," Rainer intoned. "I am arresting you on suspicion of the murder of Jennifer Watson. You are not obliged to say anything…"

Bailey left without waiting for him to finish.

Twenty Eight

"It destroyed him, keeping this dreadful secret all these years." —
Francesca Boyle

Isaac stood for a moment, looking at the frail genius that he had grown to regard as a friend and mentor over the last few years. His mind spun, seeking a more benign interpretation of what he'd uncovered. But he could find none. After half a dozen breaths, he went and lowered himself into one of the visitor's chairs and stared across the desk at the emotional husk that, until a few days ago, had been Dick Boyle.

"So tell me," he repeated. "What are you putting in the generics?"

"I think you know," Dick replied, staring into space. "Bill knows you've been through the plant here and at Wade Park. And he's examined the audit logs in the accounting system — so he knows you've been checking the invoicing. Which means that he knows that you've worked it out." Dick shifted his gaze, looking directly at Isaac. "He's a dangerous man, Isaac. More dangerous than you can imagine."

"That much I guessed," said Isaac. "But I don't know exactly what you're putting in the generics, only the effect it's having. So why don't you tell me."

Dick ignored the question. "He killed Muriel, you know. She was a beautiful woman — so full of life, such a great mother to Francesca. And he killed her."

Isaac's brow furrowed. "What are you talking about, Dick? Muriel died of can..." He stopped in mid-sentence.

Dick nodded. "Cancer, yes. Merkel Cell Carcinoma, to be precise. Very few people here know that. He infected her with the polyomavirus. No idea how, and impossible to prove of course. But he made sure I knew. And he made sure I knew who would be next if he didn't get his way."

"Francesca?"

Dick nodded. "We had a wonder cure for a cancer that very few people suffered from. Not enough people for Bill, anyway. So he came up with the plan for the generics. Just a straightforward marketing policy, he said — textbook demand generation."

"So you put something in the generics to cause the cancer."

Dick nodded again. "It's a modified form of the polyomavirus, one that survives ingestion. It's quite a difficult trick, biochemically speaking — to build a synthetic virus that could survive in the intestine, and pass through the wall of the duodenum to infect the victim. But we'd solved the problem first for the Mertusugene itself, of course. And then..."

Dick seemed lost in his own world for several seconds. Then he continued, in a frail half-whispered monotone. "It's a simple enough marketing plan, really. Millions of people are prescribed Simvastatin or Clopidogrel every year; for high cholesterol, or after a heart attack, or whatever. So we manufacture generic versions of these drugs, infected with Merkel cell polyomavirus. People take our generics, they're infected with the virus, they develop Merkel Cell Carcinoma, they get treated with Mertusugene, they get better. And Dakin Boyle Pharmaceuticals makes half a billion dollars a year from their governments and insurance companies. Would have been closer to a round billion, if we'd ever been allowed to sell the generics into the US market."

Dick ended the explanation with a barely perceptible shrug.

"Except that not everybody gets better, do they Dick?" Isaac responded. "What about the couple of thousand people who die every year because the drug doesn't work for them?"

With what seemed like a monumental effort, Dick raised his eyes to meet Isaac's gaze. "Seventeen thousand people since we launched the generics, by my estimate," he whispered. "Maybe four or five every day. And every day I think about who those people might be today — somebody's father, somebody's husband, somebody's daughter. But not my daughter. At least, not until…"

Dick's eyes were red, but there were no tears. Isaac reflected that, as emotionally shattered as Dick had been all week, he had never seen him cry.

"Did Francesca work out what was going on? Is that why Bill had her killed?"

"I honestly don't know why she was shot, Isaac. I can't make any sense of that. Bill had already killed her, long before that."

"What? What do you mean? You're talking in riddles, Dick."

"He killed her the same way he killed Muriel. Just a different cancer. Adenocarcinoma rather than Merkel Cell Carcinoma. It developed in her pancreas, the worst possible place. It was Bill's way of trying to hurry me along with our current research; to give me an incentive to come up with a cure. But we're still a million miles away from a treatment for adenocarcinomas; I'm not sure if we'll ever find one. And pancreatic cancer always ends so…" He paused, shook his head. "What happened to Francesca was probably for the best, in that sense."

Isaac started to say something, but found he had no real way to express what he was thinking; no real way to even *think* what he was thinking. They both sat there in silence.

Eventually Isaac just said: "Did she know?"

"About the cancer? Oh yes. A hell of a shock for someone at her age, obviously. Hard to even imagine. Unspeakably unfair, she had so much living to do. She did her fair share of screaming to herself alone in the forest, to start with, I can tell you. But it didn't take too long before she came to terms with it, decided to make the most of what time she had. So strong…"

"What about the other stuff? Did she know about that? About what caused her cancer, what killed her mother, about the generics."

"I honestly don't know, Isaac. She's a bright girl. *Was* a bright girl. Jenny tried to make sure she didn't get close to the truth, of course. But I'm not sure how successful she was."

"Jenny? Jenny was in on it too?"

"Yes, Jenny too, I'm afraid. Jenny was the one who kept everything running, without anyone else seeing enough of the whole process to figure out that anything was amiss. She was very young when we started, of course — and incredibly bright. But she found it hard to look past all the money we were giving her. But in recent months it was clear that she had started to find it all a bit… troubling. Both Gus and Bill began to regard her as unreliable, a liability. Of course there was no way out for her, she had got herself in far too deep for far too long. But the two of them had started making plans — 'succession planning' they called it."

"Let me guess — Russell Bridgeman?"

"Bridgeman, yes. He was always quite, shall we say, ethically flexible. Gus has been discreetly grooming him for years. He was padding his expenses from the moment we took him on. Gus made a point of not pursuing it, even encouraged him to rort a little more each time. After Russell had been on the payroll for a couple of years, Gus contrived a stock-take discrepancy and paid Bridgeman in cash to fabricate some dispatch notes to cover it up. Over time, the favours and the pay-offs got gradually bigger and bigger, until Bridgeman was right inside the tent with the rest of us."

"And Jenny became surplus to requirements," added Isaac.

"As you say," Dick agreed quietly, "surplus to requirements."

Isaac leaned forward, put his elbows on the desk and slowly buried his face in his hands. "And now she's dead as well."

Dick nodded again. "And now Jenny is dead. Poor girl. She was…" His voice petered out.

Isaac lifted his head from his hands. "You know that I'm going to have to take this to the police."

"I know, Isaac."

"This isn't going to end well for you, Dick. I'm sorry. I can't see any way around that." As he sat there, Isaac wasn't at all sure whether he really wanted to see any way around it.

"Don't worry about me," Dick replied. "This hasn't been going well for me for a long time. You need to worry about yourself. You know what's happening, and Bill knows that you know. For your own sake, you need to tell the police quickly. Nothing that they can do could possibly make things any worse for me."

Isaac looked at the frail man across the desk for several seconds. Then, without a word, he pushed himself out of the chair, turned, and walked out of Dick Boyle's office. Sixty seconds later, he was in Francesca's Audi easing into the early evening traffic.

He would, he decided, call Inspector Troy in the morning. Tonight, he needed to have some quiet time with Captain Morgan.

Twenty Nine

"Girls are nice" — Francesca Boyle

Bailey waited for a gap in the oncoming evening rush hour traffic, then turned the car into the entranceway to the forensics lab.

There was no sign to indicate what the building was — there was nothing to be gained by advertising the location of the building that housed so much of the evidence used to convict the city's criminals. It was just a slab of featureless serrated concrete, pierced every few metres by frosted glass windows surrounded by plain aluminium joinery. It sat behind a parking area roughly a quarter full of unremarkable and faintly drab middle-class cars — mid-sized sedans, hatchbacks, and station-wagons in varying shades of white, blue or brown.

Bailey parked in a vacant spot near the building entrance, one of three that had the words "Visitors Only" sternly stencilled across them in dull yellow paint. As she opened the car door, the sound and smell of the traffic of this light industrial area hit her — the occasional honking horn, the bass snarling of large diesel trucks using engine braking to decelerate, the almost subsonic reverberating *doof-doof* from ancient and absurdly over-customised wannabe muscle cars, the sooty smell of incompletely burned diesel. She wrinkled her nose in unconscious distaste and headed quickly for the doorway into the building.

Inside, the reception area was plain and utilitarian. The walls may once have been a pleasing off-white, but had long ago decayed into a geriatric and uneven beige. The linoleum floor was a scratched and faded grey. To Bailey's right, a pair of wood-veneer swing doors led into the interior of the building. Directly in front of her a single guard, his pot belly straining against his uniform shirt, sat slumped behind a broad reception desk. On the desk sat a telephone, a closed A4 ring-binder, and two ancient TV monitors. Each monitor displayed a monochrome and grainy image of what Bailey assumed to be security camera coverage of the outside of the building. Next to the telephone, a yellowing sheet of A4 paper containing what appeared to be a phone list was taped to the desk. The guard held a battered paperback in his hand and, from the look on his face, was more than a little displeased at having had his attention taken from it.

Bailey pulled her ID from her back pocket and held it out for the guard to see. "I'm here to see Dr. Doris Ackland."

The guard briefly eyed the ID, then reached forward to pick up the phone with his left hand while running his right index finger slowly down the phone list. He then punched a 3-digit number into the phone, waited for two seconds, announced "there's someone here to see you", and hung up the phone with no obvious sign of having waited for a reply. He looked up at Bailey and pushed the ring binder across the desk in her direction. "You'll need to sign in," he instructed her, then returned his attention to his book.

Bailey flicked open the binder and, finding a cheap ballpoint pen within, wrote "Troy", "Ackland", and — after quickly looking at her watch — "17:52" in the appropriate columns of the register. Then she looked around for somewhere to sit while she waited.

There were no chairs.

Just as she felt herself beginning to sigh in indignation at having to stand, the swing-doors opened with a forceful *whump* and admitted a young woman who, Bailey assumed, was the Dr. Doris Ackland she had come to see.

"Inspector Troy, I assume?"

The woman was, Bailey guessed, in her late twenties or early thirties. She wore shoulder-length hair that was blonde and, judging by the lack of dark roots and the fairness of her eyebrows, naturally so. It was parted slightly off-centre and tumbled down to her shoulders in a casually uncared for style that, Bailey had no doubt, took at least 20 minutes each morning to maintain. She was wearing faded Levi 712 jeans and a black t-shirt over a body that, Bailey noted with subconscious approval, managed to appear both athletic and curvaceous. Across the front of the t-shirt, stretched over the contours of a pair of exquisitely filled demi-bra C-cups, was the logo:

$$\left(\sqrt{-1}\right)\left(2^3\right)\sum \pi$$

Bailey nodded and held out her hand. "And you must be Doctor Ackland."

The woman reached out and shook the offered hand. "Please, call me Doris," she said.

"Bailey," the detective responded. The t-shirt logo was, Bailey decided, about as good an excuse as she was going to get to stare openly at the other woman's breasts, for a while at least. "Not too much, or too often, I hope," she continued with a smile, pointing at the logo.

"Oh, I don't know about that," Doris replied with a chuckle. "I can resist anything except temptation. Come on through." With that, she turned and headed back through the door. Bailey took a second to admire the doctor's perfectly proportioned butt as it retreated, before breathing in slowly through her nose, exhaling through her mouth, and following through the swing doors.

She understood exactly what Goff had seen in her. Understood exactly.

Beyond the swing doors was a large room that reminded Bailey of her old chemistry classroom. The room was harshly lit by three rows of fluorescent lighting across the ceiling. The walls shared the same ageing beige paintwork as the reception; the floor the same tired linoleum. There were two wide, waist-high wooden benches running the length of the room. Bunsen burners, water baths, centrifuges, microscopes, oscilloscopes, test tube racks, and equipment of every kind cluttered every work surface. Apart from Bailey and Doris, the room was vacant. The forensic scientist walked halfway along the room, picked up a pair of A4 Manila folders from the bench and waved them playfully in Bailey's direction.

"Here we are. Boyle or Watson, take your pick."

"It's really the Boyle case that I need an update on."

"Sure," Doris responded. "Fire away. What do you want to know?"

"Constable Goff has been keeping me more or less up to date with the results as they come through." Doris chuckled and pulled a mock-horrified face at the mention of Goff's name. OK, Bailey thought to herself, so it's definitely over for him. She carried on: "But is there anything new from the last twenty four hours?"

"Well, yes and no," Doris replied. "Technically, it's part of the Watson file, but I gather this evidence really relates to the Boyle case. The spent nine-mil ammo from the Dakin vehicle. We've done the fingerprints from those."

"What did you find?"

"Lots of old smudges, as I'm sure you'd expect. But there were several clear prints that are definitely from your suspect."

"From Gus Dakin? That's great to know. That will help us a lot."

"What? No," Doris interjected. "I should have been clear, sorry. Not Dakin. Your suspect in the Boyle case. Henriksen."

Bailey paused for a breath. "Okay. Let me make sure I've got this right. The spent brass that we found in Gus Dakin's car *doesn't* have Gus

Dakin's fingerprints on it, but it *does* have Lucas Henriksen's prints. Do I have that right?"

"That's right, yes. Strange, eh?"

"It does rather complicate things, for sure."

"But then it's a bit of a weird case in general, really," Doris responded. "The thing about the credit card withdrawals…"

Bailey shot a puzzled look at the forensic scientist. "What thing about the credit card withdrawals?"

"Oh, sorry. I've put my foot in it, haven't I." Doris looked genuinely flustered. "Your constable Finlayson mentioned it to me when he brought in the last batch of evidence. I hope I haven't got him into trouble."

"Trust me, Doris, he doesn't need any help from you or anyone to get into trouble. Now," Bailey continued, in as reassuring tone as should could muster, "tell me about the credit card withdrawals thing."

"It's what he found when he checked the videos at the bank branches. He said that the withdrawals weren't made by the guy whose card it was. They were made by a woman."

Bailey closed her eyes and exhaled slowly through her nose, counting quietly to five. "I don't suppose he happened to mention whether it was anyone known to us?"

"Not anyone he could recognise, apparently, no. She wore glasses, he said, and had dark hair." Doris paused and cocked her head to one side before continuing. "Not really my area of expertise, I know, but I think if I was going to walk into a bank and withdraw money to pay for an assassination with someone else's credit card, I'd certainly want to disguise my appearance first. Maybe put on some thick-rimmed glasses and change my hair colour — wear a wig or use some of that rinse-in, rinse-out stuff. Wouldn't you?"

Bailey nodded pensively. "First thing I'd do," she agreed.

She looked at her watch, 18:15. Then she looked up at Doris with an apologetic smile. "I'm so sorry. Look at the time. It's late, and it's Friday night. I should go and let you get away to your evening."

"Oh, no rush," Doris replied with a theatrical sigh. "To tell you the truth, I don't have much on this evening worth getting way for."

Bailey raised an eyebrow and smiled. "Really? I'm sure we can fix that…"

Thirty

"I always sleep like a baby afterwards." — Francesca Boyle

Bailey eased into consciousness slowly and lazily, teased awake by the faint smell of Lancôme "La Vie est Belle" perfume. Someone else's Lancôme "La Vie est Belle" perfume.

As she lay on her back with her eyes still closed, she could feel that someone else's body snuggled warmly up against her side, their arm draped lazily across her own torso, their slow and even breath delicately brushing her shoulder. She opened her eyes and turned her head to take in the still sleeping, and still achingly beautiful, form of Doris Ackland, Ph.D.

Bailey closed her eyes again and let it all — the smell, the touch, the remnants of the now six hours old post-coital bliss — wash over her. Saturday mornings simply didn't get any better than this, she reflected. She lay still, semi-hypnotised by the experience and willing it to last forever.

The phone rang.

Doris jerked awake with an "oh!" and the slightly confused and disoriented look that comes from waking up in an unfamiliar place and with an almost unfamiliar person. Bailey twisted round, grabbed the phone and looked at the callerID — Isaac Church. She flicked her thumb up from the bottom of the phone screen to reveal a list of pre-defined text messages, selected "Can't talk now, will ring you back in 10", dropped the phone back on the bedside table, and hurriedly turned her attention back to her guest.

"Good morning, Doctor Doris. Did you sleep well?" Bailey smiled attentively as she observed the other woman working quickly through the inevitable "morning after a one-night stand" thought process. The process seemed to end well; Doris smiled back, just a little shyly.

"Blissfully well, yes. Thank you."

Bailey leaned forward slightly, just a fraction of an inch, watching to see if her guest reciprocated. She did. They both continued forward, and kissed; just a touching of the lips — slow, light, undemanding.

"Blissfully well," Doris repeated, whispering. She brought her hand up and ran her fingers lightly through Bailey's hair, looping gently behind her ear.

Bailey kissed her again — quickly this time, a peck. Then she grabbed Doris's hand and quickly kissed that too. "I'm going to have to return that phone call. But I won't be more than two minutes. Don't you go anywhere."

Doris smiled impishly back at her. "I might just, erm...", she gestured towards the en-suite. "But I'll be right back, I promise." She threw the duvet back, swivelled up and off the bed and walked, unselfconsciously naked, into the bathroom.

Bailey watched her go, with an undisguised appreciation that was both aesthetic and lustful in equal measure. Goff was right, the tattoo *was* a nice touch. Once the bathroom door had swung closed, Bailey swung herself up to a sitting position, grabbed her phone from the bedside table, stabbed the call button twice, and raised the phone to her ear.

It rang three times before it was answered. "Thanks for calling back," Isaac said. "I hope you don't mind me disturbing your weekend."

"Just so long as you've got something important, Isaac," she replied. "I was kinda looking forward to some… relaxation."

"We do need to talk. I don't think it can wait until Monday, sorry."

"So talk," she replied. She heard Doris padding back from the bathroom, felt the mattress shift as she climbed across the bed and crawled over to the side where Bailey was sitting.

"Not over the phone. Too complicated. This really needs to be face to face. How about Café sur la Colline in half an hour?"

Bailey felt Doris's arm snaking around her waist. Doris's lips caressing her shoulder. Doris's inner thighs sliding forward to embrace her hips. Doris's nipples dancing lightly across her back. She closed her eyes and tilted her head back before speaking quietly into the phone.

"Make it two hours. I have something I need to take care of first."

Thirty One

"We've tried to think of everything." — Francesca Boyle

It was a sunny day, but the wind was just a little too strong, and with just too much hint of chill, to make sitting on the balcony of Café sur la Colline a relaxing experience. Consequently, they had the balcony to themselves — Isaac, Bailey and Constable Goff. Isaac sipped his flat white and observed the inspector sitting across the table, slowly processing what he had just told her. Goff sat to her left — quietly observant and with an A5 notepad open on the table in front of him, the page three-quarters full of Goff's business-like handwriting.

It seemed to Isaac that Bailey must have left her house in something of a hurry. She was wearing paint-stained and baggy sweatpants and a polar fleece, and showed no sign of having combed her hair recently. Beneath the collar of the polar fleece, he thought he could see a hickey. It looked fresh. Something to take care of, indeed…

"So, let me make sure I have this right," she said. She lifted her finger as if to start repeating back what she had learned. But instead she paused, closed her eyes, pressed the raised finger into her temple, and shook her head slowly.

"OK," she started again. "Dakin Boyle is putting something into their generic drugs that gives people cancer."

"A form of the virus that causes Merkel cell carcinoma, yes."

"And then the people who take the generics get the cancer, and Dakin Boyle sells them the drug to cure them of it."

Isaac knew from long and oft-repeated experience that, just because something had crystallised into something elegantly simple and straightforward in his own mind, that didn't mean that it was quickly going to form that way in anyone else's. He nodded patiently. "The Mertusugene, yes."

"And they do all this to make more money."

He nodded again, and smiled in a way that he hoped was encouraging rather than patronising. "The naturally occurring levels of Merkel cell carcinoma are far, far lower than the occurrences caused by people taking the generics. Without the cases caused by the virus in the generics, the sales would be a tiny fraction of what they are, barely one percent." Nothing he hadn't already said at least twice this morning; nothing, no doubt, he wouldn't need to repeat.

Bailey stabbed her finger down on the table, as if to pin down her next point. "And Bill Dakin killed Dick Boyle's wife, and threatened to kill his daughter, to make Boyle go along with it all. Killed her by giving her cancer."

"By infecting her with the virus that gave her Merkel cell carcinoma, yes. Probably an early version of the virus that they're putting into the generics now, I'm guessing. And he actually did give something to Francesca to give her cancer — an adenocarcinoma of the pancreas. Dick and Jenny developed a way of causing adenocarcinomas in lab rats to help them research a cure; worked on humans too, I guess. Francesca's cancer was terminal; it would've killed her, if she hadn't been shot."

"But then Bill Dakin *did* have Francesca shot, because she was too close to working all this out and spilling the beans. Then *Gus* Dakin killed Jenny Watson because she was in on it all along, but was starting to get cold feet." Bailey looked over at Isaac and raised her eyebrows, seeking confirmation.

"Well, we're all still guessing about that last bit," Isaac replied. "But that's pretty much it, yes."

"And what about the woman who made the cash withdrawals on Dakin's card? Who was she? And how does a woman who is so obviously not Bill Dakin manage to make a withdrawal on Dakin's card?"

"The name on the card was just W. Dakin," said Goff. "It could've been a man's or a woman's card, for all the cashier knew. Just an as-yet unknown accomplice, I'm guessing. A clumsy attempt to distance Dakin from the cash."

"Pretty damned clumsy," observed Isaac.

"Yes, yes. All right," said Bailey. "Back on topic. We know all this because…"

Isaac put his coffee down and started counting off on his fingers. "First and foremost, Dick admitted it to me — at least, the bits about the cancer virus in the generics, about Bill killing his wife and infecting Francesca, and about Jenny being in on it all."

"I don't suppose you recorded that conversation, by any chance?"

"I'm afraid not, no," he replied. But it would, he reflected inwardly, have been a smart move; he missed a trick there. He continued: "Second, the levels of Merkel cell carcinoma, are a hundred times higher in those parts of the world where Dakin Boyle ships its generics than in those parts where they don't. FDA rules have stopped them from selling their generics in the US, and levels of the cancer there are a tiny fraction of what they are in Europe. Third, the production numbers don't square with the accounts. What gets invoiced to the distributor is pretty-much exactly half what apparently gets produced at the plant. Fourth, the production processes at the main plant don't tie up with what happens at Wade Park. Half of what is allegedly active Mertusugene ingredient created at the main plant gets shipped off to Wade Park for finishing; but when it gets there it's just treated as another ingredient for the generics. That's how the cancer virus gets introduced into the generics, I'm guessing."

"So," Bailey replied, "apart from the admission by Dick Boyle, for which we only have your word, everything else is circumstantial. And I'm sure Dakin will have a queue of epidemiologists, accountants, and pharmacologists a mile long to provide some other explanation."

"True," he said. "But what you've got should be enough for you to get a warrant to seize some of the product and get it examined. If it has the virus in it, then you've got a case. A pretty damned good case, I'd say."

"We've got a case for Dakin Boyle poisoning millions of people, for sure. But I'm not sure it's enough to give us a slam-dunk for Francesca's murder. And I'm sure we'd all like to see them get held to account for that..."

"They murdered 17,000 people," Isaac responded. "All the cancer victims that the drug didn't cure. One more or less won't make much of a difference."

"Nonetheless, all those other people died somewhere else. Francesca died on my patch, and I want a result." She turned to Goff. "Now, you and I have some planning to do. We've got enough to get warrants to search both plants, plus the residences of Bill Dakin and Dick Boyle. We've already got Gus in custody, we need to grab Bill Dakin and Dick Boyle as well. And let's pull in Russell Bridgeman for good measure, since he's apparently in on the act too."

"A nice bit of overtime for a bunch of people," Goff observed. He looked at his watch. "It'll be tomorrow before we can pull it all together, too. Double time on a Sunday."

"I aim to please," Bailey replied, with mock sincerity. "Now you go and find your favourite magistrate and get the warrants. And see if you can find out who the hell we can get to test all this stuff for viruses and so on. I need to..."

Her phone rang. She pulled it impatiently from her bag and looked at the callerID. She shook her head wearily. "Finlayson," she said, to nobody in particular. She pressed the answer button and raised the phone to her ear. "Yes?" she barked. Isaac heard the indistinct tone of Constable Finlayson's voice burbling from the phone. Then he saw the inspector's eye close and her head tilt forward almost imperceptibly.

"When?"

More burbling from the phone.

"OK. Thanks. You know the drill. Get both areas secured and get a Scene-of-Crime squad in to each one. Goff and I are on our way."

She dropped the phone back into her bag and turned to Goff. "Slight variation to the plan. We won't be arresting either Bill Dakin or Dick Boyle, but I suspect that we will be adding a murder-suicide to our crime statistics for the month." She looked across the table at Isaac. "I'm sorry. I know you were fond of him."

Thirty Two

"He's not really my uncle, of course." — *Francesca Boyle*

Bailey looked impatiently across the table. "You said it was important."

It was the same prison interview room as before. The same old wooden table; the same steel door behind her; the same matching steel door across the room in front of her, again flanked on either side by guards. Different guards this time — neither portly nor muscular, neither old nor young, unmemorable in every way, just boring guys, looking bored, doing a boring job.

And, just like last time, across the table from her was Lucas Henriksen, still looking comfortable and incongruously well-presented in his prison overalls. Unlike last time, his lawyer Owen Walker was sat next to him. Unkempt as always, in no rush to get the interview finished, or even started. Being paid by the hour from the public purse.

Five seconds passed. Ten. Then Walker leant forward, with obvious reluctance. "My client has something to tell you that he believes will be of help in your investigation."

"Really? Well then you won't mind if we, erm…?" She reached into her bag, pulled out a small recorder, and waved it questioningly in the air.

"Not at all Inspector," replied Walker. "Not at all." He closed his eyes, shook his head, and slumped back into his chair.

Henriksen smiled. "You'll need to forgive Mr. Walker, Inspector. He has offered me some excellent advice, and he's quite frustrated that I'm not following it." He nodded towards the recorder. "Shall we begin?"

Bailey pressed the record button and recited the preliminaries into the recorder. "Now, what do you want to tell me, Lucas?"

"Mr. Walker tells me that you've had a busy weekend, Inspector. Lots of raids and so forth."

Bailey sighed. "Yes Lucas, I have had a busy weekend. And I've still got a lot to get through. So can we please get to the point."

Henriksen ignored her prompting. "That Mr. Dakin that you were so interested in, I gather he came to a sticky end. Pummelled to death in his own living room. With a crowbar, no less."

"Yes, Lucas. Mr. Dakin is dead, and we are investigating his murder. Now, how about we get to the bit where you tell me something I'll find interesting?"

"It would have been Dick — Mr. Boyle — who dealt to him, of course. Before he, ahh..." Henriksen raised his left hand above his head and jerked it upwards, twitching his head to the right and sticking out his tongue as he did so. "He had it coming, Dakin. Not a nice man. Not a nice man at all. But it is a shame about poor Dick." He lowered his eyes and nodded to himself. "My wife was very fond of him; we both were. And of Francesca, of course. He saved her life, you know. Henrietta's, that is."

"So we discovered," Bailey replied drily.

Henriksen smiled at her across the table, still clearly in no mood to be rushed. "His daughter, Francesca, was very sick, you know. Before...". He shrugged, apologetically.

"Before you killed her."

Walker leant forward as if to interrupt, but Henriksen reached out and gently put his hand on his lawyers shoulder, easing him back into his seat.

"And here," Henriksen replied, "is where we get to the bit that is causing Mr. Walker so much anxiety." He looked down at the table and nodded to himself. "But before we do, I'd like you to tell me one thing."

"This interview is about *you* telling *me* things, Lucas, not the other way around."

He smiled again. "No free lunches here, Inspector. Indulge me, please."

She eyed him across the table for several seconds, then nodded gently. "No promises, Lucas. But try me, what is it you want to know?"

"The Dakin boy, and that other chap, Bridgeman. You have them nailed to the wall, fair and square?"

"Why do you care? You told me you didn't even know Gus Dakin, last time we spoke."

"Ah yes," he replied. "Well, I might have lied about that. People do, you know. Especially..." He paused and looked around him before returning his gaze to Bailey. "Especially people in my situation. And, to be honest with you, Inspector, there may have been a little theatrical reverse psychology going on. But that was then, this is now, things have moved on. So tell me: are they going down?"

"I believe so, yes," she replied.

"And they'll throw away the key? Not just a slap over the wrist."

"They'll be going to prison for at least as long as you, Lucas, I'm confident of that. And I doubt they'll settle into the environment anywhere near as comfortably as you appear to have done."

"That's what I needed to know. Thank you, Inspector. Now, let's make sure you don't waste time disappearing down any rabbit-holes unnecessarily. Ask me again who shot Francesca Boyle."

"OK. Who killed Francesca Boyle?"

"I didn't say to ask me who killed her. I said to ask me who shot her."

He was talking about Francesca's cancer. He *knew* about Francesca's cancer. She decided to play dumb, let him tell his story.

"It was the gunshot that killed her, Lucas; the post-mortem was pretty clear on that. But as you wish. Who *shot* Francesca Boyle?"

"I did, Inspector. We both know that, of course. But now you have my confession there on the tape. I stole a Mazda 3, took the plates from that young lad's car and put them on the car I stole, ran a red light to make sure that you had a record of the car heading towards the scene of the crime, shot her once in the head with my revolver, and left some nine-mil brass to make it look like she was shot with the young lad's gun. And, as you know, it was me who messed up her apartment. Of course, I would rather not have been caught. But," he shrugged and smiled, "you don't get everything you want in life, eh?"

"All of which we already know, but thank you for confirming. Now tell me something we don't know. Who paid you to shoot her?"

"Now who's telling fibs, Inspector? I'm sure you have a theory on that. And I'm sure you're gathering plenty of evidence to support it, too. You will have found out by now that the money I was paid came from Dakin's credit card. And you will have found some of that nine-mil brass in the son's car, just like the brass I left at the scene. Am I right?"

"So," she responded. "Are you telling me that it was Bill Dakin who paid you?"

Henriksen laughed. "No, Inspector! Don't get me wrong, he killed her, of course. But not by paying me. He killed her long before I came on the scene."

"You're not making any sense, Lucas." Still playing dumb. "Just tell me what happened."

Henriksen smiled and shook his head slowly, staring at his hands as they rested on the table. Then he raised his gaze again and look directly at Bailey. "She was very sick. I think I mentioned that, didn't I?

Pancreatic Cancer, did you know that? Nasty business. Particularly at the end. And it only ever ends one way, sadly."

Bailey made a show of looked impatiently at her watch, then across at Owen Walker the lawyer, raising an eyebrow that shouted "how long do we have to put up with this?" He just shrugged and shook his head in reply.

"Get to the point, Lucas," she said sternly.

"Ductal adenocarcinoma, I think they call it. And they were researching cures for adenocarcinomas at Dakin Boyle, I gather. Funny coincidence that, don't you think?"

"How do you know all this, Lucas? You seem very well informed on it all, for a contract killer."

"Why, she told me, of course. Francesca told me. She told me everything"

"She told you everything? Just before you killed her? It seems like an unlikely conversation to have with your murderer."

"No, no. Not then. It was whe…"

Bailey's phone rang, the loud chirping reverberating around the room and silencing Henriksen in mid word. She pulled the phone from her bag and looked at the callerID. Goff. He knew where she was; knew not to interrupt her unless it was vital. She tapped the answer button with her thumb and lifted the phone to her ear.

"What's up?"

"I though you should know, we found a suicide note among Dick Boyle's stuff in his office."

"OK. What did he put in it that's so important?"

"It wasn't written by him, Boss. It was written by her. It's a suicide note written by Francesca Boyle."

Thirty Three

"Goodbye" — Francesca Boyle

Dearest Daddy,

Please, please, please don't be angry with me. I just can't bear to think you'll be angry with me. But I had to do this. I couldn't let them get away with what they've done. Not to Mummy, not to me, and most especially not to you. You are such a wonderful, wonderful man. They have to pay for the terrible things they've done to you, the things they've made you do.

I know what it will look like, when they find me. But please understand it really was my choice. It was really the only choice, given what they have done to me. I couldn't let it carry on. I can't wait and let this thing run its course; I can't go the way Mummy went. It scares me. I don't have the courage for that. Sorry. It's better this way. Hopefully, some good will come of it, at least.

You worked so desperately hard to save Mummy, I understand now. But you just couldn't make the drug work in time. You loved her so much, I know; but they just didn't care. And I know that you're not going to be able to save me either. The research just hasn't progressed the way it needs to. You understand this too, I'm sure.

Uncle Lucas is being so brave, I do hope they don't catch him. He would do anything for you, of course, after what you did for Aunt Henrietta; but I do feel bad about asking him to do this. Hopefully it will work out the way Uncle Lucas and I planned it, and Gus and Bill will get what's coming to them.

You tried to shield me from all this, of course; and I love you for it. But after I got the diagnosis, and knowing what you were researching, it all looked like too much of a coincidence. And once I started looking, it all became pretty clear. It's there to find in the company's books, and in the little slips that people make when they were just a little too comfortable around me. Jenny, Gus, Russell. Even you, Daddy. All that investigative journalism training paid off, I guess. Under different circumstances, it might have been a Pulitzer Prize in the making. But it's not to be.

If this goes according to plan, it's going to be a bit hard on Isaac for a while. He doesn't deserve it, he's a nice guy. But hopefully it won't take too long for the police to follow the breadcrumbs to where we want, and he'll be off the hook. Please take good care of him, Daddy. I feel bad about what we're going to put him through, but there's really no other way.

Once all this has played out, you'll understand why I spent those couple of weeks dating Gus. I know this must have been very painful for you, knowing what he and his father are doing. And he is a heartless pig in ways I'm not even going to describe. But I needed to get into his car, and I needed some opportunities to shoulder-surf his Dad's PIN number, and I needed to be close to him when he was relaxed and had his guard down.

And a girl's got to use the tools she has available, you know.

Please, please, PLEASE burn this once you have read it. I couldn't bear to leave you without making sure you understood what was going on, and why. But the police must never find this letter; it would ruin everything.

I'm crying as I write this. I really wish I could just hug you one last time; just hold you tight and never let go. But you're not here, it's nearly time, and now I must go.

I love you, Daddy.

Francesca.